TRANSCENDENT

TRANSCENDENT
The Year's Best Transgender Speculative Fiction

edited by K.M. Szpara

LETHE PRESS
Maple Shade, New Jersey

Published in 2016 by Lethe Press, Inc.
118 Heritage Avenue • Maple Shade, NJ 08052-3018 USA
www.lethepressbooks.com • lethepress@aol.com
ISBN: 978-1-59021-617-0 / 1-59021-617-2

Credits for previous publication appear on page 195, which constitutes
an extension of this copyright page.

Set in Caslon, Truesdell, and Modern No. 20.
Interior design: Alex Jeffers.
Cover art and design: Noel Arthur Heimpel.

Introduction

THIS ANTHOLOGY IS A SUPERHERO—OR HEROINE, or sometimes both or neither, or one and then the other. This anthology is a Super. It has superhuman powers that will radiate good and eradicate evil because it amplifies transgender voices and characters and themes amidst the faraway and fantastic. And, like all Supers, it has an origin story.

Not so long ago, in a coffee shop that served magical muffins and smelled of the roastery next door, a transgender writer's finger hovered over the "send" button in his email. He'd written a story with a gay couple that had been published earlier that year and earned some heartfelt reviews, so he thought he'd submit it to the *Year's Best Gay Speculative Fiction*.

With little suspense, the editor called him and offered something unexpected, instead: the opportunity to edit a new anthology, a Year's Best Transgender Speculative Fiction. The trans writer was elated by the offer and that such an anthology would even exist, but the reason seemed to be a lack of intersectionality. A worry that Year's Best Gay readers would not enjoy gay transgender characters. A separate but equal solution.

After two weeks of weighing pros and cons, of wondering whether he would betray his core beliefs by accepting the opportunity but imagining what a wonderful book he could create—he wished he'd had such a book when he was younger—he emailed the editor, heart pounding as he explained why he thought this anthology would be important but why the offer made him uneasy.

And, to his surprise, unlike many cisgender folks before, the editor listened. The editor asked him not only to edit *The Year's Best Transgender & Genderqueer Speculative Fiction* but also to draft a statement of inclusion for the other Year's Best anthologies. The writer accepted and the editor rejoiced and they worked happily ever after.

Transcendent contains multitudes. Inside, you will meet friendly monsters, book thieves, and an assassin. You will travel from the ocean kingdoms to alien planets. You will be stuck between the year 1905 and August 3, 2321—any further and you'll be marooned in time.

I have strong opinions on who should be writing transgender stories and how, but *Transcendent* challenged me to look beyond that. There are stories with actual transgender characters, some for whom that is central and others for whom that isn't. And there are stories without transgender characters, but with metaphors and symbolism in their place, genuine expressions of self through shapeshifting and programming.

We saw ourselves in those transformative characters, those outsiders, before we saw ourselves as human protagonists. Those feelings are still valid. We still see through a lens that cisgender people can never understand; we are transformation and outsiders.

But sometimes we are insiders. Sometimes the change is more a self-realization or maybe we always knew. Maybe it's not the center of our story, but just another stupid gendered pit stop on our way to slay the dragon or save the galaxy.

I experienced a wonderful sensation while reading submissions: that every story I read would have a transgender character or theme in it. We rarely see ourselves manifested in speculative fiction, and when we do it is all too often in an appropriative manner by cisgender authors. I've put down many books because of a frustrating lack of queer characters. But that didn't happen with *Transcendent*. As I read every story, I experienced the delight of seeing myself or my experience reflected though speculative fiction.

I hope that if you are trans and reading this, that you experience the same. See yourself, see your friends. See your community and your makeshift family. These stories immortalize us; I hope you enjoy them.

K.M. Szpara
Summer 2016

Contents

The Shape of My Name

Nino Cipri

THE YEAR 2076 SMELLS LIKE ANTISEPTIC gauze and the lavender diffuser that Dara set up in my room. It has the bitter aftertaste of pills: probiotics and microphages and PPMOs. It feels like the itch of healing, the ache that's settled on my pubic bone. It has the sound of a new name that's fresh and yet familiar on my lips.

The future feels lighter than the past. I think I know why you chose it over me, Mama.

MY BEDROOM HAS CHANGED IN THE hundred-plus years that passed since I slept there as a child. The floorboards have been carpeted over, torn up, replaced. The walls are thick with new layers of paint. The windows have been upgraded, the closet expanded. The oak tree that stood outside my window is gone, felled by a storm twenty years ago, I'm told. But the house still stands, and our family still lives here, with all our attendant ghosts. You and I are haunting each other, I think.

I picture you standing in the kitchen downstairs, over a century ago. I imagine that you're staring out through the little window above the sink, your eyes traveling down the path that leads from the backdoor and splits at the creek; one trail leads to the pond, and the other leads to the shelter and the anachronopede, with its rows of capsules and blinking lights.

Maybe it's the afternoon you left us. June 22, 1963: storm clouds gathering in the west, the wind picking up, the air growing heavy with the threat of rain. And you're staring out the window, gazing across the dewy fields at the forking path, trying to decide which one you'll take.

My bedroom is just above the kitchen, and my window has that same view, a little expanded: I can see clear down to the pond where Dad and I

used to sit on his weeks off from the oil fields. It's spring, and the cattails
are only hip-high. I can just make out the silhouette of a great blue heron
walking along among the reeds and rushes.

You and I, we're twenty feet and more than a hundred years apart.

You WENT INTO LABOR NOT KNOWING my name, which I know now is
unprecedented among our family: you knew Dad's name before you laid
eyes on him, the time and date of my birth, the hospital where he would
drive you when you went into labor. But my name? My sex? Conspicu-
ously absent on Uncle Dante's gilt-edged book where all these happy
details were recorded in advance.

Dad told me later that you thought I'd be a stillbirth. He didn't know
about the record book, about the blank space where a name should go.
But he told me that nothing he said while you were pregnant could con-
vince you that I'd come into the world alive. You thought I'd slip out of
you strangled and blue, already decaying.

Instead, I started screaming before they pulled me all the way out.

Dad said that even when the nurse placed me in your arms, you thought
you were hallucinating. "I had to tell her, over and over: Miriam, you're
not dreaming, our daughter is alive."

I bit my lip when he told me that, locked the words "your son" out of
sight. I regret that now; maybe I could have explained myself to him. I
should have tried, at least.

You didn't name me for nearly a week.

1954 TASTES LIKE KELLOGG'S RICE KRISPIES in fresh milk, delivered earlier that morning. It smells like woodsmoke, cedar chips, Dad's Kamel
cigarettes mixed with the perpetual smell of diesel in his clothes. It feels
like the worn velvet nap of the couch in our living room, which I loved
to run my fingers across.

I was four years old. I woke up in the middle of the night after a loud
crash of lightning. The branches of the the oak tree outside my window
were thrashing in the wind and the rain.

I crept out of bed, dragging my blanket with me. I slipped out of the
door and into the hallway, heading for your and Dad's bedroom. I stopped
when I heard voices coming from the parlor downstairs: I recognized

your sharp tones, but there was also a man's voice, not Dad's baritone but something closer to a tenor.

The door creaked when I pushed it open, and the voices fell silent. I paused, and then you yanked open the door.

The curlers in your hair had come undone, descending down towards your shoulders. I watched one tumble out of your hair and onto the floor like a stunned beetle. I only caught a glimpse of the man standing in the corner; he had thin, hunched shoulders and dark hair, wet and plastered to his skull. He was wearing one of Dad's old robes, with the initials monogrammed on the pocket. It was much too big for him.

You snatched me up, not very gently, and carried me up to the bedroom you shared with Dad.

"Tom," you hissed. You dropped me on the bed before Dad was fully awake, and shook his shoulder. He sat up, blinking at me, and looked to you for an explanation.

"There's a visitor," you said, voice strained.

Dad looked at the clock, pulling it closer to him to get a proper look. "Now? Who is it?"

Your jaw was clenched, and so were your hands. "I'm handling it. I just need you to watch—"

You said my name in a way I'd never heard it before, as if each syllable were a hard, steel ball dropping from your lips. It frightened me, and I started to cry. Silently, though, since I didn't want you to notice me. I didn't want you to look at me with eyes like that.

You turned on your heel and left the room, clicking the door shut behind you and locking it.

Dad patted me on the back, his wide hand nearly covering the expanse of my skinny shoulders. "It's all right, kid," he said. "Nothing to be scared of. Why don't you lie down and I'll read you something, huh?"

In the morning, there was no sign a visitor had been there at all. You and Dad assured me that I must have dreamed the whole thing.

I know now that you were lying, of course. I think I knew it even then.

I HAD TWO CHILDHOODS.

One happened between Dad's ten-day hitches in the White County oil fields. That childhood smells like his tobacco, wool coats, wet grass. It sounds like the opening theme songs to all our favorite TV shows. It tastes like the peanut-butter sandwiches that you'd pack for us on our walks, which we'd eat down by the pond, the same one I can just barely see from my window here. In the summer, we'd sit at the edge of the water, dipping our toes into the mud. Sometimes, Dad told me stories, or asked me to fill him in on the episodes of *Gunsmoke* and *Science Fiction Theater* he'd missed, and we'd chat while watching for birds. The herons have always been my favorite. They moved so slow, it always felt like a treat to spot one as it stepped cautiously through the shallow water. Sometimes, we'd catch sight of one flying overhead, its wide wings fighting against gravity.

And then there was the childhood with you, and with Dara, the childhood that happened when Dad was away. I remember the first morning I came downstairs and she was eating pancakes off of your fancy china, the plates that were decorated with delicate paintings of evening primrose.

"Hi there. I'm Dara," she said.

When I looked at you, shy and unsure, you told me, "She's a cousin. She'll be dropping in when your father is working. Just to keep us company."

Dara didn't really look much like you, I thought; not the way that Dad's cousins and uncles all resembled each other. But I could see a few similarities between the two of you; hazel eyes, long fingers, and something I didn't have the words to describe for a long time: a certain discomfort, the sense that you held yourselves slightly apart from the rest of us. It had made you a figure of gossip in town, though I didn't know that until high school, when the same was said of me.

"What should I call you?" Dara asked me.

You jumped in and told her to call me by my name, the one you'd chosen for me, after the week of indecision following my birth. How can I ever make you understand how much I disliked that name? It felt like it belonged to a sister I'd never known, whose legacy I could never fulfill or surpass or even forget. Dara must have caught the face that I made, because later, when you were out in the garden, she asked me, "Do you have another name? That you want me to call you instead?"

When I shrugged, she said, "It doesn't have to be a forever-name. Just one for the day. You can introduce yourself differently every time you see me."

And so every morning when I woke up and saw Dara sitting at the table, I gave her a different name: Doc, Buck, George, Charlie. Names that my heroes had, from television and comics and the matinees in town. They weren't my name, but they were better than the one I had. I liked the way they sounded, the shape of them rolling around my mouth.

You just looked on, lips pursed in a frown, and told Dara you wished she'd quit indulging my silly little games.

The two of you sat around our kitchen table and—if I was quiet and didn't draw any attention to myself—talked in a strange code about *jumps* and *fastenings* and *capsules*, dropping names of people I never knew. More of your cousins, I figured.

You told our neighbors that all of your family was spread out, and disinclined to make the long trip to visit. When Dara took me in, she made up a tale about a long-lost cousin whose parents had kicked him out for being trans. Funny, the way the truth seeps into lies.

I WENT TO SEE UNCLE DANTE in 1927. I wanted to see what he had in that book of his about me, and about you and Dara.

1927 tastes like the chicken broth and brown bread he fed me, after I showed up at his door. It smelled like the musty blanket he hung around my shoulders, like kerosene lamps and woodsmoke. It sounds like the scratchy records he played on his phonograph: Duke Ellington and Al Jolson, the Gershwin brothers and Gene Austin.

"Your mother dropped in back in '24," he said, settling down in an armchair in front of the fireplace. It was the same fireplace that had been in our parlor, though Dad had sealed off the chimney in 1958, saying it let in too many drafts. "She was very adamant that your name be written down in the records. She seemed…upset." He let the last word hang on its own, lonely, obviously understated.

"That's not my name," I told him. "It's the one she gave me, but it was never mine."

I had to explain to him then—he'd been to the future, and so it didn't seem so far-fetched, my transition. I simplified it for him: didn't go into HRT or mastectomies, the phalloplasty I'd scheduled a century and a half in the future. I skipped the introduction to gender theory, Susan Stryker, *Stone Butch Blues*, all the things that Dara gave me to read when I asked for books about people like me.

"My aunt Lucia was of a similar disposition," he told me. "Once her last child was grown, she gave up on dresses entirely. Wore a suit to church for her last twelve years, which gave her a reputation for eccentricity."

I clamped my mouth shut and nodded, still feeling ill and shaky from the jump. The smell of Uncle Dante's cigar burned in my nostrils. I wished we could have had the conversation outside, on the porch; the parlor seemed too familiar, too laden with the ghost of your presence.

"What name should I put instead?" he asked, pulling the book down from the mantle: the gilt-edged journal where he recorded our family's births, marriages, and deaths.

"It's blank when I'm born," I told him. He paused in the act of sharpening his pencil—he knew better than to write the future in ink. "Just erase it. White it out if you need to."

He sat back in his chair, and combed his fingers through his beard. "That's unprecedented.".

"Not anymore," I said.

1963 FEELS LIKE A MENSTRUAL CRAMP, like the ache in my legs as my bones stretched, like the twinges in my nipples as my breasts developed. It smells like Secret roll-on deodorant and the menthol cigarettes you had taken up smoking. It tastes like the peach cobbler I burned in Home-Ec class, which the teacher forced me to eat. It sounds like Sam Cooke's album *Night Beat*, which Dara, during one of her visits, had told me to buy.

And it looks like you, jumpier than I'd ever seen you, so twitchy that even Dad commented on it before he left for his hitch in the oil fields.

"Will you be all right?" he asked after dinner.

I was listening to the two of you talk from the kitchen doorway. I'd come in to ask Dad if he was going to watch *Gunsmoke* with me, which would be starting in a few minutes, and caught the two of you with your heads together by the sink.

You leaned forward, bracing your hands on the edge of the sink, looking for all the world as if you couldn't hold yourself up, as if gravity was working just a little bit harder on you than it was for everyone else. I wondered for a second if you were going to tell him about Dara. I'd grown up keeping her a secret with you, though the omission had begun to weigh heavier on me. I loved Dad, and I loved Dara; being unable to reconcile the two of them seemed trickier each passing week.

Instead you said nothing. You relaxed your shoulders, and you smiled for him, and kissed his cheek. You said the two of us would be fine, not to worry about his girls.

And the very next day, you pulled me out of bed and showed me our family's time machine, in the old tornado shelter with the lock I'd never been able to pick.

I KNOW MORE ABOUT THE MACHINE now, after talking with Uncle Dante, reading the records that he kept. The mysterious man, Moses Stone, that built it in 1905, when Grandma Emmeline's parents leased out a parcel of land. He called it the anachronopede, which probably sounded marvelous in 1905, but even Uncle Dante was rolling his eyes at the name twenty years later. I know that Stone took Emmeline on trips to the future when she was seventeen, and then abandoned her after a few years, and nobody's been able to find him since then. I know that the machine is keyed to something in Emmeline's matrilineal DNA, some recessive gene.

I wonder if that man, Stone, built the anachronopede as an experiment. An experiment needs parameters, right? So build a machine that only certain people in one family can use. We can't go back before 1905, when the machine was completed, and we can't go past August 3, 2321. What happens that day? The only way to find out is to go as far forward as possible, and then wait. Maroon yourself in time. Exile yourself as far forward as you can, where none of us can reach you.

I'm sure you were lonely, waiting for me to grow up so you could travel again. You were exiled when you married Dad in 1947, in that feverish period just after the war. It must have been so romantic at first: I've seen the letters he wrote during the years he courted you. And you'd grown up seeing his name written next to yours, and the date that you'd marry him. When did you start feeling trapped, I wonder? You were caught in a weird net of fate and love and the future and the past. You loved Dad, but your love kept you hostage. You loved me, but you knew that someday, I'd transform myself into someone you didn't recognize.

AT FIRST, WHEN YOU TOOK ME underground, to see the anachronopede, I
thought you and Dad had built a fallout shelter. But there were no beds
or boxes of canned food. And built into the rocky wall were rows of doors
that looked like the one on our icebox. Round light bulbs lay just above
the doors, nearly all of them red, though one or two were slowly blinking
between orange and yellow.

Nearly all the doors were shut, except for two, near the end, which
hung ajar.

"Those two capsules are for us, you and me," you said. "Nobody else can
use them."

I stared at them. "What are they for?"

I'd heard you and Dara speak in code for nearly all of my life, jumps
and capsules and fastenings. I'd imagined all sorts of things. Aliens and
spaceships and doorways to another dimension, all the sort of things I'd
seen Truman Bradley introduce on *Science Fiction Theater*.

"Traveling," you said.

"In time or in space?"

You seemed surprised. I'm not sure why. Dad collected pulp magazines,
and you'd given me books by H.G. Wells and Jules Verne for Christmas
in years past. The Justice League had gone into the future. I'd seen *The
Fly* last year during a half-price matinee. You know how it was back then:
such things weren't considered impossible, so much as inevitable. The
future was a country we all wanted so badly to visit.

"In time," you said.

I immediately started peppering you with questions: how far into the
future had you gone? When were you born? Had you seen dinosaurs?
Had you met King Arthur? What about jet packs? Was Dara from the
future?

You held a hand to your mouth, watching as I danced around the small
cavern, firing off questions like bullets being sprayed from a tommy gun.

"Maybe you are too young," you said, staring at the two empty capsules
in the wall.

"I'm not!" I insisted. "Can't we go somewhere? Just a—just a quick
jump?"

I added in the last part because I wanted you to know I'd been listening, when you and Dara had talked in code at the kitchen table. I'd been
waiting for you include me in the conversation.

"Tomorrow," you decided. "We'll leave tomorrow."

THE FIRST THING I LEARNED ABOUT time travel was that you couldn't eat anything before you did it. And you could only take a few sips of water: no juice or milk. The second thing I learned was that it was the most painful thing in the world, at least for me.

"Your grandmother Emmeline called it the fastening," you told me. "She said it felt like being a button squeezed through a too-narrow slit in a piece of fabric. It affects everyone differently."

"How's it affect you?"

You twisted your wedding ring around on your finger. "I haven't done it since before you were born."

You made me go to the bathroom twice before we walked back on that path, taking the fork that led to the shelter where the capsules were. The grass was still wet with dew, and there was a chill in the air. Up above, thin, wispy clouds were scratched onto the sky, but out west, I could see dark clouds gathering. There'd be storms later.

But what did I care about later? I was going into a time machine.

I asked you, "Where are we going?"

You replied, "To visit Dara. Just a quick trip."

There was something cold in your voice. I recognized the tone: the same you used when trying to talk me into wearing the new dress you'd bought me for church, or telling me to stop tearing through the house and play quietly for once.

In the shelter, you helped me undress, though it made me feel hotly embarrassed and strange to be naked in front of you again. I'd grown wary of my own body in the last few months, the way it was changing: I'd been dismayed by the way my nipples had grown tender, at the fatty flesh that had budded beneath them. It seemed like a betrayal.

I hunched my shoulders and covered my privates, though you barely glanced at my naked skin. You helped me lie down in the capsule, showed me how to pull the round mask over the bottom half of my face, attach the clip that went over my index finger. Finally, you lifted one of my arms up and wrapped a black cuff around the crook of my elbow. I noticed, watching you, that you had bitten all of your nails down to the quick, that the edges were jagged and tender-looking.

"You program your destination date in here, you see?" You tapped a square of black glass that lay on the ceiling of the capsule, and it lit up at the touch. Your fingers flew across the screen, typing directly onto it, rearranging colored orbs that seemed to attach themselves to your finger as soon as you touched them.

"You'll learn how to do this on your own eventually," you said. The screen, accepting whatever you'd done to it, blinked out and went black again.

I breathed through my mask, which covered my nose and face. A whisper of air blew against my skin, a rubbery, stale, lemony scent.

"Don't be scared," you said. "I'll be there when you wake up. I'm sending myself back a little earlier, so I'll be there to help you out of the capsule."

You kissed me on the forehead and shut the door. I was left alone in the dark as the walls around me started to hum.

Calling it "the fastening" does it a disservice. It's much more painful than that. Granny Emmeline is far tougher than I'll ever be, if she thought it was just like forcing a button into place.

For me, it felt like being crushed in a vice that was lined with broken glass and nails. I understood, afterwards, why you had forbidden me from eating or drinking for twenty-four hours. I would have vomited in the mask, shat myself inside the capsule. I came back to myself in the dark, wild with terror and the phantom remains of that awful pain.

The door opened. The light needled into my eyes, and I screamed, trying to cover them. The various cuffs and wires attached to my arms tugged my hands back down, which made me panic even more.

Hands reached in and pushed me down, and eventually, I registered your voice in my ear, though not what you were saying. I stopped flailing long enough for all the straps and cuffs to be undone, and then I was lifted out of the capsule. You held me in your arms, rocking and soothing me, rubbing my back as I cried hysterically onto your shoulder.

I was insensible for a few minutes. When my sobs died away to hiccups, I realized that we weren't alone in the shelter. Dara was with us as well, and she had thrown a blanket over my shoulders.

"Jesus, Miriam," she said, over and over. "What the hell were you thinking?"

I found out later that I was the youngest person in my family to ever make a jump. Traditionally, they made their first jumps on their seventeenth birthday. I was nearly five years shy of that.

You smoothed back a lock of my hair, and I saw that all your finger-nails had lost their ragged edge. Instead, they were rounded and smooth, topped with little crescents of white.

UNCLE DANTE TOLD ME THAT IT wasn't unusual for two members of the family to be lovers, especially if there were generational gaps between them. It helped to avoid romantic entanglements with people who were bound to linear lives, at least until they were ready to settle down for a number of years, raising children. Pregnancy didn't mix well with time travel. It was odder to do what you had done: settle down with someone who was, as Dara liked to put it, stuck in the slow lane of linear time.

Dara told me about the two of you, eventually; that you'd been lovers before you met Dad, before you settled down with him in 1947. And that when she started visiting us in 1955, she wasn't sleeping alone in the guest bedroom.

I'm not sure if I was madder at her or you at the time, though I've since forgiven her. Why wouldn't I? You've left both of us, and it's a big thing, to have that in common.

1981 IS COLORED SILVER, BEIGE, BRIGHT orange, deep brown. It feels like the afghan blanket Dara kept on my bed while I recovered from my first jump, some kind of cheap fake wool. It tastes like chicken soup and weak tea with honey and lime Jell-O.

And for a few days, at least, 1981 felt like a low-grade headache that never went away, muscle spasms that I couldn't always control, dry mouth, difficulty swallowing. It smelt like a lingering olfactory hallucination of frying onions. It sounded like a ringing in the ears.

"So you're the unnamed baby, huh?" Dara said, that first morning when I woke up. She was reading a book, and set it down next to her on the couch.

I was disoriented: you and Dara had placed me in the southeast bed-room, the same one I slept in all through childhood. (The same one I'm recovering in right now.) I'm not sure if you thought it would comfort me, to wake up to familiar surroundings. It was profoundly strange, to be in my own bedroom, but have it be so different: the striped wallpaper replaced with avocado-green paint; a love seat with floral upholstering where my dresser had been; all my posters of Buck Rogers and Superman replaced with framed paintings of unfamiliar artwork.

"Dara?" I said. She seemed different, colder. Her hair was shorter than the last time I'd seen her, and she wore a pair of thick-framed glasses.

She cocked her head. "That'd be me. Nice to meet you."

I blinked at her, still disoriented and foggy. "We met before," I said.

She raised her eyebrows, like she couldn't believe I was so dumb. "Not by my timeline."

Right. Time travel.

You rushed in then. You must have heard us talking. You crouched down next to me and stroked the hair back from my face.

"How are you feeling?" you asked.

I looked down at your fingernails, and saw again that they were smooth, no jagged edges, and a hint of white at the edges. Dara told me later that you'd arrived two days before me, just so you two could have some time to be together. After all, you'd only left her for 1947 a few days before. The two of you had a lot to talk about.

"All right, I guess," I told you.

IT FELT LIKE THE WORST FAMILY vacation for those first few days. Dara was distant with me and downright cold to you. I wanted to ask what had happened, but I thought that I'd get the cold shoulder if I did. I caught snippets of the arguments you had with Dara; always whispered in doorways, or downstairs in the kitchen, the words too faint for me to make out.

It got a little better once I was back on my feet, and able to walk around and explore. I was astonished by everything; the walnut trees on our property that I had known as saplings now towered over me. Dara's television was twice the size of ours, in color, and had over a dozen stations. Dara's car seemed tiny, and shaped like a snake's head, instead of the generous curves and lines of the cars I knew.

I think it charmed Dara out of her anger a bit, to see me so appreciative of all these futuristic wonders—which were all relics of the past for her—and the conversations between the three of us got a little bit easier. Dara told me a little bit more about where she'd come from—the late twenty-first century—and why she was in this time—studying with some poet that I'd never heard of. She showed me the woman's poetry, and though I couldn't make much of it out at the time, one line from one poem has always stuck with me. "I did not recognize the shape of my own name."

I pondered that, lying awake in my bedroom—the once and future bedroom that I'm writing this from now, that I slept in then, that I awoke in when I was a young child, frightened by a storm. The rest of that poem made little sense to me, a series of images that were threaded together by a string of line breaks.

But I know about names, and hearing the one that's been given to you, and not recognizing it. I was trying to stammer this out to Dara one night, after she'd read that poem to me. And she asked, plain as could be, "What would you rather be called instead?"

I thought about how I used to introduce myself after the heroes of the TV shows my father and I watched: Doc and George and Charlie. It had been a silly game, sure, but there'd been something more serious underneath it. I'd recognized something in the shape of those names, something I wanted for myself.

"I dunno. A boy's name," I said. "Like George in the Famous Five."

"Well, why do you want to be called by a boy's name?" Dara asked gently.

In the corner, where you'd been playing solitaire, you paused while laying down a card. Dara noticed too, and we both looked over at you. I cringed, wondering what you were about to say; you hated that I didn't like my name, took it as a personal insult somehow.

But you said nothing, just resumed playing, slapping the cards down a little more heavily than before.

I FORGIVE YOU FOR DRUGGING ME to take me back to 1963. I know I screamed at you after we arrived and the drugs wore off, but I was also a little relieved. It was a sneaking sort of relief, and didn't do much to counterbalance the feelings of betrayal and rage, but I know I would have panicked the second you shoved me into one of those capsules.

You'd taken me to the future, after all. I'd seen the relative wonders of 1981: VHS tapes, the Flash Gordon movie, the Columbia Space Shuttle. I would have forgiven you so much for that tiny glimpse.

I don't forgive you for leaving me, though. I don't forgive you for the morning after, when I woke up in my old familiar bedroom and padded downstairs for a bowl of cereal, and found, instead, a note that bore two words in your handwriting: *I'm sorry.*

The note rested atop the gilt-edged book that Grandma Emmeline had started as a diary, and that Uncle Dante had turned into both a record and a set of instructions for future generations: the names, birth dates, and the locations for all the traveling members of our family; who lived in the house and when; and sometimes, how and when a person died. The book stays with the house; you must have kept it hidden in the attic.

I flipped through it until I found your name: Miriam Guthrie (née Stone): born November 21, 1977, Harrisburg, IL. Next to it, you penciled in the following.

Jumped forward to June 22, 2321 CE, and will die in exile beyond reach of the anachronopede.

Two small words could never encompass everything you have to apologize for.

I wonder if you ever looked up Dad's obituary. I wonder if you were even able to, if the record for one small man's death even lasts that long.

When you left, you took my father's future with you. Did you realize that? He was stuck in the slow lane of linear time, and to Dad, the future he'd dreamed of must have receded into the distance, something he'd never be able to reach.

He lost his job in the fall of 1966, as the White County oil wells ran dry, and hanged himself in the garage six months later. Dara cut him down and called the ambulance; her visits became more regular after you left us, and she must have known the day he would die.

(I can't bring myself to ask her: couldn't she have arrived twenty minutes earlier and stopped him entirely? I don't want to know her answer.)

In that obituary, I'm first in the list of those who survived him, and it's the last time I used the name you gave me. During the funeral, I nodded, received the hugs and handshakes from Dad's cousins and friends, bowed my head when the priest instructed, prayed hard for his soul. When it was done, I walked alone to the pond where the two of us had sat together, watching birds and talking about the plots of silly television shows. I tried to remember everything that I could about him, trying to preserve his ghost against the vagaries of time: the smell of Kamel cigarettes and diesel on his clothes; the red-blond stubble that dotted his jaw; the way his eyes brightened when they landed on you.

I wished so hard that you were there with me. I wanted so much to cry on your shoulder, to sob as hard and hysterically as I had when you took me to 1981. And I wanted to be able to slap you, hit you, to push you in the water and hold you beneath the surface. I could have killed you that day, Mama.

When I was finished, Dara took me back to the house. We cleaned it as best we could for the next family member who would live here: there always has to be a member of the Stone family here, to take care of the shelter, the anachronopede, and the travelers that come through.

Then she took me away, to 2073, the home she'd made more than a century away from you.

TODAY WAS THE FIRST DAY I was able to leave the house, to take cautious, wobbling steps to the outside world. Everything is still tender and bruised, though my body is healing faster than I ever thought possible. It feels strange to walk with a weight between my legs; I walk differently, with a wider stride, even though I'm still limping.

Dara and I walked down to the pond today. The frogs all hushed at our approach, but the blackbirds set up a racket. And off in the distance, a heron lifted a cautious foot and placed it down again. We watched it step carefully through the water, hesitantly. Its beak darted into the water and came back up with a wriggling fish, which it flipped into its mouth. I suppose it was satisfied with that, because it crouched down, spread its wings, and then jumped into the air, enormous wings fighting against gravity until it rose over the trees.

Three days before my surgery, I went back to you. The pain of it is always the same, like I'm being torn apart and placed back together with clumsy, inexpert fingers, but by now I've gotten used to it. I wanted you to see me as the man I've always known I am, that I slowly became. And I wanted to see if I could forgive you; if I could look at you and see anything besides my father's slow decay, my own broken and betrayed heart.

I knocked at the door, dizzy, ears ringing, shivering, soaked from the storm that was so much worse than I remembered. I was lucky that you or Dara had left a blanket in the shelter, so I didn't have to walk up to the front door naked; my flat, scarred chest at odds with my wide hips, the thatch of pubic hair with no flesh protruding from it. I'd been on hormones for a year, and this second puberty reminded me so much of my first one, with you in 1963: the acne and the awkwardness, the slow reveal of my future self.

You answered the door with your hair in curlers, just as I remembered, and fetched me one of Dad's old robes. I fingered the monogramming at the breast pocket, and I wished, so hard, that I could walk upstairs and see him.

"What the hell," you said. "I thought the whole family knew these years were off-limits while I'm linear."

You didn't quite recognize me, and you tilted your head. "Have we met before?"

I looked you in the eye, and my voice cracked when I told you I was your son.

Your hand went to your mouth. "I'll have a son?" you asked.

And I told you the truth: "You have one already."

Your hand went to your gut, as if you would be sick. You shook your head, so hard that your curlers started coming loose. That's when the door creaked open, just a crack. You flew over there and yanked it all the way open, snatching the child there up in your arms. I barely caught a glimpse of my own face looking back at me, as you carried my child-self up the stairs.

I left before I could introduce myself to you: my name is Heron, Mama. I haven't forgiven you yet, but maybe someday, I will. And when I do, I will travel back one last time, to that night you left me and Dad for the future. I'll tell you that your apology has finally been accepted, and will give you my blessing to live in exile, marooned in a future beyond all reach.

into the waters I rode down

Jack Hollis Marr

HHHHHH

??

hhhhh

well this is fucking useless isn't it

kkkkkkkkkkkkkkkk

that's worse Romaan STOP IT

kkkkkkeyesn'tkkkkkanyoukkkkkus?

there's something now

kkkkkkkaliyekkkkkKKKKKK

fuck that hurt!

what was that

was that my name

try again

kkkkkkaliye?aliye!kkkkkk

YES I can hear it now /// I can HEAR it (guess this is hearing?) this is fucking weird i tell you

kkkkAliyeogdwekkkkiditdkkkkknowwhatthismeans?

Of course I know what it fucking means. I've been working on the project as long as any of them; longer than many. I guess Romaan thinks my work didn't count because none of it's been said aloud, only input through computers. Well, screw him. He's never spoken to anyone working on this back on Earth in person either, only in text relay, but I suppose that's different, right. After all, I'm only the fallback after none of

17

the hearing walking people's brains could adapt to the neural linkage, aren't I?

Must fucking *burn* Romaan, that I could do this and he couldn't, just cos my battered old brain's had to adjust to so much fucking adaptive tech over the decades. *Neuroplasticity.* Nice little word. I suppose it's nice to have something they're jealous of, for once. God knows several degrees don't do it, not when you're old and a woman and deaf.

The hearing's secondary, of course, a side bonus of the main task: that neural linkage between my brain and an animal's. I've been working on it most of my life, this fake telepathy, trying to match the other side's advantage in this strange war.

We tried between people, but it was too overwhelming. We—lost people, in that stage.

(Saira, my dear Saira, who will never be the same; I see her each week, her in her bed and me in my chair, and she smiles and touches my hand, and doesn't speak. Leish, Persis; oh, my dead dears. I reread that poem this week, before the linkage that might have done the same to me, thinking of you. *Rock-a-bye baby, washing on the line.* The drowned dead voices asking, *How's it above?* I imagine your voices in those lines, the white bone talking: *When she smiles, is there dimples? What's the smell of parsley? I am going into the darkness of the darkness forever.* My lost darlings all, I'm so sorry, I am. I think of your sinews in the far-away earth, and how I'm not enough. I can't give you back the world, the smell of parsley, anything at all. Would you have been pleased that we succeeded, in the end?)

My Romaan was the one who worked out the audiovisual part; he's brilliant, if annoying, and being able to promote this sort of shit to civilians always does the Service good, doesn't it? Look at how helpful we are. We can even give veterans back some of the senses we cost them. Know he'll expect me to be over the moon (ha, there's an old-fashioned phrase, now) over *actually hearing* for the first time in my life. That's what I'm supposed to be excited about, isn't it? Noise, or the simulation of it, in my skull. Big deal. Bunch of hissing and clicking and the odd weirdly three-dimensional word that hurts and echoes. I'd stick with text, if it wasn't for the rest.

But. The rest. To get *down there*, and not in a clunky suit but slipping easy as fish through not-water through the strange thick air, resting light in alien animal mind, witch-riding a foreign familiar in a world no human's ever *touched*, not with skin and eyes and nose—and ears, I suppose, those too (do the otterfishcatsnake things they showed me *have* ears?)—this extraordinary modern magic that will, if it goes right, let us eavesdrop on the other and its hidden world… For that, oh God, for *that*. That's worth all the hissing and clicking inconvenience, the drilling in my skill, all the years of different aids.

And, I mean, it's war. Doing my bit for the Effort. All the shit I was meant to do, defective daughter of a military family. Daddy would be *so proud*, the old bugger. Thank fuck he's dead. Last thing I need's him being proud that his broken little girl's able to be a spy.

THEM THE ENEMY THE BAD GUYS *the invaders* (though how they're invading planets that used to be *theirs*…but you don't question that, do you, old woman? Not if you've got the sense you were born with) and worst *the aliens*. NotOfUs. The Others. Headless freaks, The Blob. Spooks, Dad called them. You'd think he'd've been less shitty, given the crap people in his own beloved military called him in his day, but I reckon there wasn't much that'd make Dad be less shitty. Whatever they are, they can move easy through that thick weird air down there, and we can't. We can protect our mining interests in vehicles and suits, missiles and lasers and bombs from space, but we can't walk among them. And we can't do what they can, use our minds as weapons, not directly. Neither of those things.

Well. *I* can, now.

THE ANIMAL THEY BRING ME'S AS high as my knee, as long as my body lying flat. It *does* have ears, little hollow dents. I wish I could reach through the clear glass or plastic and touch it, see if those are thin scales or strange fur, if it's warm or cool against my own smooth skin. Its head is small, sharp-nosed, its legs short like a ferret's, its back supple as a cat's. Its gill-like orifices pulse gently. It looks at me through one nictating eye and then the next, turning its head like a bird. I can't remember its scientific name; we've been calling it the catsnake, and it fits.

I look for the implants but they're invisible, hidden in the scale-spike-fur. My own make my head throb, pried between the plates of my skull. I wonder if it's afraid. I can see its sides expand and deflate slowly as it breathes; maybe it's sedated. Lucky bugger.

we're goingkkkkkto trythelinkage hhhhhere first, Romaan says. The existing link, the one through the computer, is working so much better now, though I'm still adjusting to (the illusion of) actually *hearing* words in my skull. Whatever part of my brain that input stimulates *aches*, a constant weird throb. I'd rather he just used my old text relay, but he's too fucking proud of his invention. And I don't want to look *ungrateful*, do I? That doesn't look good for the cameras that've been trained on me these recent weeks, on and off, for this marvellous breakthrough: hearing to the deaf! Sight to the blind! Pick up thy bed, and walk!

This isn't being filmed, though. The Service doesn't like too many records of its little failures, and we've had too many of those in this long project. I'm very aware of that as I close my eyes, let them wire me up yet again, little clips and clamps, the vibrations that used to be my sound. I move my hands on the padded arms of my chair, feel-hear them run through me: bass throb, treble sting. Familiar and easing, beneath the godawful **kkkkkHHHkkkk**ness they've given me.

And then, the linkage.

Not much at first: sharp little zap all through me, leaving a dull ache in my back teeth, heavy sort of throb in my balls that could almost be pleasure. And then—falling. Not like falling in dreams, not like the sick whirl when you miss a step (I remember that, so clearly), but vertigo, everything spinning, no up no down and nothing to hold onto (somewhere my fingers clench, but I can't feel it, I can't *feel* it, oh god the old paralysis, please no—) and darkness and lights all mixed and through the computer feed my own *screaming* fed back to me on and on and on, ringing through me so that I batter myself against glass, supple body thrashing helplessly between panes like a sample on a slide somehow living and aware, the noise must stop the noise must *stop*—

—and this is not my body and these are not my ears that hear, this is not-i and i together, pulse of gills and beat of strange slow blood. catsnake is this you, i, i-thou, we? catsnake is frightened, and so is aliye. hush, hush. rock-a-bye. you're hurting us, we're hurting us. see, the screaming has stopped. see, there through the distorting glass, the woman in the chair. when she smiles, there's dimples. there, the slow breathing, the calming blood. i-thou-i, resting nested. nest-memory, slow weed-breathing thickness by the slow river's bank, dark hole hollow, infant scale-skin against adult fur: so we are twice mother, thou and i? so I held my baby. how soft her tiny fingers were, her soft and dented skull! so; so. we are together.

—and then we are not, and I am in my chair with everything *hurting* and my fingers tearing at the implants, Romaan shouting **kkkkkk** and the catsnake thrashing panicked in its narrow tank. I get myself free and wheel myself across to it, press my hands against the glass. There are alarms somewhere: I can feel them. The film on its eyes is flickering fast in panic. I have never touched an animal that wasn't human before—how strange it is that I still haven't, when I've been in its bloody head! I wish I could hold it to me like the baby we remembered, touch its strange pelt.

So. Hush. Rock-a-bye. The prick of a needle in my neck, putting me to sleep. Rock-a-bye, Aliye, falling into vertigo-darkness. Rock-a-bye, catsnake. Silence all.

It's months before we're ready, catsnake and me. I'm never able to make it—her?—us?—understand what it is we're doing, and I'm glad. It's its planet down there, after all, that I'm going to be creeping over in its head, when it's released, its planet that we're filleting with mining gear in the cause of Need. There are less of them now than there used to be, I'm told: rivers dammed or dried, swamps drained, and a war zone besides. I wonder what became of the kits in the nest, the thick quiet hollow, if they died or throve. There's no way to ask it. Its animal-brain works in *now* and glimpses, flashed sense-memory. We can't communicate, not properly, though I can stir or soothe it in its glass box.

What's it like to walk again, Mum? He does care so much, in his own way, doesn't he, my Romaan, though he doesn't understand a thing. Desperate to have *given* me that, like he tried to give me hearing I didn't want, had never had. To have given it *back*, as if I ever ran on four stubby legs beneath a wiggly back and tasted electricity in the air. Blinked back through my text relay: It's not so bad. It shuts him up, for a bit.

But there are always others: **You must be so happy, Aliye. Ms Parlak, it must be so liberating for you. Will you tell our viewers what it's like?** No one fucking saying: "Well done, Aliye, you and your team've fucking cracked a military and scientific problem we've been working on for a couple of lifetimes, you genius woman. How does *that* feel?" Romaan's shaking hands, accepting the awards. Saira would be furious with him, our son pushing me into the background like that. She would have understood, my Saira. She would.

I asked Romaan to turn off the noise. He didn't want to—he's been angry, the little shit—but he did it. Eventually. I suppose it hurts to have your mother reject what's meant to be a gift, even an incidental one, a side-effect. He took it better when I explained it helped me with the catsnake, that its hearing from inside is strange and muffled, the underwater booms and bangs close to what I feel through skin and bone without my ears.

It's got another sense, too, strange to me: electric zaps and tingles with nowhere to go, leaving it confused as I was in my vertigo. I've insisted they give it a bigger box, a tub of water to wallow in. It pings its electricity off the plastic sides of the tub and hums to itself constantly, a discontent whining thrum. Everyone in the lab's starting to hate it. Bet they wish *they* could turn off their hearing now. They only get peace when we're hooked up, it and me, curled together in memory-dark, sharing half-memory without words. Smell of a baby's head, taste of riverweed and strange fish, Saira's hands on my skin, sharp sweet jolt of a barbed dick inside us. I'm filling in all sorts of facts for the xenobiologists: they're the ones who really love me now. Not sure what good it does anyone, this knowledge of a dying species on a torn-up world. Seem to be getting even more bitter these days, don't I? And people think old ladies're sweet.

AND NOW. AND NOW WE'RE GOING down. My body in close orbit, catsnake's down to the surface. In the linkage still, and I'm caught in its confusion, the horrible pressure. Both of us screaming. Thick air of its tank shaking. Our bones are splitting—

—and then there is freedom, the wide soft air in which to run far and fast and then free of all the strangeness to leap and twist, dancing delighted loops under a double moon in doubled shadows, there is the river and its taste, familiar-unfamiliar home at last all full of whiskered things that swim and we are in the bottom-mud all stomach-wriggling hunting in hunger for the savour of real food after immeasurable incomprehensible long and homehomehome here an abandoned den to nest in all tail-over-nose and warm and safe **parlakparlakyouhavetomoveit** for time without measure in the slow warm dark.

parlak can you hear me. you have to move it. north-west, their camp is north-west.

in the slow. warm. dark.

parlak.

warmdarkwarmdarkwecan'thearyou

parlak. aliye.

no.

mum.

romaan? (catsnake confused: no names here.) (the kit, the kit that survived.) romaan. What?

go north-west, parlak. mum.

moving confused-obedient, body bending to the river. romaan like this? **yes mum.** deep drumming of machines. taste of metal in not-water, vibration, electricity all wrong. up out of the water, almost-voices, strange smells

there, parlak, there, we're recording. go further in.

shapes moving, vast and almost-formless. not one looks at catsnake, another animal slinking along. ones closelike to catsnake chained up, yowling protest at intrusion. pets? guards? humans've never been this close. only glimpses on screens

lightblare sudden, handshapes reaching, sirens all piercing skin and it

hurtshurtshurt **pull back pull back parlak get out they've detected our signal**and PAINPAINPAIN whiter than light all bloodsmell and *run* go go go waterseeking dive deep engines on water vibrating following. bowels voiding sudden sharpwater stink. deeper twist and flee, swamps shallow and streams thin, up and over down again twisting, catsnake-and-woman flee flee flee and there is

so

much

pain.

darkplace found, hiding now. i'm sorry, i'm sorry, i did this to you, we did, the pain, i'm sorry. this is our fault, oh god, our fault. are we dying?

our belly hurts so very much

and then

…shhhh, otherperson, rider, it tells us without words. shhhh forget, come back to riverlair safe and sleep, safenest dark and silence shhh. come back to dreams of kitsandbabes, lullaby quietsoft sleep. shh now forever

silence dreams, no more machine loudshouting no more the headvoice
intruding **mum** and we are back in riverdeep **mum** metaltaste slipaway
silence song and home to lair and we are back in rock-a-bye memory and
we are **mum** we are we are we.

river is taste softdreaming always. remember whiskerfish crunch
tasteonthetongue and home to lair, curl around. tail over noseyoursand-
mine, share again the memory of scaleskin and babysmell, little fingers
counting lullaby sheep baabaablack and piggies gone to market. what
pigssheep, otherself? and we show though we have never touched, share
pictures once on screens of pink and woolly shape, otherworld wonder to
us both. mothermother curled in dark, otherother nested minds together
away from war

(what is war, otherself)

(hush, hisst, rock-a-bye quiet. goodbye to all that. glad I am to say it)

**aliye, we have to break the linkage. that thing's dying, we have to get
you out. you have to wake up. aliye.**

do you remember/we remember. this is the taste of parsley, catsnake/
this is the winter dreaming, otherself. we remember. we. we do. (I will.)

kkkkkk

Mum. Mum kkkou all right?

*fuck off, romaan. just—fuck off/// i told you before to turn that thing off///
go away. i'm done. i quit i quit. leave me be.*

Rip the connections out of the metal holes in my skull, wheel away
fast. Get away, get away (deeper twist and flee through swamp and river),
nails prying at the implants, ripping pain but they won't come out. I don't
want to hear or walk, not again, never wanted to, that stupid side effect
of war-usefulness that I was supposed to love. I can't I won't. Not part of
that world ever again (sorry Daddy not sorry), not used as a warmachine
instrument, soft furscale or skin body (Saira Leish Persis me) become a
weapon and lost.

Another voice forced on me all **Parlak this is insubordination** and
courtmartial and **lost her mind.** I hunch down in riverdark memory and
rock, as best I can. I'm sorry. I'm sorry.

Oh, my dead dear, forgive.

Everything Beneath You

Bonnie Jo Stufflebeam

You don't know me, but I changed the world.

I have held many names. If I had my choice, I would be known as Zhou, but names cannot be stolen; they must be given, and when your true work is secret it is not easy to be granted the name you deserve. So here I tell this story in the hopes that you, givers of names, weavers of stories, might pin the name to my breast like a badge of honor. And that in doing so, you will also bring my legend into light.

"Zhou" means boat. It means rocking on the water with little beneath you, with everything beneath you. I did not always have my ship, my *Dragon's Bane*. Once, I lived in a fishing village where others had boats but never me. Women were to cook the food and swell with child and stay away from the water, for we were told that the sea dragons had a particular taste for woman's flesh. I too had that taste.

This is a common story. Women who want to be other than woman. For I had a woman's life hunger but a man's mouth, and as I grew older I found purchase in men's company. I was one of them for all but the fishing. Because I would still one day trade my tongue for a child. Because I would be expected not to waste a womb.

I did not explain correctly, for it is complicated. I did not wish to be a man. What I wished was to be wombless, to never be forced to carry that burden. To not have this empty part inside me waiting to be filled. That is what I wanted. To go out on the water. To have no reason to fear the calming crash of waves.

Instead I had parents who did not understand but tried their best. My father bought me miniature wooden boats from the time I was a little girl. I displayed them upon my bedroom shelf, and when I brought home girls, which my parents also did not understand and did not ask much of, the girls asked after my collection. They laughed at my explanation: "One day I will have my own." They did not let my hands cross the skin of their bellies. "You'll jinx me," they said. "No touching." So I touched them elsewhere, and loved them, but never more than the dream that woke me from sleep each night, drenched in salt sweat, smelling of seaweed. The girls beside me held their noses. "You stink," they said, laughing. "Are you sure you're not a man? You smell like one." They teased my neck with their fingertips, pulled me down to them. I did not tell them about the sometimes starfish I found beneath my pillow, about the mornings I woke from dreams so deep my bed was soaked with fishy water.

The gods unwove my parents from this world when I was twenty, both of them together, one day apart. My mother caught the sickness women often caught; she died in childbirth, her body too weak to bear another daughter. My sister too did not survive. My father followed them across the wall. Other children might have hurt at this, that they were not enough to keep their father alive, but I was glad of their passing, for since I had been old enough to bleed between the legs I had thought to leave upon my twenty-first year and never return. I packed up what little I desired of my parents' home: two pairs of clothes, my mother's jade medallion, my father's tangled fishing net, a single wooden ship. I left in the night, walking the stone path out of town. I did not tell the woman sharing my bed that I was leaving. I did not want to worry her, for she was beautiful and kind and would fare better without her love stretched thin between a husband and a lover.

I followed the shore until I could not walk any longer. I slept on the beach, the waves licking my skin. I did not worry for dragons; even the young keep to the deep. My clothes were always wet, my skin bloated and wrinkled.

On my second month of walking, eating only washed-up fish and the sea's weeds, I woke to a woman panting over me, hands on her hips. Her hair was braided with seaweed, her skin beaded with salty sweat.

"I have been searching for you," she said.

"For me?" I said. "I think you are mistaken."

"I am not." She extended her hand. I took it and pulled myself up. Her fingernails, I realized, were made of seashells. Her braid, I saw, did not end but stretched on and on and on, as far down the beach as I could see. The seaweed grew from her scalp. Her hand in mine was grainy, as though she were made of compacted sand. I stood eye to eye with her. Her eyes were the unearthly blue of the ocean, and like the shoreline, the blue throbbed against the outer limits of her pupil. I let go of her hand.

"Where did you come from?" I asked, wiping the grainy residue from my hand.

"Where do you think I came from?"

I knew, of course; there was only one place she could have come from. "How did you get across the wall?" I asked.

"When my father was not watching, I climbed it with my bare hands. Then I followed your footsteps." She gestured back where the ocean had washed all trace of my steps away. As she did so, crabs crawled from the water and arranged themselves in the shape of my prints, scuttling one to the next as I stared. "Your footprints and your smell."

Here is what I wanted, then: I wanted to go, but I did not know where I was going. I wanted to stay and rub my hands all over her belly, but I did not like the thought of all that sand in the creases of my palms. I wanted to ask her more questions, about the way the world was made, about death and dreams, but did not want to know the answers, should they distract me from my destined future. Here is what I said, then: "How far did you walk?"

She waved her hand. "It is not a good question," she said. "Listen, I have been watching you. I have seen your parents and how you did not leave them until the very end. How kind that was, to put your life on hold. How human."

I didn't correct her. I didn't tell her about the plan to escape, parents dead or not.

"I watched you with those women, giving and giving and never taking. Letting them tread on you, so that they might have a moment of happiness, while you had none. I have come here for you. I want what all women want: love, happiness. I want to be yours, forever. I want to live here, on earth, until our end days, and I want you to care for me as you did your parents, though it will be better for you, because I will never die. I will give you everything you have ever wanted."

"Everything?" I wanted so much. The sea, a wombless body, a life of my own.

"You have only to speak it."

I knelt into the sand and rummaged through my sack, pulled out the wooden ship, no bigger than my fist.

"A ship," I said.

She snatched it from my palm. "You call me Huan," she said. "I will make you a ship."

She set the toy at the water's edge. The ocean took it, and as the water touched its wood the ship grew until its prow loomed before us, larger than me, larger than Huan, a great dragon with its mouth hanging wide, forked tongue emerging.

Huan grabbed my hand. Together we jumped aboard before the ship grew too large for us to climb. I looked out on the blank beach and felt a solid deck where before there had been shifting sand. A home where before there had been no hope of home for miles, for weeks. I gripped the railing's edge.

"What now?" I whispered.

"We ask my sister to weave the wind that will push us to sea," said Huan. The wind picked up and beat against the front of the ship, the *Dragon's Bane* come to life.

As the ship slid out from shore I turned to Huan. "What do you weave?"

"I do not weave anything but wool in your world, for I do not have the right loom."

"And behind the wall?"

"What else?" she said. "I weave the sea."

The beach disappeared into the distance as we moved toward the horizon. Huan took my hand in hers. "It is time," she said. "You have promised yourself."

That was not what I wanted, but it was what I had promised, she was right. It would not be such a poor trade, forever for all my desires made true. I squeezed her hand. She clamped her nails into my skin. I winced but did not let go. Blood welled up in the jagged nail marks. She let go. My body ached below my belly, the place those other women would not let me touch, and I doubled over from the pain, my knees on my ship's deck. I felt a pulling in the space between my legs. I grabbed there and found not the vee I had stared at so curiously in the mirror as a child but a knob of flaccid flesh that flopped in my fingers and a thin-skinned sack behind it, much like I had seen on my childhood boy friends when they stripped down on the beach to dive into water I was not allowed to touch. I looked up at Huan; she did not look back at me but instead at the wood grains as though she were studying a pattern.

"What have you done to me?" I said. I did not say that it was half-good, half-bad, for I did not want to give her any sliver of hope that this was what I had wanted. If to be without womb one must also be without the rest of a woman's form, then I was not certain that the trade was worth it.

"It has to be this way," she said to the floor. "I cannot love a woman. It is forbidden."

I wanted to cry but found it difficult. Huan pulled me to my feet. My new body throbbed. She took me into her arms and kissed my lips for the first time. Then she dipped her hands over the ship's side, and a spray of ocean fountained up into her cupped palm. She brought the palmed water to my lips and bade me drink. I did so; it tasted of rice wine and made me drunk with giddiness. I kissed each of her fingers as she sipped the rest from her palm. She kissed me a second time, and as she pulled back a single red string stretched between our lips, wrapped around my tongue. "Swallow," she said in garbled speech, her own tongue tied too. I unwrapped the string and swallowed it down my throat. She did the same, and we moved closer as the string coiled in our bellies. At our third kiss, the string dissolved between us and left a red line down the front of both our lips.

"We are bound," she said when we parted once more.

The ocean wine had not left me. I watched the ocean dance upon the ship's sides. Huan retreated to the stern. I gazed upon her standing there and thought, *Maybe I can love you.* I twitched under my pants and re-membered who I was now. I felt a great drop in my belly like falling. She was beautiful, though, there was no denying that, and the water, too, more beautiful than anything I had laid eyes on. What had I lost to get here? I no longer knew.

Hours later Huan met me in the moonlight, stripped bare of her elabo-rate dressings. She unpeeled me, and I stood naked and ashamed of my new body until she ran her hands down the length of my spine. I felt the surge of blood that gave me a confident strength. We made love on the deck, with Huan astride my waist, and as I came inside her I felt through my body spasm an electric jolt like nothing I had ever felt. Huan pinched the skin around me until I was ready once more and moved until she too screamed into the night air. I never knew one so unearthly could make so human a noise. I held her as she shook back to herself.

It was not easy to see how this would end. It was not easy to feel glad at earning two of my life's dreams in one day. Would I ever not want, would I ever be full? There was no womb in my body, but still there was an empty space I longed to fill.

WHEN I ASKED HUAN ABOUT THE danger of dragons, she laughed the throaty laugh of one with power.

"Do not worry about dragons," she said. "They are not drawn to women. And even if they were, do you see a woman aboard this ship?" She cupped her breasts. "I may look like a woman, but a dragon is no match for me."

Huan told me other things, other truths, other stories. She told me of her six weaver sisters, how they had encouraged her to go when they saw how heartsick she had become. They did not laugh at her love of a human. They did not tell their father. They helped her cross the wall and come to me.

"Don't they miss you?" I asked her.

"No," said Huan. Her seashell fingernails snuck up my legs, cutting the skin as they passed. "My sisters have their weaving to keep them busy. They weave the wind and the sky and even the birds." Huan peered at the sky, right into the sun. "Those birds, there," she said, pointing to a patch of black moving in shadow against the light. "She is watching over us. You have nothing to fear with me, my wife-husband."

I did not fear with her. I did not think about sea dragons or death or even much about the body I had lost, though still I did not feel as though I were myself. My fingers itched for Huan's skin when she was not beneath them. I gripped the ship's stern when I could not hold her for her sleeping. I gripped my new body until she woke and called to me. I loved her stories and fell asleep dreaming of her world behind her wall.

Unlike the other women, she let me touch her belly. Unlike the other women, she did not ask me if I loved her. Then one day she squinted at the sun and frowned. We had been lying across the deck, watching the blue pass us by. She sat up and searched frantic about the clouds.

I shook myself awake. How long had it been since we'd been one? I ran my hand down my beard, which seemed to have grown overnight past my navel.

"What's the matter?" I asked.

"The birds," she said.

"I don't see any birds."

The way she looked at me, one would think there would never be birds again.

She cupped my face in her palm. "No matter what," she said, "come find me."

A crash of thunder cracked the sky and split the ship in half. Splinters showered the water. Huan was gone.

I clung to the ship's corpse as long as I was able, but it sank fast into the sea. I grabbed hold of a plank of wood, the last remnant of my beautiful ship, and tried to slow my breathing so that I would not choke. I searched the water but did not find her. A great pain struck my belly, and I stilled as my body changed again, from man to woman, the flesh between my legs receding.

"Never again will you steal one of my daughters," said a voice of nowhere, no one. It was the squeak of shattered wood planks against one another making words that sounded human. It was the crash of far-off waves upon a far-off shore. "I'll watch you drown where the sea dragons will feast upon your bloated body."

What I worried of in that moment: that Huan was wrong about the sea-dragons, that I would drown, that I would die, and all that I had not said to her would go down with me, buried at the sea's bottom, that I loved her, that she was my sea.

I DID NOT DROWN OR DIE. I wept all the water out of my body, and when it was gone I floated in wait for death to wrap its crooked fingers around my throat. Instead I woke like a beached whale, belly-up in the sand, with a sea-dragon breathing down my throat.

"Don't eat me!" I cried upon waking.

"Eat you?" The dragon huffed salt spray down onto me; it stuck to my skin like mucus. "You're thin as dry muscle. You're the least appetizing thing I've ever seen, though your smell," it said, pressing its nose against my cheeks, "is intoxicating."

"You are drawn to women," I said. "Huan was wrong."

"Women?" The dragon slunk back into the surf, wetting its back. "What is women? I am drawn to those wet things down your cheeks. I am drawn to the gut empty feeling in your stomach. I am drawn to the denial of your desires."

I remembered the women who lay across the sheets of my bed, their night whimpers, how they did not allow me to touch them across the belly, where their future lived. Some of them wanted that future. Others did not, I am certain.

"Did you save me?" I asked.

The dragon blew more spray upon me. "I could not let you drown. Those that drown smell of the sea."

The dragon's back was broad and expansive, a landscape stretching into the ocean: a deck, the dragon's rows of spikes lining both sides like a railing.

"Will you save me again?" I said, imagining myself even then as Zhou, the rider of sea dragons. Only a creature great as this could ferry me to the wall, where I would beg for Huan's hand once again, only this time as myself. I would ask her to remove the womb, and nothing more; there was no more space in this world for the old who spouted lies like the dragon spouted ocean. We were daughters, and we would take what we wanted and give back the rest.

THE DRAGON TOLD ME THIS: THAT it would ferry me until I gained back my desire. That it would be difficult for it to leave until I was satiated. That it would not carry me forever but would carry me for a little while.

"Fair enough," I said. "Take me to the wall." I climbed aboard its back.

The sea we rode upon was not the same sea; purple light danced across the sky each evening, and soon after setting sail I glimpsed in the distance strange little ships off to our sides. The sea appeared as we sailed; to look too far into the distance was to look into nothing. The little ships, we came to know, were giant swallows, and they sailed to either side of us, a flock of them, leading our way forward. I watched them glide across the otherwise-still ocean and listened to them twitter to one another each morning, speaking their secret language. I remembered the birds in my other journeys, and I knew that Huan's sisters were watching over us.

I saw the sea unfold and knew that it was Huan who weaved it, that she still loved me.

The dragon demanded nothing more from me than that I cry upon its skin each night. I did my best, but soon I was too dry for tears. I became thin as paper, until I was paper pressed against my dragon ship's sides. I had to unpeel myself from its edges to move across the bright blue skin.

The sky grew lighter as we grew closer, until it was only purple, untouched canvas, unwoven. The wall came into view. We reached it in three days. It was high and made of jade. As the dragon crawled to shore, my stomach tightened. How would I climb a wall so high? The sparrows circled me until I realized; they were meant to lead me over.

"Goodbye, dragon," I said, letting it bury its face once more in the stink of my clothes.

"Your sorrow is lighter already," said the dragon. "I am both happy and sad."

I climbed a sparrow's back and grabbed tight to its feathers. I looked down upon the sea glistening blue and white and black; my body called out to return to it. The air was too dry. But there was no going back, not without Huan.

On the other side of the wall massive trees stretched into an endless white sky, their leaves made of gold bells that rang in a soft wind. The trees did not stay in one spot, as trees did in our world, but moved with me, their roots sliding along the ground. They swatted at us with crooked branches. I clutched at the swallow's feathers as she jerked to miss them. Finally we came to an area free of trees, where instead wooden pavilions as tall as the trees swayed in silver light. Inside the open-sided pavilions we passed up-close, weavers and other creatures slept standing up, leaning against the beams.

The sparrow slowed and descended onto a carpet of red moss that stretched below us. I climbed off its back and stood looking up and down the rows of buildings so tall I could not see the tops from the ground, wondering where to go. I did not have to wonder long, for from one of the pavilions stepped a giant man-god in bright red robes that I realized formed the moss at our feet. His eyes were wooden and creaked as they moved. He was this place, and so I knew that he must be the king.

"Climb," he said, and he grabbed hold of the white beard that reached to his shins and shook.

"What?" I said, shrinking back from his booming voice.

"I expect you have come here to talk, and so I am telling you to climb, so that we might be face to face and can speak like two who are equal." I grabbed hold of the beard and began to climb. He lifted the beard once I was halfway up, plucked me from his hairs, and sat me on his shoulder. "Though we are not equals at all," he said. "We will never be equals, as I am sure you know. Why have you come to me?"

"Your daughter," I said, holding a strip of his robe so that I would not fall. "I want to be with her."

"You have come a long way," he said. "And you do smell like a man, it is true. You have been at sea. You have much in common with men. But you did not want to be a man when my daughter made you so. You are a man no longer, and your marriage is revoked. Should you go back to being a man, your marriage would be restored."

"I can't do that," I said, for I knew that I would not be happy. I would have his daughter's love, but what of my own love? Was there a reason he could not give me everything I wanted? He was tall, and loud, and weaved the world. He weaved us into being. I could hardly speak I was so angry. Why wouldn't he just give us all we wanted?

"Yes, you humans cling to what power you have. You want more than you deserve. Fine. I am impressed by how far you have come. I will not make you leave without reward. I give you two choices, then. Your first: you may have all that you ever wanted. You may keep your womanness, your womb. You may be with my daughter as you are. You may have another ship with which to sail the seas."

I could taste it, the satisfaction of all my life's dreams met, like salt water on my tongue.

"Or, your second choice, you can give it to all of your kind. You cannot have my daughter's hand but can instead gift choice to others, to all of your humanity. I will make this man-woman power malleable. I will give you control of what you are. I will give you all blank slates to work with as you please."

It was not a fair choice, to pit my desires against those of my fellow people, against those of the women I heard cry at night, who could never be with me forever always, the way some of them wanted. I would be lying if I said I did not want both things but wanted the first more. My belly ached with the weight of this decision. How dare he.

But one cannot change all the world in one day. One cannot take all the power at once. I would do what I could. I would give up Huan, beautiful Huan, who must be waiting for me, who had asked me to come for her, who I would never see again, to give my people their own power.

"You know what my choice is," I said.

"I knew," he said, "that you were a fool when I saw you riding your dragon to meet me."

"Can I see Huan?" I said. "One more time? Can I see her?"

"It will upset her," he said. "You have chosen your people over her. I cannot be sure that she will forgive you that. No, I think it best you leave the way you came." He picked me up with his too-large fingers and dropped me upon the swallow's back. "I hope you enjoy the complicated nature of the world you wrought. I made things simple for a reason, you know." The swallow lifted into the air. I was grateful that I could no longer see him, though I could still hear his calls. "You will regret the ambiguity. You will regret the confusion. Things will not be as you think they will."

When we reached the wall, his voice disappeared, and I sank my face into the bird's back and screamed out Huan's name.

MY NEW *DRAGON'S BANE* WAS WAITING for me. The smell of my sadness, it said, was impossible to ignore. I did not go back to my homeland to check on the women there; those I met across the sea told me stories, of the confusion, of women making themselves men making themselves women again. Of in-between people. Of people of neither. I was no longer part of that world. Maybe I never had been.

The sea brought me to you all, though neither I nor my ship led the way. We sailed on waves unfolding before us and washed up on your shore. You who bestow legends. You who weave stories into the world. I ask you for my name. I ask you for a legend never-changing, where Huan and I may be together in story if not in life. This is what I believe she wants, why she wove the sea to take me here.

Give us this, please. A story that ends in happiness, a story of love. Give me a name that suits me.

Contents of Care Package to Etsath-tachri, Formerly Ryan Andrew Curran

(Human English Translated to Sedrayin)

Holly Heisey

IN THIS PACKAGE:

1. Three letters. (With our instructions on opening order, per Human dating system.)
2. One musical instrument, harmonica.
3. One plastic package containing three toothbrushes.
4. One tube of toothpaste.
5. One cloth Earth mammal, bear (unsure of further classification), filled with synthetic material. (We are sorry for the lack of symmetry, the cloth mammal was obviously damaged and repaired at some point. We were told not to modify it.)

First letter:

July 18, 2041

DEAR RYAN,

They told me you'd get this after, so you won't really be reading my words, will you? And you told me yourself you'd forget your own language, though I hope to God you don't forget your planet, and your wife. And your daughter.

Ryan, how could you? I know this was supposed to be a nice letter to settle you into your new life, to bridge the transition, and God knows you tried to talk me into doing it, too—

I'm sorry.

No, I'm not fucking sorry. You left me for another species. Not another woman, Ryan, or even another man. Another fucking *species*.

If this is supposed to be the last letter, I guess I should say I love you.

Are you dead now? Can I mourn you?

Fuck.

—Sophie

Second letter:

July 19, 2041

HEY, BRO.

The Sedrayin consulate people said you'll be travelling in a bubble-ship that breaks some sort of theory, and time will move faster for us than it does for you. That's okay, I get that.

I just wanted to tell you that I support you in this. I don't understand it, and I've asked the pastor what she thinks, if it's even in the Bible. She quoted me some nonsense that had nothing to do with anything, and then just said the best thing I could do was accept you where you're at.

I like that.

Because I've always looked up to you, you know? You were so different. I used to make fun of you for sneaking out at night to go and look through your telescope, especially when there were a lot more...ah, entertaining things you could be doing while sneaking out. And you just smiled, and said it made you feel calmer. And maybe I didn't press too hard, because I didn't like when you were so restless. I knew you weren't happy.

But man, coming out as another species? Bro, I'm still trying to wrap my head around that. I look at the Sedrayin in their enviro suits, with their blue skin and ~~weird~~—sorry Bro, I still have a hard time, I'll get better—oddly shaped oval eyes, and the way they kind of walk with that forward slant, like they're coming at you with all they've got.

Dude. You have always walked that way. Oh my God, I never noticed that until now.

Bro, I guess you look different now.

Anyhow, I hope you remember me. Meet a hot alien babe and fall in love. Have lots of alien babies. (Whoa, Jenna will have alien siblings???) I'm sorry they couldn't come with you. Man, I know that's hard.

I love you. I hope you're happy, now. And, you know, have fun seeing the stars for real, and living on another planet! Dude, how cool is that!

—*Gabe*

P.S. Oh, I found your harmonica the other day and thought I'd send it along. Maybe that wasn't the best idea, because do you even have lips now? Well, something's gotta blow air.

Third letter:

July 20, 2041

MY DEAR RYAN,

Oh, I'm sorry. I should call you Etsath-tachri now, right? Yes, I checked the spelling.

Etsath. I'm sorry I waited until the last minute to write this letter, I almost didn't make it in time, but they held the courier shuttle at the consulate so I could write this.

I just wanted to say, I love you, son. This is all so new to me, the aliens being here at all—what are there, twenty-something species we've now had contact with? And I saw on the news that there's another ship inbound from outside Jupiter. But honey, it's hard. This isn't the world I grew up in. The world I grew up in was having a hard enough time accepting people like myself and Leanne, but I—we—love you so much that we're changing, too. We're changing the way we look at the world. Or any world, if I think about it.

We always knew you were special. You spent hours with your science books and games, and you loved your art, though the galleries said it was too symmetrical. I guess that makes sense, now. I won't ever let anyone paint over your mural of the stars in your bedroom.

I packed some toothbrushes and toothpaste, I know you always forget those.

I know we've already said our goodbyes. I will miss you like nothing I've ever missed before.

Thank you, son, for being my son. For being born to me. You were the greatest gift the universe could ever give me.

~~Be the best damn Sedrayin you can be.~~ Be yourself.

Love,

Mom

P.S. Please forgive Sophie. I've talked with Jenna. She misses you, but she said she knows you'll be watching over her in the stars. She wanted to send something, too. She said to hug her teddy bear whenever you're feeling sad or lonely, and you'll remember how much she loves her daddy and be happy again. The kids, they are so quick to understand.

The Petals Abide

Benjanun Sriduangkaew

IN THE WOMB-TANK CODED WITH THOUGHT and memory, Twoseret learned three things: that her life will be full of peace, that she will never die, and that she will know precisely one tragedy. These facts are absolute, untarnished by chance and impregnable to intervention.

After that, petals started blooming in her mouth.

THEY COME AT DAWN AT A regulated hour; she knows to be awake with her mouth empty so she does not choke. A tickle in her throat, a pressure against tonsil, and they emerge fluttering: the shape of hands with spindly digits, the color of unlit space that demarcates empires. She likes to speculate whose hands they might be modeled on, or whether they are the quintessence of hands, a mannequin standard.

They are pristine and velvet, untouched by teeth and untainted by saliva: like no part of the body at all, no effort to resemble tissue or keratin.

Here Twoseret finds her orders, in the capillaries that call to the light of accretion disks and press against her nerves in synesthetic licks. The petals are the flowers of prophecy, the blooms of destiny. As long as she follows their instructions, like any memorialist Twoseret stands deathless.

She arranges the petals, four, radiant—fingers pointing out, fluttering in the low salted wind, the heels of their palms held down by mosaic stones. A murmur of sun slants across unlight velvet. She bends to read, sibyl to her own fate.

The city ground is a canvas, the avenues brushstrokes, history a palette. An avian view yields faces gone to carcass and archive, some self-portraits, others celebrating personal affection and past deeds—the war heroes, the founding scholars, the beloved siblings. Within these walls, nothing is forgotten. Outside them, everything is.

Twoseret walks through parabola gates of porphyry and persimmons heavy on the bough, down bridges whose curves follow theta-rhythms. The petals have given her a course, a target.

It will be a channel, she expects, through which she may monitor a life and from that material suture together a new person. Broad edits are crude: a wholesale revision of a planet's chronology, a rearrangement of civil wars and epidemics and sundry. The work she does, however, requires more finesse. In identity reassignment the subject must feel at home in their new path, natural to a strange career and family and spouse as though they have always lived this life. The more moving pieces there are, the more skilled a memorialist has to be. Twoseret counts herself one of the best in the city, if not the very best.

The only one to whom she conceded supremacy was Umaiyal, but ey is long gone.

She stops at the basin of faces, where bone dunes in a hundred twenty-seven colors—most visible, a few not—rotate hourly, resolving into the faces of the first memorialists. There, at the border of grinding femurs and fibulae, she finds a casket.

The edges of it are sharp as invasion, its casing radiant as war-beads, its lid heavy as regret. Around this a homunculus of encryption hovers, epidermis full of paradoxes clenched shut. She coaxes them open, by intuition and determination. Her routines grant her a surplus of leisure, and she's spent it on dead languages, ciphers, puzzle-solving.

She expects a soldier, a spy, a politician of high standing. Those are ever the first to develop a taste for sedition. But once the homunculus has been whispered and peeled off, she finds instead a foreign assassin.

Beneath a canopy of chameleon fish and isometry rosettes, she thaws the body. Their face is blunt, singed at temple and jawline by ecclesiastic tattoos. Their neck looks as though branded by bird beaks, their biceps abraded by bird claws. The marks of the Cotillion and the divine Song under which they march.

The assassin is armed too, but Twoseret is unconcerned, for the petals did not forecast that she will die today. When the fluids have been drained and the cryogenic phase deactivated, the assassin wakes: all at once, without the transitional stage between occluded cognition and full alertness. The gaze that latches onto Twoseret's is clear and iridescent with corneal implants.

They jackknife and heave. A splat of saliva and bile, so black, so blue. Waking up this way is never pleasant, no more than being decanted from a tank. Twoseret has vivid recall of her own birth, her first breath and emergence, of volition beyond the crèche-parents.

She reads their name and gender as they come online. "Sujatha Sindh." The name susurrates like parched leaves, from a language spoken on several Hegemonic constituents. Not entirely foreign, but the two empires have regular exchanges; citizens of one flee and become refugees in another, diasporic. Their descendants repeat the cycle.

The assassin gains their composure in turns, gray and shuddering, on their back, then on their knees. Twoseret offers a hand; they take it. Long fingers, velvet where synthetic dermis has replaced fingerprints.

"You have been sent to abduct or kill one of us," Twoseret murmurs, off the dossier. "Did you choose a specific target or would any of us have done?"

"My instructions were not discriminating." Sujatha's voice is a blasted echo, its wealth and timbre gouged out. Cotillion personnel wield their voices for sacred music, better than any weapon. Without that the assassin's bite is much blunted.

Because they do not ask what their fate will be, Twoseret does not provide. Perhaps they already know, as surely as if they had read the same petals Twoseret did. She gives them her shoulder, her arm around the heft of a torso honed to swift retribution, limbs trained to kinetic poetry. Those too have been weakened, ligament augmens snipped off, bone enhancement ripped out. Where once there was puissance, now there is brittle mortality.

Muscles spasm in Sujatha's cheeks as they walk. It's not the only part of them that trembles in withdrawal from the destruction of their voice. Twoseret imagines how it was done. An operation, painless. An appointment with precise instruments during which Sujatha was awake for every minute, nerves primed to open wounds. Dilated time.

Sujatha's prison is a palimpsest of deep-sea salt and abyssal cold. Its frictive patterns convert to musical notations, echoing the voice of a deceased memorialist. The assassin gazes at the water. Their mouth parts, habit, but they press it shut.

"It isn't really a song," Twoseret says.

"All ordered sound is part of the eternal symphony. The birth of universes. The end of them. Entropic culmination and singularities." Sujatha touches their throat. "I will not sully any of it with the voice I have now."

Twoseret does not present a secular objection—that sound is merely sound, can be synthesized and reproduced; that sound has no purchase without air, and what is a deific verity that cannot cross stars? She helps Sujatha settle into their bed of solid-state husks and slaughtered engine cores. Battle salvage is material for art. It speaks of Hegemonic peace spreading abroad, a reminder of the army's might. What are memorialists and their city without the commanders and the troops, their strategies and victories?

That thought dogs the heel of another. "Who captured you?" For someone must have, an act of heroism and advancement.

Sujatha takes a cracked breath, perhaps weighing their tactics: to tell, to withhold. "A soldier. Oridel Nehetis."

Twoseret's expression must have spoken louder than her silence. She corrects that. "I see," she says, and seals the oceanic palimpsest between them.

"Do you remember," she asks one of her age-mates, "Umaiyal?"

His answer is interrupted by a trio of petals. He catches them as they fall, fans them like a spread of cards on the gameboard between him and Twoseret. "Yeah," Riam says, reading his instructions, not disclosing them. "How goes it for em? The exception."

The exception to have punctured the city's skin from the inside. The exception to have left. Twoseret will never know how this was done, what deal was brokered, what Umaiyal's petals spoke; whether this was mandate or Umaiyal's volition. She only knew—knows—the loss like a suppurating hurt. Out there ey goes by Oridel, a good elegant name. Ey wears eir face differently too, sharp-boned and pearl-pale, chased in nacre that traces and wraps eir skull in place of a scalp. A short clip that Twoseret plays, over and over, with Umaiyal caught mid-chuckle. Wry and polished in dress uniform, eir throat a choker of respiratory implants for work in toxic battlefields. She wonders how many deaths ey has logged.

Umaiyal once asked her what name she would take, out there, if she could leave. On a whim she picked Nehetis.

Twoseret moves her piece, desultory, not much caring for the game's result. "Ey's as well as can be expected. Alive, certainly."

"So you don't know either?" Riam flicks his head, apologetic. "Uncharitable of me. Not as if they would have let you keep in touch. I always thought if anyone got out, it'd be Umaiyal. And ey would take you with em."

Umaiyal never asked. One day ey was there, the next gone. Even eir clothes, eir jewelry: the nexus-choker of corneal opals, the eigenvector jacket she gave em.

"I'm content here," says Twoseret. "Aren't we all?"

The petals yoke her to the prisoner's cycles. She comes to know the palimpsest's smell as well as that of her own bed, and Sujatha's face as well as her own reflection. The questions she puts to the assassin are broad and she's rarely interested in the answers, so much so it provokes Sujatha to say, "You aren't what I would call an adequate interrogator."

Twoseret sinks her hand into the water, warm and viscous as gestation plasma. She imagines pulling Sujatha through it and the assassin coming out her side reborn, a blank canvas numinous with possibility. "I'm no interrogator. Would you like to talk about something else? Tell me secrets. Not state matters, just little things."

Sujatha sits cross-legged, and despite the palimpsest distortion they look much better: they'll never have their old strength back, nor their voice, but their colors are healthier. Umber rather than jaundiced sepia. "Why would I do that?"

There is an acid-edge of animus that Twoseret finds strangely personal. "To pass the time, as I can't persuade you to sing and you wouldn't learn origami or any of the games I've brought you."

"I play nothing well behind a prison cell, and I'm not a graceful loser." The assassin cranes their neck back, looking up. From their perspective the world entire is sunlight filtered through depth, exegesis by fiber-optic sharks and hydrogen anemones. "There's a dessert of egg yolk shaped like gilded drops that I indulge in to a fault. From each of my bed-partners I've collected a necklace, a scarf, a collar; as long as it's been close to them like a garrote. In all my life I've fallen in love only once."

"Yes?" The barrier is permeable up to a point. Twoseret encounters soft resistance once her hands have sunk through to the wrist. "Tell me about love."

They laugh, a stutter-bark of actuators guttering out. "You've never been happy. No species of love would be known to you."

"If happiness is freedom from deprivation and pain, then I've never known anything but."

"Happiness," Sujatha says, "is more than that. You haven't seen—"

"Beyond this circle of existence," Twoseret says, drawing up her knees and resting her chin on them, "the calculus of being distills to this: rule or be ruled. Under Hegemonic peace your past is robbed; under the Cotillion your future is sealed. There are only so many places for power, and most will never rise to them nor even see the path."

The assassin blinks, a play of lamplight on black pearl in their irises. "You aren't what I expected."

"Mindless, you mean? As long as I follow the petals, nothing is forbidden. The province of my mind belongs to me alone, and in *that* I have what most outside this city never will."

Perhaps some of that turns a key in Sujatha's heart. For the assassin says, "I'll tell you of my love. Much you won't comprehend and have no basis with which to compare, but I'll tell you."

"And I'll tell you of mine." Twoseret leans forward, her nose almost nuzzling the vertical tide. "We may surprise each other."

"The person I love is absolute, untarnished by loneliness and unsullied by lust. They require no justification to exist; they are beholden to no outer forces or obligations. Like the drive of a warship, but those require guidance and crew, hull and superstructure. Like a sun, but those has a finite age and obey greater forces. So," Sujatha says, softly, "they are like the Song, given human body, human visage. And to think that is to blaspheme beyond absolution."

"Today, the person I love is shaped like a hole. But once upon a time that they had arms like polished teak, cheeks like bathyal amber, and eyes like lodestars." Twoseret unrolls permutative paper in her lap, tears out a precise square. "When they couldn't sleep they liked to keep their hands busy, and they'd fold this into animals neither of us has ever seen. Lava alligators and polar butterflies, thunder wasps and aquatic bees. They kept their hair very long, dipped in an attar of comets. I'd try to braid those paper things in it, but the hair was difficult of temper, just like their owner."

Sujatha has flinched as though each of Twoseret's sentences have pierced them, needle by needle under the nails. "That isn't a person," they say, voice tight. "That's a childhood."

"Childhood is formative; no person springs into being fully-formed, like a sun or warship or holy music. Everyone has a past. That's the *definition* of personhood."

"The larval stage of it, perhaps. The person someone *becomes* is honed by time, tempered by experience, the true shape." The assassin frowns. "Do you fence, wrestle, or box? I feel the need to test you in combat."

Twoseret laughs and gazes with interest at the hard lines of Sujatha's body. Umaiyal was built like a willow, but out there ey would have received combat augmens and assiduous training would have changed em. "I don't do any of that, and in your state you wouldn't be able to defeat a child. I'll play you any sort of game, conquer you in any sort of puzzle."

"You're trying to offend me."

"Yes. No. But tell me more about your personal blasphemy."

The assassin's mouth curves then, tracing the arc of a blade. "The person I love has far more in common with me than you, than this city, than anything you know."

It is, perhaps, not wrong. Twoseret puts two calligraphic avenues between them before she allows her hand to press against her sternum as though to staunch a wound. But her palms come away clean.

In her room, roofed by silver beaten chiffon-thin, she composes. On the malleable walls that submit to her nails, on the permutative paper that yields to her thumbs. She sketches the same figure again and again, an outline of slender limbs and rounded narrow shoulders. Then it becomes more sinuous and muscle-dense, shedding the eigenvector jacket and robe for something more martial. Close-cut uniform that gloves the body, a long coat with severe hem. Twoseret leaves out the sidearm.

A visualization is not required, but she has always found it helpful. The petals give instruction and goal, but the means to achieve them are her own. She begins scanning her own memory segments. A person is gestalt. There is past, present, and the potential for the future.

Now that Umaiyal is gone, of the entire city she is the best memorialist alive.

TWOSERET GAZES THROUGH SUJATHA'S EYES. SHE is almost Sujatha, for a while. Total immersion has its risks, but the best of her compositions often arise from that.

Sujatha's meetings with Oridel-Umaiyal began at a distance, observing a figure limned in pale light through a corridor of spiral glass. A figure tall and compactly made, unrecognizable to Twoseret. Over weeks the assassin observed, followed.

Was noticed, one day.

An eel-twist of the street where Umaiyal disappeared. The assassin sidestepped, turned in time to catch Umaiyal's knife on an armguard. The blade locked; Sujatha pulled. Fell with Umaiyal as ey went down, hand on throat—precise pressure—and knees straddling arms.

Both held still: aortae marching to the same adrenal tempo, muscles stretched taut. Then Umaiyal smiled. "You're very good," ey said. "Galling as it is to admit, I'm no match for a Cotillion assassin. Had you wanted me dead, I would have been cremated a week ago. So what is it?"

Sujatha drew back slightly, caught by frankness. "Captain."

"Shall we get a drink? My treat."

They did, and more than once. An uneasy negotiation, tenser for Sujatha than for Umaiyal. By their fifth meeting in a club of enameled ice, Umaiyal leaned forward and pulled the trigger on a question both of them had always circled around. "You targeted me for my background, didn't you?"

In that club, at a table laden with conch-shell bowls, Sujatha stopped eating. Curved a hand around a glass, took a long, deliberate sip.

"I can give you a way into *that place*. Only you'll have to trust me." Umaiyal drew closer. "That will be my gift to you."

It takes Twoseret two heartbeats to realize *that* had been spoken to her. Meant for her ear, not Sujatha's. It is not the only instance—many other times Umaiyal couched eir messages in conversations with the assassin. *There's a childhood place I miss, where the bones resolve into faces* or *Have you ever seen upside-down gardens?*

Where I was born, Umaiyal said as ey stood watching the breaking of Sujatha's voice, *there's a palimpsest that sings.*

As Umaiyal put a stunned Sujatha in the casket, ey held the assassin's hand, saying, "This is the closest I can get to going back." A harsh breath inhaled. "This is the closest I can get to talking to you." The lid clipped.

"I'll never be able to go back, I'm sorry, I didn't say goodbye. And I can't explain. There are no petals here, but even so some things are forbidden. Some things are prophecy, and to disobey them is to accept death."

The casket slipped shut.

For hours after, Twoseret is not herself. She remembers being in a stronger body; she remembers parts of the surgery that took her—*their*—voice. An immersive link to the subject's memory doesn't give her the subject's feelings.

Nevertheless Sujatha's want is plain, blazing gold across the fabric of their recall. "The person I love is absolute," she says softly, startling herself when what comes out is not in Sujatha's voice. The original voice brimming with Song, one with the code of existence.

The next time she visits the assassin, she brings a small drawer of perfumes captured in vials of chameleon jade. One takes on the texture of Twoseret's palm as she handles it. "Do you know the scent?" she asks, opening a window through the prison-tide. "I've no idea if this is available outside. Probably it is. Some of us have hobbies but I don't think anyone distills perfumes, so this must have come with a supply drop."

Sujatha edges forward. Stiffens in recognition. "What of it?"

"The person I love—" The euphemism, still. "Left this behind, even though they were some of eir favorites. No time to pack it, I suppose, and these bottles are so fragile. I don't wear perfume, though. Do you?"

No answer.

"It'll spoil eventually, go rancid." Twoseret pulls more vials out of their slots, idly rotating one between her fingers. "I could have the containers recycled. The perfume though, that's a bit of a waste."

"Then I might as well accept them."

"There are other things, too." Talking around and keeping up the pretense, like *Umaiyal* is the forbidden secret: profane or else too pure and wondrous a word to utter. "I'll bring them. Clothes that don't fit me, jewelry, and so on."

Two sets of petal later, Sujatha smells and dresses a little like Umaiyal. They must know this, but do not object and seem content simply to have Umaiyal's belongings next to their skin, scenting their clavicles. When Twoseret brings them a lattice necklace, their breath hitches: an object that's lived next to Umaiyal's throat.

She cannot claim to understand their terrible longing for Umaiyal; it seems so much, and burns so bright, for such distance and so little return. But it is there, their shared knot, and she makes use of it.

Desire complicates, between *to love* and *to want to be*. A certain affinity between those two, she thinks, a bridge that can be built and directed. She makes more sketches of Sujatha, of Umaiyal as she remembers em. She compares and finds herself not dissatisfied. *That will be my gift to you.*

One day she lets down the prison, which after all was for effect rather than any real intent to cage. As the water cascades away and the kaleidoscope of sharks evaporates, the petals come. Twoseret cups her hands for them, spends half a minute absorbing their directives; when she looks up she finds the assassin staring at her, appalled. "It's nothing," she tries to explain. "It doesn't hurt. This is only an artist's whim made real by a biotech."

"It's not all right," Sujatha says then surrenders to silence, as though even that thread of anger exhausts.

"It's more *interesting* than receiving messages the conventional way." She folds her petals into her dress. By nighttime she will have to dispose of them properly, a ritual.

Sujatha tires easily, has to be eased down onto benches and soft grass. Twoseret eventually lets them rest at a fountain that gurgles gossamer pennants, translucent kites, streamers in soft copper and gold.

Eyes shut, the assassin says, "You don't feel the limits of your world? You don't find it confined, claustrophobic even? This place isn't even large enough for fifty million. What's up there isn't a sky. This is all you will ever see, all the air you'll ever breathe. What you do, how you live, it's all bound up in those fucking flowers. Doesn't it chafe? Doesn't it *choke?*"

"You are very angry," Twoseret observes, "on behalf of someone you don't know and hardly like. I have no illusions that you'd choose my society, given other choices. How can it matter if I live a constricted life, or one whose limits of liberty you disapprove?"

"The person you love—" The words come out like retched poison. "Did they live like this?"

She catches a twist of streamer; it convulses around her wrist, prehensile, rose-touched platinum. "To that you already know the answer or you wouldn't have asked. It's a life. For most of mine, I never lacked for

anything. I still don't see why you were sent here, though; you obviously
can't get out."

The assassin smiles a rictus. "As I came, I was transmitting my location.
That stopped at a point, but the approximation is sufficient."

"This entire city can be moved."

"Very slowly. With considerable difficulty. It'd be a feat of years. Our
ships are much faster, inescapable, will not be outraced. Of course ne-
gotiating the gravity snarl that protects this place would be a trick and
a half, but the same maze that safeguards you also makes relocating the
city...vexing."

Twoseret strokes Sujatha's head the way she might soothe a distressed
animal. The assassin's hair used to be shoulder-length, in those memories,
but it's been growing since. Someday it will be long, serpentine, and she
will find an attar of comets to anoint it full of light. "Will they attack?"

A short laugh, that same noise of failing machines. "No. We only wanted some idea of where this might be, just in case. For that I gave my life,
without regret. Acquiring this information for the cost of a single person
is an extravagant bargain."

"Patriotism is very nice." Twoseret has never experienced such a concept,
but she means it. Belief—faith—in some vast, grand ideal must be reassuring. The notion that after one has passed, one's contribution will live
on as part of that ideal or, in this case, system of brutal oppression. Still,
it's certainly a greater thing than a single human being or even a billion.

"You're mocking me." But this too is said listlessly, the annoyance per-
functory.

"No, I think fervor is admirable. Passion is its own virtue. It animates.
It can give an otherwise ordinary thing a terrible magnetism, an ensnar-
ing brilliance..." She unties the streamer and casts it forward, where it
catches on an updraft, snapping toward the sky-that-is-not. "Oh, that's
why. All this time, you've been so weakened but there's been this—fire?
This gravity, this pull. I think that's why ey decided on you."

Sujatha's head rises a fraction. "*Decided* like a calculation, the way you
say it."

"It probably was. But not an exact thing, no, eir variables were more
organic than numbers. Perhaps it had to do with how you moved, the
way you sang, how your face was limned in profile at sunset. And always
the fire that burns within you, visible between your teeth, behind your

eyes." She helps them to their feet. "Do you want to see the gardens? Ey loved those."

Twoseret continues sketching in her head, drawing points of like and unlike. A framework of contrast and potential markers for synaptic joints. In the swaying garden with its inverted field, she picks clusters of edible hydrangea, mangosteens the size of her thumb, syrup oranges with thin ripe peel about to burst. These and more she puts in Sujatha's lap, absent the assassin's interest. As the pile grows they pick at it, a bite here, a lick there. Inevitably they have juices running down their fingers, their chin, sticky and fragrant.

She thinks of kissing them away, drop by drop. In the end she unthinks it. Not the right person, not the right time. As of now they are both in love with an idea.

Twoseret stirs to the city quaking and Sujatha's shadow lying across her like whip-scars. "I know you're awake," the assassin says in that fractured, devoured voice. "We're under attack."

She peers up at them through her eyelashes. "From whom?"

"Must you ask?"

"But they'll kill you too," she points out calmly as she pushes to her elbows, dislodging sheets, baring shoulders and breasts. Baring, too, the places on her ribcage and waist where the incisions were made and implants seeded so she would be able to receive the petals each morning.

Sujatha's gaze snags on those places and the cartography of their features shifts, sideways, to that region between disgust and fascination. It makes Twoseret want to say that the scars are quite all right: she chose to keep them when they could have been operated away to smoothness, leaving skin unmarred. Of course their horror is really for Umaiyal's sake, the thought that Umaiyal once lived like this, bore these same scars. Still Sujatha is nearly tender, as though she's a small child prone to spooking. "Are you in shock?"

"Oh, no." Her bed trembles as though a beast shaking itself from hibernation, sloughing off sleep and matted grass, or whatever it is that animals coming out of hibernation do. Paper moths flutter from their shelves. "I'm in full command of myself." She doesn't say that the petals came early today, and they did not instruct either Twoseret or the city to die. No doubt pointing that out will only distress the assassin.

Twoseret stands all the way up, knows as she turns her back that Sujatha stares at the tiger-stripes up her spine that culminate at the top—below her nape—in a dainty port, flourished in nacre and tiny citrines. "You believed I'm incapable of love because I have never experienced its prerequisites. Is it so hard to believe I'm not panicking because I've had no experience of terror, of illness or fear of dying?"

"Even a creature like you must retain her survival instinct."

"How wrong you are." Twoseret shrugs into her dress of suede cuffs and amethyst whorls, the fabric whispering like origami in fire as it molds to her. "Umaiyal used to help me dress, pick my clothes. Ey had—still has, I should think—these long fingers, with calluses from the wood-carving ey used to do as a hobby. Ey wasn't much good at it, though ey tried to make me birds." The calluses would be different now. Imprints from wielding a chisel and from wielding a gun are nothing alike, she imagines.

"Who?"

"The person you and I love. Pretending further is obscene, isn't it? I don't know if ey ever gave you eir birth name." She slides her shoes on, lavender gray, texture almost petal-like.

Sujatha presses their lips into a hard line and leads her by the hand. Twoseret is startled at the force of their grip, the limber grace of their stride, their familiarity with the puzzle-paths. An assassin would of course be able to map a place from memory, with speed and attention. Even so the unerring way with which they negotiate the city fills her heart, and their recovered strength makes her glad.

"My superiors have given me up for dead," Sujatha says as they emerge into artificial morning under the sky that is not. "So have I. For all intents and purposes I'm no longer alive; my presence makes no difference."

"But we're running somewhere rubble can't fall on us. A corpse doesn't run." Though ultimately the city's swarm-bounds can shatter; the ceiling of Twoseret's world is an unbearable weight, upheld by a thread of synaptic aegis. If it falls there will be no escaping it.

"My sense of self-preservation hasn't deserted me. Flight or fight." But their expression creases as though they'd said something different, a thing of ache and thorn cupped on their tongue.

A sudden ruthlessness seizes Twoseret. "This city holds the memory of the only person you've ever loved. While you breathe you won't permit its destruction."

Sujatha doesn't meet her eyes. "I need a node I can broadcast from. This isn't a full assault—a veilship or two, not much more. Just scouts."

Other memorialists have poured into the streets, as calm as Twoseret, intrigued by this new development. A few crèche-parents lead their charges by the hand, clear-eyed children from five to nine in various stages of wiring. By twelve they will be tested, and on success granted the petals. The sight of them draws a smile from her, reflexive and un-complicated.

"There are consoles we use for supply drops." Routine communications for assigning and dividing up the items. There's always abundance and most memorialists can have their pick, tools and luxuries and raw mate-rial with which to feed fabricators: steel for hair-ribbons, glass for skirts, a hundred type of gemstones for belts and bedspreads. Everyone wears jewels, is sheathed in it until skin and facets are one.

Twin shadows press against the unsky, each the shape of a hornbill's head. Another tremor sweeps through like a racking cough, or so Twoser-et imagines, never having seen hypothermia in action. There are defenses, but she supposes absently that those must have been breached: they are automated, and while some memorialists know them well—Umaiyal did—most of them never train themselves to battle. The nearest military outpost is too far to make it in time. The city's greatest protection has always been in its secrecy and location rather than firepower. She finds a wall and activates the console, feeding it a cluster of authentications like grapes, and steps aside.

Sujatha bends close, their breath fogging the obsidian curlicues that frame the console. Twoseret watches with avid interest as they connect to the Cotillion channel with a lover's intimacy. "Veilship couplet, identify yourselves."

The shaking pauses. From the console comes a low note, strain of music made by sighing woods and running currents.

"Remotely piloted," Sujatha murmurs, "as I thought. That'll be easier."

"Yes?"

The assassin straightens and inhales. More affectation than any real need for oxygen, Twoseret expects. And they sing.

Sujatha's voice makes a dirge for extinguished suns and singularistic contractions that kill worlds, for defeat in empty reaches that will go unknown and uncommemorated. It jolts Twoseret's nerves, constricts her throat, pries at the seams of her flesh.

When it ends Sujatha turns away, trembling slightly. "They will leave. It's the only command override I can access now, with my voice the way it—in any case it won't work a second time."

"It was exquisite."

"It was nothing of the sort." The assassin sags, as though the song has leeched their arteries dry and drained their limbs of strength.

Up above the shadows have disappeared. Twoseret catches the assassin. "You're exhausted. Let's get you somewhere to rest."

Sujatha doesn't resist or push her away. "I've been sleeping on grass, under trees."

"Then come to my bed. I'll tuck you in."

In the street, the crowd thins, memorialists returning to their duties and routines now that the excitement is past. Riam nods to Twoseret, perhaps guessing at her intent, giving tacit approval or merely mute in-difference.

She frees the assassin from their shoes and vest, and eases them down between the sheets. She holds them until they fall limp and asleep, and very gently kisses their brow, their eyelids, the tip of their nose. Sujatha smells so right.

When she is sure they are deep in dreams, she gathers up her composi-tion and resumes her work. Making a person—an identity—is delicate labor, but it is a labor of love. She thinks she will keep the singing, to retain the best of both worlds, and sends out a request for the casket.

TWOSERET WATCHES THE SKY FOR SILHOUETTES of insects, vast, their wings enveloping half the city, their antennae slashing the horizon to segments. The outpost has become more attentive and sent them guard-ians since the attack. She never sees any of the soldiers, though she can imagine them helmeted and carapaced, animated statues of lustrous ab-sence. Faceless, voiceless, nameless. She wonders if, far away, there is a war going on. A real one, sparked off by the assault here. On that the petals are silent.

The weather is getting warm, though never humid or uncomfortable. She's taken to seed-pearl sandals and lighter dresses with skirts that snap like prayer flags in an assassin's memory.

She kneels. A casket on the pavement, surrounded by mosaic pieces. The person in it has been sleeping a long time, nested in dreams of being reared by crèche-parents and of being wired; of pride when the first petals came. The casket is like the tank, incubating, preparing a sacred genesis.

Twoseret begins to unlatch the lid. A fetus must push through eventually or be stillborn. That is rare, but she's seen it happen. The locks and puzzles fall away quickly this time, decorative more than protective.

Eir hair has grown to eir waist. Thick frosted lashes twitch in sleep. A curl of cool breath, body temperature artificially lowered, rises to meet the thick air. Crossed wrists coiled in origami vipers. She runs her palm over eir forehead; she imagines to em the contact must feel like a flame tickling candlewax. In this way she thaws her dreamer, waking em with her own warmth. No fluid to drain, no instrument to detach—this was, almost, a simple and natural sleep.

Ey turns on eir side as though wishing to rest a little longer. Twoseret brushes eir hair, her fingertips grazing the side of eir neck. When eir eyes open, they are terribly clear: irises deeply brown, circumference gilded in amber. The scent of eir favorite perfume wafts, the angular folds of eir favorite vest rises and falls to eir breathing.

"You always slept so heavily." Twoseret takes em into her arms, helping them out of the casket. "Do I call you Oridel now? Captain Oridel Nehetis. It sounds all grand."

Ey rubs at eir eyes, groggy, one of those slightly childish gestures—she's never been able to break eir habit. "No, of course not. It's been a while, hasn't it? When did we have hornet fliers guarding our sky? God, I miss piloting those."

"Recent addition. I find their silhouette very charming. There's so much to tell you." She pecks em on the lips. "Welcome back, Umaiyal."

And Umaiyal laughs, in what is nearly eir voice, straightening to eir feet and taking her hand in that light-firm way that belongs to Umaiyal alone. "I'm home."

AT THE MOMENT OF HER BIRTH, Twoseret learned three things: that her life will be full of peace, that she will never die, and that she will know precisely one tragedy. These facts are absolute, untarnished by chance and impregnable to intervention.

As she walks arm in arm with Umaiyal up the puzzle-paths, her tragedy falls away like pale chrysalis, dissipating on the mosaic tiles and dispersing in the low salted wind.

When her next petals come she reads them and smiles, and casts them aside.

Treasure Acre

Everett Maroon

HE PEERS INTO THE ROUGH HOLE, dabbing at his brow with a damp handkerchief. The shovel has found every large stone in this three-square-foot area. Beating down on the two of them is the early summer sun, but he, much older than his companion, feels it a lot more, especially in his knees and the middle of his back.

She squats down easily, inspecting the rough sides of what looks like an overgrown divot in the grass. At only twelve years old, she has much experience with the central New Jersey soil and rock in her mother's backyard. With nimble, dirty fingers she retrieves a stone, rolling it over as if it signals some clue they need.

"You haven't gotten very far," she tells him, brushing dregs of red clay onto her jeans before standing up. She is only about six inches shorter than him.

"I realize that." He takes care not to sound sharp with her.

He stabs at the ground, and again the spade bangs against stone, making a sound that irritates him. Without meaning to, he grunts as he digs. Now the sweat and humidity have wilted his shirt collar. This is not the way he envisioned the afternoon would proceed, but he's not sure what he should have expected, really.

He asks her if she's sure this is the spot, making sure he's quiet about it because he knows her feelings are easily hurt.

"Yes, I'm sure." She pulls a wrinkled map out of her back pocket.

Faded blue lines streak across the paper, with broad brown writing upstaging the rules where she was supposed to practice her penmanship. Instead she'd gotten excited by an episode of *Mr. Wizard's World* and as soon as she'd learned she could draw a treasure map in lemon juice, she put off her math homework and attempted to fashion directions to something terrific. Except she didn't have anything important to bury, and for sure she'd need to sneak this project under her mother's radar. Danielle looks at the number of paces again, using her index finger to keep focus as she calculates. Steps are drawn off to the side, in clumps of five hash marks, an inch or so above a simple compass guide. She should not have tried to draw a dragon in lemon juice with a toothpick, because it looks horrible blurry and not at all like a dragon.

"It should be right here," she says, pointing to the disturbed earth at their feet, but lacking the confidence she had just a moment earlier.

"May I see it?"

She wonders when he got so mannerly, because she couldn't be less interested in that Dear Abby nonsense.

She passes it to him and stifles a grumble because she knows how to read her own map.

"So this is the tree here?" He tries to remember if this was always the way the backyard met up with the woods. It's been so long.

Danielle leans in, and they study the slip of paper together. Everything has become so absurd, but she has put in too much energy now to back down from locating the box. Filled with something like a hundred Susan B. Anthony dollars and whatever else she can't recall, he's apparently desperate for it.

"Come to think of it, maybe it's this tree." She walks back to her starting point, sixty yards away, where the uneven bricks of the patio end and sod picks up. He tries not to stare at her gait or watch for any tell-tale signs from her. Soon enough Danielle is back across the lawn, now standing about thirty feet further west from his location.

"Try over here, Derrick," she yells. His name feels funny in her mouth, unreal.

He hurries over, worrying about how all of this activity must look to whatever neighbors are around.

This time the shovel sinks easily through the grass and he tilts the long handle back, bringing up a good measure of earth. Finally a smile breaks across Derrick's face.

"I think this may be it," he says, as sweat rolls past his temples. It's not long before he feels the lunch pail, and gets on his knees, creaky as they are, ignoring that it's time to take his pills. The green and orange picture of the Scooby Doo Mystery Machine van peeks out at them.

"Yay," Danielle says, grabbing the handle of the lunch pail. It hangs on by only one side, the other end having dissolved away into the ground. She catches her breath. What if what he said is true?

"Don't be scared," says Derrick, brushing black dirt out from between the seams of the lid and box. "We can put this back in a couple of minutes." He walks over toward a tree near them and sits under it, noticing that the cancer inside him is pushing on his bladder. Danielle walks up and sits beside him, feeling the rough bark through her t-shirt. It's a new shirt that she got at the mall, having selected the Ghostbusters logo from the lineup of emblems on the wall at the small store. But she didn't actually believe in ghosts or magic before today.

"I still think it's weird that you did this," she says, unable to refrain from bringing up the subject again.

"I know." He opens the box, a rough prospect after so much of the hinge has rusted shut. Wrapped in newspaper are the coins they expected, and he brushes past them, still looking. Guatemalan worry dolls, far from where they could provide any help. They're supposed to be placed where they can resolve problems.

"I don't remember putting it in there, you know," she says.

Danielle has told him this already, but he knows it's here. He sees a corner of plastic. It found its way to the farthest corner of the box. He holds the clump of baby hair up to the light—delicate, thin brown hairs wrapped in cellophane.

Danielle wants to hold it, but Derrick says she can see it from where she is. He gives her a sideways glance and asks if she's nervous. She nods.

"I believe that I become you, but why can't we just let it happen the way it did? Why can't you just get to a doctor before you get so sick?"

It's a perfectly good question, and a smart one from a pre-teen, but intelligence has never been her, or his, problem.

He sizes her up, considering how much he should tell her and how much he's obligated to say. Because they're the same person, does he need his earlier self's permission?

"I like my life right now," she says, not exactly looking for a defense. Maybe he has just imitated her scars on his own body. Maybe he's a hoax.

"Yes, I was pretty happy until my body started changing in puberty," he says. He doesn't want to overwrite the child's attitude, or show her too much of the future.

"It's really that bad?"

"It solves a lot of problems if we just do this." Derrick knows when the hair was taken, his first day home after the birth. It's the best time anchor, a new start.

Danielle frowns at the lock, which reminds her of an ancient bug trapped in amber like the one that sits in the glass case in the science classroom.

"I just wonder, maybe I won't be the same person if I start out as a boy."

Too smart, he thinks. Derrick nods his head. He's come all this way, at great risk and expense, and yet, he's forgotten to ask the simplest of questions.

She takes his hand and compares the folds in their palms. His are deeper, his skin less elastic.

"You're dying?" she asks.

"Yes. It's not your fault, or mine."

"Doctors refused to treat you?"

"It's the law where I come from. We're on our own, so resources are limited."

"If you change our history, will we remember who we used to be?" Danielle feels her own palm instead of looking at him.

"I honestly don't know. Probably not," he says, laying his infancy on top of the Mystery Machine.

"I don't want to die at forty-seven," she tells Derrick.

"But I want to be my me at least for now." She grabs the packet of hair off of the lunch box and bolts into the woods, knowing he can't keep up with her. Only once Danielle has scattered the clipping in the creek does she walk back to the boundary of her parents' property. He is still under the tree, looking somewhat grayer than before. She apologizes, and Derrick waves her off.

"I'm sorry," she says.

"I would have done the same thing," he says, managing a small smile.

Splitskin

E. Catherine Tobler

Gugán was always my *khaa yahaayí*, my soul bound into the flesh of another while yet part of my own. From beginning to the end, Gugán's bones were my bones, his breath my breath. He moved as sun and I as moon, reflecting and eclipsing the other in eternal dance, one standing brighter for the other's shadows. The immortal ghost of him—*khaa yakghwahéiyagu*—remains with me even as I speak these words. Hear him speak with my voice if this pleases, using my tongue as if it is his own, because it is. We were born with two spirits, never only male or female, but revered for the way we walked both paths, each unable to exist without the other.

My love reveled in winter's sunbroken days, when the light spills to the fresh-fallen snow to stab a person in the eyes. Gugán flitted from path to stone, a trickster comfortable with his Raven heritage. I, as Eagle, startled at every shift of snow, caught always unawares in the bright sun as he pelted me with clumps of melting cold.

It was one of these days when we witnessed our mothers taken from us, lifted into the sky and away where we could not yet reach. After failing to take the deer we had tracked the morning through, our mothers brought us to the wild wet of the river slicing through the woods. The doe skipped into the forest shadows and our mothers let her go, because the forest is an uncertain thing, but the water known and trusted. There, we emptied the woven fish traps, cooked a meal, and ate in a pleased silence.

We did not yet lick each other's fingers clean—we did not yet understand such a thing was possible, well content to press thigh-to-thigh upon a cold log while our mothers harvested more fish from more traps.

It was then Raven swallowed the sun. Raven-as-clouds descended upon the running river and made the air thick, unknowable. The day around us turned as night, as if the forest itself had dissolved and spread across the river, leaving it strange and unsettled. I leaned into Gugán, not for warmth but to know I was not alone in witnessing this. *Give way,* something inside me whispered, but the terror of that whisper was deeper than even the sight of an empty river.

When the clouded dark retreated, our mothers no longer stood within the rushing waters. The baskets of wriggling fish remained, but nothing else. We crept to the river as one and looked to the clouded sky, as if they might be suspended there, laughing as birds were wont. The sky hung empty and silent.

That our mothers were thunderbirds; we had known this for all our days. Each and every one knows the story, has heard it spoken around crackling fires. But there remains within me a deep joy at speaking these words—my words, with the echo of his voice—in allowing myself to remember all he was, all we were, and how the thunderbirds came to break the sky.

Gold brought the men to the mountains, invading the way ants will swarm upon a fallen morsel, crawling one over the other with little re-gard for the body on the bottom of the stack. The coming of men meant the coming of trains, and there is a joy in the recollection of their black iron stench even as much of what we had known was changed. They broke our quiet world with rail and axe, shining innards hauled to more distant shores.

The men who came wanted to know more than we could tell them. We were asked to be guides—we were natives and must know the mountains as we knew the ridges of our own interlocked knees. They asked for but shunned our suggestions as to how the land might be conquered. Many men went their own ways, and many died, and we did not mourn—not because they were unlike us, but because we knew this was the way. Every person carries with them their own story and creates with their own hands their own ending. This rests inside until it can no longer remain contained, until it bursts into being and ignites the world. Some were taken by cold, some others by the greed in their own hearts. Some asked us of their endings; even when we spoke of them, we were never be-lieved.

We had taken to living near the routes into the highest mountains. Getting closer, but still not daring to walk into them. Frightened of what we would sacrifice. We lied to ourselves, saying that if we could acquire enough money, we could make the journey to free our mothers. But we knew the mountains the way we knew the forest, from a respectful distance, always more comfortable near the placid flat of water, be it lake or ocean. If we had possessed the courage of our mothers, perhaps we would not have waited so long. Would not have sought to make a living among the white men who sought to make *their* livings from the gold buried in the hills.

They wondered: where may we easily find the gold? Will you lead us to the river where the gold sits upon the banks as ducks do? There was no explaining that ducks did not sit on riverbanks as gold. The men were firm. They had traveled a long distance, a distance they said we could never fathom. They had heard of the way the water washes the gold onto the shores, the way the world shines when the sun splits the clouds. The world did this, I could never argue, but it was rarely the gold that gleamed.

For them, we burned our grasses into sweet smoke that made their heads spin, and within the smoke trails we saw images, possible paths into the hills where one might prosper. For one man, this meant discovering a hollow in the world, a hole into which he fell and was discovered by ladders of mushrooms and pillows of fungus. These crawled over him in riot until they made him one their own, digesting him even to this day. For another man, this meant discovering the great brown bear who parted his skin with her ragged claws to free his *khaa yahaayí* into the world forevermore. These paths did not always lead to the gold the men desired. But these men believed so fiercely that they would. Felt the weight of the rocks within their packs already.

Jackson, when he came to my table in the local tavern, was more knowing than any of them in combination. He was bent by the cold air, shoulders hunched, hands often curled into useless claws at his side. While he possessed the exterior body of any man—skin, reddened cheeks, mussed hair—he was never in these moments human. He was an ending, struggling to burst from the flesh that confined it. He was a creation of tentacle and fire, a serpent bound into flesh he didn't yet understand despite the years that marked him. He looked as old as we two, when he came to hear us tell fortunes.

I was allowed this table at the local tavern, beside the window hung with lace, hired to ply my fortune telling because Soapy knew that the curiosity of me, and my "magic," would lure more drinkers. These drinkers often thought I was a prostitute—so many in those days were, and Soapy said I was more than welcome, but this was not my way. Soapy surely knew I meant to leave as soon as I was able—every person in this place meant to.

Jackson had the means to carry people away, his train like something from a vision, a beast that could carry anyone away. He joined me at my table, sitting not in the chair opposite my bench but on the bench itself, his thigh warm against my own. He brought whiskey; I was drinking water. He was smoking a cheroot; I kept a length of sweet grass resting between us.

He stubbed out his cheroot and a grimace crossed his lined face from the pressure on his crooked hand. He made no sound of complaint, only looked at me with his eyes, behind which I saw swimming other eyes, the eyes of the bound creature he was. Men called my sight magic because they could not explain it; they called it magic because they made no effort to understand it. When you know the world in such a plain manner, it is not magic. It is breath and it is being.

I reached for my matches, but Jackson dared touch me to prevent me from lighting the length of sweet grass. His fingers were rough, hooked into claws, and while the touch was tender, it was not hesitant. He did not fear me, even dressed as I was in a woman's clothing, with beads knotted into my long dark hair and tied around my wrists. He was not repulsed even as I drew his hand beneath the table to the hard flesh between my legs. Was *this* what he had come for? Would he demand that such be given in trade to travel upon his train? It was only flesh, after all; it was not the heart of me. Jackson leaned in and took a breath of me and did not stare as if I were a thing to break apart and better understand. He looked at me with reverence, seeing my female spirit within my male skin.

You are more than this skin, he told me, and beneath me I felt the stirrings of the thing I could not yet embrace. *Give way*, it whispered. I said the same of him, that he was more than his grasping, hooked hand, but deep down I felt that his hand was him—he wanted every precious thing he could scoop into claw and mouth. When he nuzzled deeper into the hollow of my throat and asked for a guide into the hills, I kept my silence. There was something in this meeting that told me Jackson already understood I was not a guide as most men expected me to be. The warmth of his once-broken fingers told me he understood what I had to offer, that he was making an offer all his own. Then, he mentioned our mothers.

He did not know then what the thunderbirds were. The greed within his voice was plain; he either did not know or care that it came so easily across. He was a man who wanted something—just as other men here wanted gold and would obtain it by any means. Jackson's treasure was a different sort, and he told me a story I knew too well.

He spoke of the women at the river, their leathers soaked with the icy rush of water. They could have been sisters with their ebony hair and eyes, but they were not. They were closest of friends, knowing they had to stay close so their sons could foster the friendship that turned to the love that turned to the devastation which would free them.

These women, Jackson said, stood in the rushing waters up to their knees and felt the cold burrow into the bases of their brains, their hearts. They became of the water as they stood counting the fish their traps had collected. They came to not notice the cold, so much a part of it they were. They knew their sons were close, but something else was closer, pushing down from the sky until it opened its hooked mouth and swallowed them.

Raven scooped them into his claws—gentle this time, because these two were not unknown to him; they were a similar creature, birds who drew the thunder down with their wings, beasts whose claws dragged the lightning from the vault of the sky. Raven scooped them into his mouth, his blue tongue startlingly warm against their chilled skins—then, *then* they felt how cold they themselves were. Raven drew them up and away and gone and my Gugán blamed himself, believed *he* had called Raven because he shared a kinship with the trickster and his ways.

I reached again for the grass; Jackson's hand again forestalled mine.

Raven bore the women ever up, Jackson said. Took them so high into the winter sky they could no longer breathe or struggle. Raven bound them into the stony mountains, but they were not women as anyone knew women; each contained a spirit that could not be caged. No such thing can be caged eternally, Jackson said. You may possess a thing for a moment in time, but such things cannot be claimed for a lifetime.

The way he spoke was a shock. He was not a white man, though looked such to anyone else. Who else would look beyond the surface? Those like me, but the men of the world? They would not. Jackson spoke of the world's deeper truths, said its bones could not be mined until hollow. Perceived that I was not entirely what I appeared to be; contained larger depths that, like the unending forest, could not be seen even in brightest sunlight, because something would always be thrown into shadow. Into *khaa yahaayí*.

He leaned into me so close I could see the fork in his tongue. He meant to release the birds from their cages, he said, and there was a long lisp around that word: *cagesss*. Birds that were not birds but still wanted to fly, wanted to slap their wings to the water and bring the thunder into being. He spoke of these women, of my mother and Gugán's, and tried to weave a spell around me. Tried to conceal his intent.

I was too old to be misled and knew Raven would demand something in return for what we sought to take. I had been down far too many paths not to see the wrong one lain fresh before me. This path would lead into the mountains, a place far removed from the waters of home. But it was the place we sought, the reason I saved money from the pathetic work of telling men what they wanted to hear. Jackson's hands slid doubled around mine, cupping me like he might a lover, but even in this he was allowing me to grasp his bent hands in return and hurt him if I so wanted. His voice slipped lower, that tongue ever forked.

Take us, I said.

There are tellings of this story where I ask Jackson what he wants of me in return. Where we bargain late into the night, until the tavern is empty and it is only we two in the candlelit darkness. These tellings are untruths even as they bring more comfort. The idea of me making certain of every feature along the path before I set foot upon it is better than me launching myself with desperation into the mountains I feared.

I did not ask Jackson anything, because I already knew. He believed the thunderbirds were true and he wanted their power for his own. He felt that with the double-spirited children born of the thunderbird's own bodies, he might achieve this. This was visible to anyone who looked into the depths of his eyes. The serpent wanted to wrestle the birds, wanted to claim them even as he knew he could not. In this, Jackson was like any of the other men, willing to expose themselves to any horror. In this I resembled these men as well, but this time, I held to the belief that I possessed my mother's courage and would put it to good use.

I left the tavern alone, having made an accord with Jackson, and went to the small house along the river where Gugán and I made our home. The scent of roasted venison greeted me; my love was elbow-deep into dinner and welcomed me with a kiss, a nuzzle into the beads that adorned my hair. He smelled like dark oiled cloves I knew from the general store, and I wanted to bury myself in that scent, the way we had once buried ourselves in sun-drenched snow drifts.

There is a man, I told him, and his head came up sharply, as if I said I had given my heart away all in the course of an evening's conversation. I threaded my fingers into his hair, loosening it from its long tail. He listened to me but did not immediately hear, and only when I mentioned our mothers did his heart quiet. *There is a train we can take into the mountains; he does not want coin, for you know our blood is coin and key for the mountain. He means to capture them,* I said. And then came the laughter, as if capture were possible when a mighty creature was loosed into the sky.

I put on my best dress for dinner and after let Gugán twine my long beaded hair around his fist. His teeth sank into my shoulder, as if he meant to suckle the ink out of me. Is it any different, to write a story upon a body or a sheet of paper? My body tells its own story, less permanent than pages upon which words fall.

I cannot leave to anyone the ink that his teeth sank into, but I can say his hands were the hands to needle it into my skin. He wrote upon me and I across him and we still never spoke quite the right words. *I love you* is a construct, a triad of words that can never encompass all one feels. In the end, words will fail—just as they will fail to tell this story and what became of us in the mountains so far from the lake and the river and the sea.

Jackson's iron train remains rooted in my memory, next to that of my mother. I can no more forget the lines of the train than I can forget my mother's eyes, her smile anchored there instead of within her mouth.

The train was long and black, and when we walked up to it Jackson was bent against the old locomotive, cheek pressed to metal. His eyes were closed, hands splayed flat against the arch of the engine body. His body swayed into the engine and he nodded, as if listening to a voice no other could hear. This behavior was familiar to me and Gugán, so we did not linger; we looked instead to the others who worked to load the train for its journey.

One could call them a family; we eventually did. They had less in common than our own people, for they were every color and size and shape, but what bound them was their differences. Where the world would have shunned them, they made their own space and way upon this train of Jackson's. The first to see and greet us were the Silver Sisters. Gemma and Sombra moved as we did, two separate beings clearly bound to each other. One was light upon water, the other shadow within forest, and sometimes they were exactly opposite of that. They were inseparable, drawing us into the train with four hands that felt somehow like six.

It was the last car we entered where a woman sat peeling the skins from rarely seen citrus fruits. She did not discard these peels but instead let them fall into a green-yellow-orange riot in the bowl braced between her knees. Despite the chill in the air, she was barefoot and wore a dress of thin cotton. She looked at us with a welcoming smile, all fierce teeth. Something in the air here spoke to the division between elements; as the water is divided from the land is divided from the forest, this is how the train car felt.

We were given warm rolls slathered in lime marmalade. This was a shock to us; we had never tasted its like and were warned that it might cause us to remember things we rather wished not to. In that first bite was the bitter moment of my birth, when there were whispers, how there should have been two children, so they had always said, but there was only one. One possessed of two spirits. This sticky lime marmalade conveyed more of my childhood with each and every bite, and I could only wonder what Gugán was made to recall with its sweet tang. It was a thing we never spoke of, those early moments on the train. I suppose in all the nights that were to come, we already knew we had both been pulled backwards, into memories that were forever a part of us even if not present every day.

Gemma and Sombra guided us through the train as it prepared to leave the city; it was a circus train, they told us, though "circus" meant little to us. They were performers—this we understood—and had com-

pleted a series of shows meant to entertain those gold-rushing men. I
saw the glitter of money in their eyes and a transformation as the light
sister became the dark sister, and knew we had found our path into the
mountains.

This path was not easily had. There were gold-seeking men upon the
train, having asked for passage to Dawson City. They were possibly as
eager as Jackson to reach the depths of the mountains on these narrow
rails, crowding every car with bodies and equipment, wedging themselves
against performers and animals alike. The animals.

I cannot say how many train cars there were, for unless my memory
fails, this number changed over the course of the journey. The train itself
changed based on what Jackson and its people required of it. Of *her*. I
felt a kindred spirit inside this metal body, a thing I have felt in no other
place. I might compare her to what I felt in my partner, that spirit beneath the flesh being opposite of the flesh itself—but this train had no
flesh that I could see. (If I had known then of the severed hand within
her engine, I would have understood that indeed she possessed such flesh
yet another doubled spirit, she of metal and woman.) She was a creature
bound to travel the tracks of the world, but sometimes she skimmed
through sky and cloud.

Some of the train cars held animals that we did not know and each car
appeared to change its shape based upon their occupants. The cars looked
entirely normal on the outside but inside, each and every beast or person
was properly housed according to their needs. The animals did not need
cages when they had small landscapes to roam.

Among the beasts, we discovered lions, sirens, and one pale bear that
Gemma and Sombra said would soon be in its proper place. The sirens
drew us because of their bird natures, their train car spackled with glittering fish scales from their many meals. We saw in these striking women
our mothers and wondered if they were why Jackson had such a hunger
for the thunderbirds. Did he seek to mate one spirit to another? We did
not ask, only burned sweet grass in the small compartment we had been
given and clasped our hands as we asked for a safe journey, for guidance,
for the ability to know what would need doing in the moments to come.

Those nights, I heard thunder through the hills, felt the rattle of windows as wind tried to invade. I dreamed of our mothers bursting from
the snow-laden mountains, cracking the world apart until it was buried

in white. Unable to sleep with such thoughts, I watched the dark world pass beyond the train windows beyond my own reflection.

Eventually, the train slowed, stopped. I left our cabin to understand what had happened.

I found Jackson easily enough. I expected him to be concerned—surely a train stopped upon tracks was bad luck—but his face split with a grin. *Come,* he said, *watch them work.*

It was one of the most magnificent things I have witnessed. Jackson guided me to the cab and sure-footed his way up the ladder that led through a roof hatch. I grasped the ladder to follow, but this is when I saw the woman's hand. Severed at the wrist, partly bundled in cloth, it spilled threaded fatelines into the world, its palm crossed with gold. I felt its eternal heartbeat, the rumble of the train even though we stood still, and climbed my way up and out through the hatch.

Gemma and Sombra, Jackson told me, had a way with metal, in the finding of it but also in its manipulation. Beyond the train, the tracks lay heavy with ice and snow, and though the women could not move these directly they reached with their essences to the buried rails. They warmed the metal, which sheared the ice; as stars fall from the night sky, bright shards of ice plummeted down the dark valley over which we stood on the elevated track.

The whole hour through, the women worked tirelessly, digging their spirits into the ice to reach the metal, to make it simmer with a warm, unearthly light. In its own way, this avalanche of ice sounded like thunder, and I looked to the sky above, wondering if our mothers could feel our approach.

Gugán, roused by my absence, soon joined me, and we sat upon the cold engine cab roof with Jackson, watching the ice's destruction. Gemma and Sombra were illuminated by the glowing tracks, water sputtering into the air as more ice broke violently free. Jackson asked nothing of us; he knew as I did that all had been agreed to in the tavern. He would take us into the hills; we would call our mothers down. What the thunderbirds did then was out of our hands. He knew this but dared it anyhow and some part of me loved him for it.

Morning saw the train in motion again, deeper into the hills that rose on either side of us. The snow-draped heights reminded me how far we were from the water, from our home. I watched them with unease, but it was Gugán's hand upon the back of my neck that grounded and calmed me. This was what we had come for, he reminded me. This is what we longed to do. Free our mothers and then— We could see nothing beyond that moment, could not even see that moment, truth be told. It was cloaked in the clouds Raven had used that day to steal our mothers away.

Being *of* Raven was not controlling Raven, I told Gugán. It was folly to think any could control such a creature. I could see that this weighed on him even now. That moment of loss, always floating in the depths of his eyes. This was the path that tethered him, and even had I known (I knew—do not listen to this untruth), I would not have stopped what came.

I came to see many forms within the cloaked mountains as we passed northward; the tail of our kin the whale, the rough-cut edge of a wing lifted in flight, the pointed nose of a leaping salmon. It was the wing that drew my eyes time and again until we were far out of its arching height. The train wove her way through tunnels of rock, breaking once more into sunlight falling through bruised clouds. It was those clouds that gave us concern, that made us feel Raven closing in to protect what he believed was his. They were not snow clouds but the clouds of storm and rage. In this way, they were also of the thunderbird.

Snow and ice on the tracks stopped the train again midday. Before Gemma and Sombra could begin their work, the gold-rush men expressed their frustration by daring to exit the train—they swarmed out of the cars, walked the length of the train, and leaped down to the ice-coated metal. They began to chip at it with picks and boots. The sisters stared at them but made no move forward. They only looked at Jackson, who stood silent upon the engine roof.

But he also made no move toward the men, and I watched him turn a slow circle, studying the mountains. The peaks traced a jagged line against the clouded sky, a line like none I had seen before. Only the clouds were familiar, possessing the rounded bounty they'd had that day in my youth, when they had dipped to the river and carried our mothers away. In my heart, a notion was given breath, was given space to stretch and explore, and I reached for the hand that should have been at my side, only to find that it was not.

Gugán had gone already, feeling that breath a moment before I had. My hand curled into the fist of a man who wants to strike a thing. I didn't look to the sisters or Jackson. I fled the engine, threading my way through the train to the strange cars that changed their shape based on need. Here, I found my other half, kneeling before the great pale bear. I felt certain the beast would lift a paw and spill Gugán's spirit to floor, but instead it leaned its massive head against his own in acquiescence.

Another breath filled me. Gemma and Sombra had said this bear would soon be in its proper place. Not necessarily its home, but proper. I watched Gugán settle onto the bear's broad back and offer me a hand to do the same. The bear heaved beneath us, the train car split wide, and we were gone, running along tracks that should have been iced but were not.

As the metal rails cleaved the mountain in a sure and sweeping curve, the bear leaped with similar certainty. He knew where he was going, muscle and bone bunching beneath our grasping thighs. Our hands curled knuckle-deep into the oily fur, and we moved as one creature with him, up and up the rock-strewn mountain. Here, the trees were sparse and the ground more rock than dirt; there was little shadow to cloak what we sought: the peak of the mountain, so far from the river, the ocean, the lake.

In tintypes, lightning appears to have split the mountain's crest in two, leaving a gaping mouth of ragged stone. But a closer look reveals the yawning V of a beak. This mouth possessed no blue tongue—this mouth was not Raven but thunderbird, and we rushed headlong toward her, caring not what would happen, only knowing it must.

We plunged into the stony mouth of darkness. This darkness rushed absolute, and we had only the cascading wind to tell us we still moved. The pale bear was invisible within this darkness, until I realized that pieces of the beast were coming loose in the dark. Strands of oily white hair pulled free from its hide, bursting into flame the deeper we ran into the mouth. These flames hovered and provided no light to see by, only a strange illumination that seemed to stretch into feathers, into beaks, into talons.

Beaks snapped at my arms. Talons raked my spine. A cooling rush of blood signaled the unraveling of the ink that marked me, upward into the dark. Pain clawed my throat as every inked thread that spoke of my double-spirited nature was ripped from my skin. The blood in the wake of the stolen ink turned to momentary fire, a burning river that flowed upward against the wind.

I saw too how my love came apart, how the flesh that confined him was peeled away, to reveal bones and heart, to expose his clove and salt soul, his *khaa yahaayí* as he became the ghost that would never leave me. I watched Raven pluck my love's heart and swallow it whole. The warm breath that once flowed from him became the wind around me; his breath channeled my blood, which became the water, which broke the stone.

When you have known darkness and are thrown into light, you are blinded. I was blind and still knew everything. The mountain shattered up the length of my arms, an eruption of snow and trees and stones spewing into the clouded sky. I was thrown upward as our mothers shook the stone from their trapped wings, to push free as if being born. They clawed the sky in jubilation, jagged streams of lightning illuminating the air. Everything crackled with energy and when the thunder rolled beneath their wings, I gloried in that sound even as I spiraled uncontrolled far through the air, landing flat against the train's roof.

Raven came as black fury through the bruised clouds, but he could not pin our mothers, could not claim what had been released with the blood and breath of our doubled spirits. Our mothers circled Raven, beat him down with beaks and wings, until he tumbled loose and flew up and up and away, screaming with his blue tongue aflame.

And then, the strange silence. The absence of mothers and lovers and every inky line that had ever burrowed into my skin. When our mothers returned, they crouched above me, studying me with eyes familiar yet unknown. They balanced on the edge of the metal train and screamed fire when Jackson meant to come closer. With shrieks, they dared me to split my own skin, to give way to that which I had not.

My Eagle spirit emerged from its slumber within my body, parting my skin like water to take the sky as her own, and I thought to see muscle unfurling in her—*my*—wake. This was the second spirit within me, the woman I had never fully unleashed, even with Gugán—*oh, my lost Gugán.*

Now that I had given myself over to her, Eagle cried her freedom as our mothers had, wings trailing fire, which ignited lighting, which caused me to pull the cool clouds closer. I wove a gown from them and floated safely to the ground where I crumpled and shook as newly born. The resuming rumble of train and thunder alike were both far distant, and I was in an unknown space dark and dappled like forest.

There, you found me, wiped the soot from my skin as though you smoothed feathers down. How, you wondered, had I come to be naked in the dark forest when I was a creature of the bright water. You brought me back to the water, for surely a story was to be shared, my skin bare of ink but still showing pale traceries of what once had been. The breath of Eagle expanded my lungs, made me steady beneath your regard.

Your inked fingers contain the shapes of all possible things and your black eyes hold a glimmer of more beneath their surface. Was it my Gugán I saw in them, moving as sun within the shadows, or only the hope of him? Either way, why you want a story is plain. You have not split your own skin. You wish to understand and carry the words—my voice, his tongue. You wish to carry our ghost, our *khaa yakghwahéiyagu*, into the future.

All things have a beginning, we would say. Split the skin. Give way.

The Need for Overwhelming Sensation

Bogi Takács

I AM STARING AT THE FACE from a thousand newscasts—the gentle curve of jaw, the almost apologetic smile. Miran Anyuwe is not explaining policy. Miran Anyuwe is bleeding from a head wound, drops falling tap-tap-tap on the boarding ramp of our ship, the sound oddly amplified by the geometry of the cramped docking bay bulkheads.

"I'm looking for a ride out," they say. They are not supposed to be on Idhir Station. They are supposed to be three jump points away, heading the accession talks, guiding Ohandar's joining of the Alliance.

I uncross my legs and get up to my feet—one quick, practiced motion. I bow my head briefly. "Esteemed, I will inquire."

They nod. Their smile intensifies just a little, as if someone repainted the lines of their mouth with firmer brushstrokes.

I dash inside, my entire torso trembling with fear of the sudden and the unexpected. I take a sharp corner and crash into Master Sanre. They steady me with both hands.

"Iryu, breathe."

I gasp.

"Slower. In and out."

Their presence calms me. It only takes a few breaths.

"Iryu, look at me."

I stare up at them. Their eyes narrow, the lines of silver paint that I so carefully applied to their face in the morning crumple like spacetime clumps around a planet. The glass beads in their hair clack together.

"Explain what's wrong."

I mutter, still tongue-tied from the sudden fright. Miran Anyuwe is outside and injured. Miran Anyuwe wants to hire us. Miran Anyuwe—

"Ward the ship, then come outside. I will talk to them."

They hurry outside, boots clanging on metal.

I exhale again. I focus on the power inside me, direct it outside and into the wards. My remaining tension eases up. I'm not missing anything—I will be able to look at my master's sensory logs later. I turn around and return to the open airlock.

I stop for a moment as I see the two of them together. They look so alike, and the resemblance goes beyond gender, appearance, the light brown of their skin and the dark brown of their braids. They have the same bearing, the same stance. It's clear both are used to effortless command. Miran Anyuwe commands an entire planet. My master commands only me and the ship.

Is my master more powerful?

It's not about the head wound, it's not about the desperate urgency in Miran Anyuwe's gestures. It involves something innate that goes to the core of being.

I knew my master was powerful. But did I overestimate Miran Anyuwe?

Both of them look up at me, nod at me to come closer. I approach, unsettled.

MIRAN ANYUWE IS UNWILLING TO EXPLAIN. Details are elided, skirted around. Anti-Alliance isolationists, terrorist threats, an attack on Miran Anyuwe's life. I don't understand why they abandoned the talks and went back to their planet—surely they knew they would present a better target there? Were they trying to pull off some populist maneuver? I find myself dismayed that my thoughts are moving along less than charitable pathways, but Miran Anyuwe clearly has something to hide.

I tell myself it is only the bitterness of disillusionment. But did I really want them to be that glorified, polished figurehead from the political news, that semi-deity with a charmingly pacifist stance?

I excuse myself; I start preparing for launch. My master can keep Miran Anyuwe company.

THESE SHIPS DO NOT RUN ON pain; that's a misconception. They run on raw magical power. It can be produced in any number of ways. Pain is just easy for many people.

Of course, it's a matter of choice. Even those who find it easy don't have to like it.

I like it. I need it. If I go without, my body protests. Maybe it's about the need for overwhelming sensation; I'm not sure.

As I'm checking the equipment, I wonder why I'm having these thoughts—I think because of a foreigner on the ship, a potential need to explain. For all the newscasts and analysis articles, I know little about Ohandar. The focus is always on Miran Anyuwe, and the progress of the negotiations. I wonder if that means the Ohandar isolationists have already won.

I slow my all too rapid breathing. There will be time to get agitated later. First to get away from the gravity wells, to a relatively clean patch of spacetime while still on sublight. Then we can decide—the client can decide. Miran Anyuwe has all the reputation credit in the world to pay. Of course, my master would nix all the dangerous maneuvers. I just hope Miran Anyuwe isn't up to something wrong.

I tug on straps, lean into them with my full bodyweight. They hold. They always hold, but it's best to check.

I undress. A lot of magic leaves through my skin surface—I'd rather not burn my clothing. I never have, but it heats up and that makes me worried. I've already adjusted the ambient temp a few degrees higher, so I'm not feeling cold.

The chamber is mostly empty—my master is a minimalist, and I like this: distractions do not help. The lines carved into the bulkheads—carefully, by hand—are the same off-white as the bulkheads themselves. One day it would be pleasant to have wood, but I like this surface too: it reminds me of ceramics, some of our tableware from down planetside.

Master Sanre is setting up the frame: pulling it out from storage inside the bulkheads, affixing it. They work quickly; we've done this so many times.

I say I'm ready. I'm eager to begin; we were stuck on Idhir Station for days upon days, our time consumed with administrative tasks. I'm starved for a run, and we have the client of clients, safely ensconced in one of the bedchambers, but probably not yet asleep. Out on the corridor I felt their jitters, but this chamber is the best-warded on the ship. No distractions inside, no stray power leaking out and causing disturbance outside.

I lie stomach down on a fixed-position pallet and my master straps me in. I wriggle a bit—everything seems to be in order. I smile up at them and they run a hand along the side of my face, smooth down my curls. I close my eyes for a moment and sigh a little. They chuckle.

"So dreamy. What would you do without me?"

"I would be sad?" I volunteer, my voice thin and little.

They pat me on the shoulders.

They start with their bare hands, slapping, grabbing and pulling at the flesh. It is all quite gentle. I relax into the restraints and my muscles unknot. Whatever Miran Anyuwe is doing, I couldn't care less.

Heavier thuds on the sides of my back. I can tell the implements by feel. I wish we would go faster—aren't we in a hurry?

Master Sanre fusses with the tool stand. They turn around, change stance. A whizzing sound through the air, a sharper pain. I yelp. Sound is good, it also helps release. We go on. On. My back burns. I groan at first, then scream. Tears and snot. I—

"What's going *on* in here?"

Miran Anyuwe. How— The door was supposed to be locked—

Did you forget to lock the door? My master sends me a private message.

It locks automatically once the frame is disengaged, I think back over our connection. It should be encrypted, but now I am uncertain about everything.

Miran Anyuwe strides up to us. "What are you *doing?*" Their voice wavers with anger and fear. I try to crane my head to see—I can't, but Master Sanre disengages the straps with a quick thought-command. I sit up, trying to suppress the shaking caused by the sudden halt. I'm not sure where to put all the magic. I clumsily wipe my face and hug myself. Why is Miran Anyuwe so angry?

They stare at each other. I wonder if I ought to say something.

You may speak, my master messages.

"Powering the ship," I say. My voice is wheezier, wavier than I'd like. This voice is not for strangers. My vulnerability is not for strangers. Not even for Miran Anyuwe.

"You did not say you would do that!"

Do what? I am baffled. "Powering the ship?"

They glare at Master Sanre. "You are hurting him!"

"Em," my master says. "Different pronouns."

Miran Anyuwe looks startled; they know they of all people are not supposed to make assumptions. I feel they are gearing up to apologize, then thinking better of it. Some of their anger dissipates.

They hesitate—I've never before seen them hesitate, then turn to me. "It will be all right," they say.

"Could you please leave?" I am trying to be courteous, but the magic is pushing against my skin. This is not a point to come to a sudden stop. What is their problem?

"I am not letting them torture you," they say, with a sudden shift of tone into media-proof reassurance.

I wish I could hit Miran Anyuwe. With so much magic, it is dangerous to even think of violence. I force down the thought. "They are not *torturing* me. Please." I wave my arms. My motions are increasingly jagged—I know I'm losing control. "I need to release the magic, please, could you *please* leave? It's dangerous. You shouldn't be in here."

"I would listen to em if I were you," my master says quietly. "If you're not leaving, I will escort you out." They step forward.

Miran Anyuwe recoils. "You—you brute!" they yell at my master. Then to me: "I will protect you!"

This would be annoying or even amusing if I weren't about to explode. I hug myself into a ball. I think I am making a sound...?

I don't see how my master grabs them and drags them physically out of the room. I can hear their huffs as they manually turn the lock.

Hurried steps across the room. My master is practically flying. Toward me.

Arms around me. I feel very small. "It's all right. It's all right. I'm here. I'm here for you." Holding me tight. "You can let it go now. I will guide it. You can let it go."

I howl, convulsing, weeping. The magic tears at my insides as it rushes out. My master will have things to repair—I am suddenly angry at Miran Anyuwe for this, but then the thought is swept away; thought itself is swept away.

Outside, the ship is moving.

My master is so furious *they* have excess. They run up and down the length of the room, then just groan and push magic into the structure.

"Next time I'll have to do that out the airlock or I'll just fry the controls," they say. Calm enough to sound cynical. They shake their head. Clack, clack. "I'll fix you up once I'm steadier," they say. "It didn't seem to leave lasting damage. I would've torn them in half!"

I seldom hear my master talk about violence. But I understand the source of their fury now.

I query the systems. Where is Miran Anyuwe? Pacing the corridor outside, apparently.

I close my eyes and lie back. I don't think I can face the client. I don't think I can face anything. How could things go this wrong?

"I'll talk to them," my master says. "You can rest. I'll bring you your heavy blanket."

They cover me up. I wriggle into the warm, weighty duvet, grab armfuls of it. Some things are eternal, unchanging. My master briefly caresses my head, fingers playing with my short curls. My muscles loosen up. I can feel that some of the tension leaves my master, too. I turn my head, peek out from the blanket to gaze at them. They look like Miran Anyuwe; but they also look like me, and this time I just want to focus on the latter. People have mistaken us for relatives before, and there is something deeply comforting in this.

"It's not your fault," they say. "None of this is your fault."

"But… the door?" I find it hard to move my lips and tongue. My mouth doesn't work.

"There was a malfunction." They frown. "Don't forget that Miran Anyuwe is a magical person, too, if not so powerful as either of us."

The message, unspoken: *Be on your guard.*

I'm back in our room, still resting, the soft upper layer of our mattress bending obediently around my aching flesh. Master Sanre repaired what could be repaired right away, then set the rest on a healing course. I'm halfway to sleep, drifting in a white-fluffy haze, when the alarm sounds.

I get out of bed, hastily dress, walk to the control room like a baby duck unsteady on its legs. Teeter-totter. My master looks up at me, and so does Miran Anyuwe. I feel they had been arguing.

"Warships on our tail," says Master Sanre. "We'll need to jump soon, and hope fervently that they can't follow us."

We're still on sublight, and moving much slower than our target velocity due to the unwelcome interruption. I grimace, try to gather my wits. The warships must be after Miran Anyuwe; we ourselves don't have enemies.

I sense my master's gaze upon me. "How soon can we jump?" they ask.

"I can start preparing right away," I say. I know the healing won't be able to run its course, and I know that's also what my master has been thinking. But if we are hit by a mass-driver, there won't be any healing in the world to repair our bodies.

Miran Anyuwe has stopped protesting. I want to grab them, snarl at them: *If you think what you saw was bad, just see what happens now. Just watch. Will you turn your head away?*

A shot whips past our ship: the sensors tell me everything in minute detail. I shudder.

Master Sanre tries to hail the warships. No response, just another shot. Deliberately missing? Intended as a warning?

Then a third, aimed head on—

My master jumps up from their chair. "We need to get out now!"

They tackle me, hug me to themselves, push me down on the floor. My face flattens against the cold floorboards, my mouth opens. I gasp for breath.

"Now!" they yell, and even without the familiar trappings, my body responds instantaneously, my mind rushes through the preparations of matter transposition.

Magic rises in me, floods me, streams outward, suffuses the ship. I scream with the sudden expansion of awareness, the pain of white-hot power running along my spine, I keen and convulse as my master holds me down, grabs hold of my power to direct it outward—

—we jump. Arriving clumsily at our target destination, off the ecliptic, too close to the system's star. I cough, close my eyes to better focus on the sensors. I try not to focus on my body. Something feels broken, not a bone or two but a process itself; something biochemical knocked askew.

Master Sanre rolls to the side, still holding me close. We remain there for a few breaths, ignoring Miran Anyuwe. We get up, holding onto each other.

"We need to jump into Alliance space," my master says, "who knows how fast they can follow us?"

Very few people can make an entire ship jump as rapidly as I do; my magic simply has an uncommon shape that's well-suited for this particular task. Miran Anyuwe doesn't know this. Our pursuers don't know this.

"I'll request a permit right away," I say.

"I'll do it. You get ready to jump again."

My master is still trying to get through to an Alliance comm station when the warships show up. I can't even make it to the power chamber. Pain unfurls, spreads out as I raise power; I flail and claw against my master who holds me strongly. The ship jumps.

I'M HALF DRAGGED, HALF CARRIED. Two voices wheezing. My master and...Miran Anyuwe?

They drop me down on the pallet, and the shape, the sensation identifies it to me. I'm in the power chamber. Straps are pulled, tightened across my body.

"Can *you* do it? Can you do it again?"

It takes time to realize my master is speaking to me. I nod, teeth gritted.

"Can you do it?" Miran Anyuwe asks them.

"Oh—" My master suppresses a curse. "Don't bother about me!"

"You're shaking."

"Of course I am—" They raise their voice and it trembles. Suddenly I am worried: I need to bring this to a close, I can take the magic, but what about my master?

I grapple with words for a few moments before I am able to speak. "I can jump us to Alliance space without a beacon."

"Without a permit? It's illegal," my master protests, but inwardly I know they are already convinced. The Alliance goons ask first, shoot second, not the other way round like the jockeys of these warships are wont to do.

"I'd take Alliance Treaty Enforcement over these people any day," I say, knowing full well that they have magic-users just like me. I used to be one of them. I wouldn't be able to get out of harm's way fast enough. More effort and I won't be able to do anything at all, but one more jump I can manage, even against the gradient, against the odds—

The warships are back.

I strain against the straps and clutch at my master, scream at them to pull, pull because I can't generate enough power in time, and after their initial hesitation they do it, and I can feel myself pulled apart, space itself getting fragmented and torn, unraveling at the edges—

We are in orbit around Andawa, second-tier Alliance population center. We know this planet well. It's easy for us to jump here.

It will take the Alliance more than a moment to mobilize their forces. Andawa is peripheral, but not so peripheral as to be without protection. The enforcers will simply take a bit longer to arrive, jumping in probably from Central.

My master undoes the straps, their fingers working as their mind is busy hailing Planetside Control. I try to stand, fall into their arms. Miran Anyuwe is silent this time, but I can tell they are shaking, and not just with the side-effects of back-to-back jumps with no jump point, no beacon.

I make a motion toward them, then slowly collapse and fold into myself as my legs give way. My master topples down on the floor together with me, cradles my head.

The warships soon follow. I can't move. I can't jump. I can't think. I gasp and wheeze, try to push myself upright. My master pushes me back. "Don't," they whisper next to my ear.

The enemies can't quite jump into our ship—the wards still hold. They board the old-fashioned way, with lots of clanging and metal being cut. Where is the Alliance? Why are they so slow?

Before my vision gives in, I see black-clad commandos stream into the room. I see Miran Anyuwe crouch on the floor next to me, taking cover behind the box of equipment.

I don't understand what the commandos are saying. I only understand what my master is thinking.

On their signal, I roll to the side, bump into Miran Anyuwe, my arms around them. They smell of marzipan. I hold fast. Then I fall through space, through time, through awareness itself.

SHARP, PRICKLY GRASS. THE SUNLIGHT SCRAPES at the back of my head when I open my eyes; I close them and shiver despite the warmth of Andawa's sun. I grapple with the earth as I try to get if not upright, then at least on all fours. I can't even pull myself up on my elbows—I lose balance, smear my face and arms with rich dark dirt. Andawa is a garden world.

Miran Anyuwe is speaking, has been speaking for a while now. I can't make sense of the words. They reach under my armpits and pull.

GAPS IN CONTINUITY.

Miran Anyuwe dragging me on some backcountry path and yelling at me, preaching that I shouldn't live a life of slavery. I try to say that I am not a slave, I serve my master voluntarily, without coercion. My speech turns into mush—my mouth is too uncoordinated—and in any case Miran Anyuwe refuses to listen. I can't walk unassisted, I can barely parse sentences and yet they are preaching to me, about how I ought not to be running away from freedom but toward it.

Who's running away, I want to say, but my systems checks are failing one by one, my biosensors are screaming.

WORDS. WORDS. MORE WORDS. COMPLETELY OPAQUE.

I'M LYING ON THE SLIGHTLY CURVING floor—a ship's bay? Entirely unfamiliar beyond the reassuring calmness of Alliance-standard. Miran Anyuwe is sitting next to me, their left hand on my forehead. I try to bat it aside; my entire right side spasms. I gasp, force steadiness on my breath, ignore all the warnings.

Miran Anyuwe speaks—the sentences elude me. I want to turn and see, observe the crowd whose presences I can feel pressing on my mind, but I can't move; even my motions to shoo away Miran Anyuwe are little more than twitches.

Someone, a sharp bright voice, finally: "…a medical emergency, Captain, we need to intervene." I miss the answer. Then the same person, slower, pausing after each word: "Captain, you need to allow me."

Miran Anyuwe withdraws; I sigh in relief. Someone crouches down next to me and oh I know this mind-template, so familiar I fight the urge to grab and latch onto it, in this sea of incomprehension where in every moment an eddy or whirl can cause me to drift away. Ereni magic-user, delegated to the Alliance; they don't call it magic, they have their own words…

"Ssh." A touch on my chest. "You are almost completely drained. I will help you if you let me."

I murmur something, hoping it will be enough, hoping the intent would be clear. I reach to the Ereni's hand on my chest, but my fingers fail to connect. I'm not quite clear about where my body parts are situated at any given moment.

Warm egg-yolk-yellow power floods into me through their hand and my cells drink it in, desperate for nourishment. I can move. I can live.

Speaking doesn't come as fast. Where is my master, I think at the Ereni now that my thoughts can move forward, *Is my master safe?*

ETA another twenty-five minutes, the Ereni thinks in my head. *We are short on people to jump them here. The Isolationists have been apprehended and are being ejected from Alliance space.* I look up at the Ereni—their appearance matches my mental impression of them. Black, thick-set, gender-indeterminate. They are still clenching their jaw. I know it takes a lot of effort to get exact numbers across—this is not a high-magic area. I nod, appreciating the effort. They hold my hand, squeeze it. Just as I understand them, they also understand me, through the shared demands of magic and the hierarchies it often creates.

I sigh, look around. Across the room, a short, sharp-featured officer in the uniform of Alliance Treaty Enforcement glares at—me? No, at Miran Anyuwe. My interface works again, the error messages recede. The officer is a man, by the name of Adhus-Barin, with about half a dozen more lineage-names after his first. A nobleman from the Empire of Three Stars, one of the more socially conservative members of the Alliance.

"Maybe we can try this again," Adhus-Barin says. He looks about as angry as a noble in a mere Alliance captaincy position can be expected to look, his auburn-brown skin darkening further. His systems are probably frantic, trying to avoid a stroke. "You might wish to rephrase what you've just told me."

Miran Anyuwe seems proud as ever, but as my body processes the influx of magic, I can already tell the politician radiates fear, apprehension and…brokenness, somehow. An impression of someone caught in the act.

"I was escaping from the Isolationists who were after me," Miran Anyuwe says, "I wouldn't have made it to Alliance space if not for these excellent people." They nod at me. Am I supposed to smile, murmur thanks? I remain silent. They continue: "One of whom doesn't even understand the Code of Life and Balance, I must say."

What is that? If I hear one more word about how I'm supposed to be some kind of slavery apologist...

Adhus-Barin also glares at them. Is he waiting for Miran Anyuwe to incriminate themselves?

The politician continues, shifting pace as if realizing they are no longer talking to their home crowd. "As you are no doubt aware, the Isolationists oppose our negotiations to join the Alliance, negotiations that I am leading..." They pause, uncertain for a moment. "Between two rounds of talks, I returned to Ohandar, where I was summarily attacked, and after my attempted escape, even my security detail deserted me at Idhir Station, so I had to seek out a private vessel for help..."

"Your security detail betrayed you?" Adhus-Barin turns oddly mild, almost gentle. I don't have to pry into his thoughts to sense a trap being readied.

"They were all Isolationists, they turned against me—" Voice rising. Miran Anyuwe is losing their cool.

"Oh, those kinds of roughshod mercenaries don't appreciate going unpaid," Adhus-Barin nods with empathy.

"What could I have done? The talks were almost over and the funds—" They halt mid-sentence.

I stare. At Adhus-Barin smiling, his thin mouth turning up in almost a sneer, at Miran Anyuwe standing statue-still, with only stray tremors breaking through their rigidity.

The security detail going unpaid. Isolationists going unpaid.

"Thank you," Adhus-Barin says, "I do believe this will be enough."

As if a dam breaking through, Miran Anyuwe starts blabbering, words tumbling over each other. The statue falling apart. "The Alliance has to understand, the Alliance knows—isolationist sentiment has always been strong on Ohandar, we had to show the populace that isolationism was extremism, we had to—"

"So you backed the Isolationist movement, steered them into violence," Adhus-Barin says, one step away from gloating. "Created and funded your own rivals, so that you could point a finger at them and say, we are not like those people. So that you could revel in the position of the peacemaker."

"The Alliance knows! Don't deny it! The Alliance knows!"

"May I?" the Ereni says, then waits for the captain's nod. "The Alliance knows. That doesn't mean the Alliance assents."

"Exactly as Officer Enisāyun has it," the captain nods at them again. "Undesirable allies often incriminate themselves during the accession process, as we have found." He says it as if the Empire was innocent of all possible wrongdoing, and I wonder if Miran Anyuwe knows how the Alliance had taken its present shape, what had prompted the member states to create Treaty Enforcement, back it with real power and threat. I sneak a look at Enisāyun, and the Ereni glances back at me, shrugs.

Miran Anyuwe mutters word-fragments, all sense lost in overwhelming anger, directed at us who thwarted the plan. We all gaze upon the spectacle. I pull my personal wards tighter around myself in case Miran Anyuwe lashes out.

Officer Enisāyun asks to speak again, then gestures toward me. "The esteemed leader might wish to thank the young māwalēni here for saving their life."

Adhus-Barin makes a face. The meaning is clear—he would rather the politician would have perished, murdered by their own erstwhile allies. Let alone called esteemed leader, but then again the Ereni are fond of formality... and its ironic flipside.

Enisāyun smiles softly. "We will make sure that the young māwalēni receives all due payment for services rendered—though from whom might be uncertain at this point..."

Miran Anyuwe collapses.

"It wasn't me," Enisāyun says, voice shaky. "Captain? It wasn't me, Captain."

"I thought they were warded from all outside—" A voice from the back of the Alliance crowd, then another, "I warded them!"

A door seal hisses, and my master dashes in, the familiar clang of boots on ship-metal. "Were they threatening anyone? I felt they might be threatening someone, so it seemed safer to shut them down."

"Excuse me?" Adhus-Barin seems utterly lost. *It's that kind of day*, the Ereni thinks at me and I suppress a chuckle.

"I have a policy of not interfering with clients' minds, but they severely disrupted my ship, interrupted the jumping procedure—"

Officer Enisāyun is shocked in the back of my mind.

"—so I thought it would be safest to plant my safeguards on them just in case. They had no defenses to speak of."

An understatement, recognized by everyone present as such. When did my master have time to do this? I consider the events of the day, fail to find the exact moment. An intervention performed off-hand, with a stray thought...

As Adhus-Barin regains his calm and goes through the motions of the cleanup, organizing transport for Miran Anyuwe to Alliance Central where they will no doubt have to endure another round of castigation before getting booted out of Alliance space, my attention is elsewhere. I knew my master was more powerful, I tell myself, but I understand at the same time that it's not about power—or, rather, that power entails more than raw control. It entails being straightforward, honest, upright.

And I know that between the two of us, we don't need a planet.

Master Sanre offers me a hand and I stand up—then they grab me, hold me tight to themselves, their tears trickling down my curls.

The Scaper's Muse

B R Sanders

I MET HIM FIRST AT A New Year's party. It was my friend Arthur's party. Friend is not quite the right word—Arthur was promoted and was then a few rungs above me; upper-management. With Arthur's promotion came more money, and thus better champagne at his parties, so I was happy to keep getting invitations even after he left me in the dust. It was a swanky party—women dripped in jewelry, the canapés catered, the whole nine yards. Everything shone; everything was crystal or diamond or mirrored. Light bounced around the room like a ricocheted bullet. It was getting on near midnight, and I had my eye out for an acquiescent girl to kiss when the clock rang in the new year. Arthur, freshly married, stood in the center of the room laughing with his new wife.

It was 11:57 PM, and in he walked: a wiry man, all long and rakish black hair, wearing a thickly cabled green fisherman's sweater over a pair of olive-drab pants he might have picked up at an army surplus store. His face was bruised; I remember the greenish-purple smear of it across the left side of his jaw. And his eyes, his eyes were jade and emeralds—a deep, enraged piercing green. Where everyone else in the room, myself included, reflected the light this man in monochromatic green seemed to drink it in, to absorb our reflections and with them our sense of merriment. He stepped inside Arthur's foyer and slammed the door behind him. The force of it rattled a chandelier. Conversation ceased. Arthur turned to see what the commotion was. "You!" he breathed.

And the man in green stepped forward, that accusatory bruise catching the light, holding the light. "Yes. Me."

Arthur sputtered into speech. "What are you—"

The bruised, plainly dressed man held up a key. "I'm returning this," he said. "I hear you married."

Arthur's wife asked who the man was. We all wanted to know. The numbers on the clock turned to 11:59 PM. Arthur stiffened; the interloper let out something like a disgusted growl. The possibility of violence shimmered in the air. And I, propelled by I still don't know what, stepped forward and took the interloper gently by the elbow. Some residual loyalty to Arthur maybe. Some petty hope that he would see and pull me up the corporate ladder with him. Some alchemy of all of that plus the champagne. I can't say. I took the man's elbow, and he turned his burning green eyes on me. "Come on," I said very softly, very gently. "I'll walk you out."

His mouth twitched. He cut a final vicious look at Arthur and allowed me to escort him out. All throughout the city the clocks struck midnight as Arthur's front door closed behind me. Shivering slightly in the cold, the man I'd escorted out paced back and forth, full of unsettled energy. "That lying fuck," he hissed. He lit a cigarette and tucked his free hand into his armpit for warmth.

"That's a nasty bruise," I said. The man let out a mirthless laugh. The clocks still sang of the new year around us. He peered at me. He smiled a wild, manic smile. He grabbed the collar of my shirt and pulled me to him, kissed me full on the mouth. His tongue slid against mine, intrusive but not wholly unwanted, and I tasted the acrid smoke of his cigarette. The surprise of it, the rough scratch of his stubble, the heat of his mouth contrasted with the frigid air outside, all of it set me spinning.

He pulled away when the clocks stopped singing. He smiled and took another drag of his cigarette. "Well," he said. He said the single word like a full sentence: *Well.* "Well. At least we made the deadline. A kiss to hold off a year of loneliness." And then he was gone, off into the black birth of the new year.

IT'S STRANGE THE WAY A TERRAN tradition followed me out of Terra's orbit. The months that followed Arthur's party were accurately predicted by that first moment of the new year: it was unexpected, and masculine, and far from lonely, and far from safe. The year that followed was green through and through.

I speak, of course, of my lived year; in the actual passing of hours it was at least twice that. It took less than a month after the party for Arthur to get me transferred off-world. He sought me out for a lunch meeting and asked a handful of nervous, probing questions about my interaction with the green-eyed man in the green sweater at his party. Three days later I was promoted and sent to "oversee emerging markets" a few stars over. I was an ideal candidate—demonstrated loyalty to the company, a definite sense of adventure, useful but ultimately expendable skill set, and the sort of immediate mobility that comes with being youngish and in good health and socially untethered. I knew very little of outbound life when I left Terra. I knew only what you see on news reports, what you glean from cousins of friends whose aunts once went on an interstellar cruise. They didn't prep me; they told me to keep an open mind, paid my way onto a Versa-steered interstellar craft, and impressed upon me their faith that I would do well out there.

They sent me to Stahvi, which back then few Terrans had heard of and fewer had been to. I realized when they woke me from craftsleep that what had happened was less a promotion than a banishment. I—and the knowledge I'd accidentally gleaned—had sent me far out of the way, well beyond the scope of scandal makers. I've never been an ambitious man. I've organized my life to ensure I live comfortably, and that's really been the driving force: a comfortable life scraped out with my decency more or less intact. And the banishment was comfortable. The company paid for my apartment. I had a generous living stipend. My work was so vague and undefined that virtually anything I did counted. There was no oversight; I had no one to report to. I was supposed to be "gauging interest" and "building relationships" and "laying groundwork" for when the company decided to set up a satellite economy there on Stahvi. I was in exile, but it was a very accommodating exile. It really wasn't that bad a deal.

Terrans are behind the curve when it comes to intercultural exchange. Stahvi is what I've read Tangier was like way back before the Cultural Exchange, back when aliens were humans born a different shade of brown. Stahvi sits on a rare habitable world equidistant from three life-infested star systems. The Versa are there, obviously, but Stahvi plays host to the Lii and the Silvans, as well. At the time I was exiled to Stahvi Terrans had a solid working relationship with the Versa, had begun to forge some relationships with Lii mercantile ships, and had only heard stories of the Silvans. Stahvi was an oddly polite place despite its lawless nature. In a mark of the difference between Terran psychology and alien psychologies I was rarely hassled. The Versa more or less ignored me since they'd gathered on my trip over I had no money or intel. But I made many Lii friends—friends I still have. I learned two or three Lii dialects. I was paraded around at Lii garden domes on one Lii's frond or another, passed back and forth between them like an in-vogue accessory. Of all the aliens, the Lii looked most at home on Stahvi—they were as green as Stahvi's sky. They had the same silky fineness of Stahvi's smooth soil. They weren't from Stahvi, but it was hospitable to them. The Silvans mostly kept to themselves underwater. There are amphibious markets on Stahvi, places where the land-dwellers can go haggle with the aquatic Silvans, but I've always been scared of drowning and I confess I did little "relationship building" or "interest gauging" with the Silvans. Who knows what "emerging markets" I lost for the company there. My most sincere apologies to the shareholders.

As I said, when I got there Terrans were rare on Stahvi. It was months before I encountered another Terran. I heard her before I saw her: a human woman's laugh trilling in a Lii garden. It was so strange, and yet so familiar, so immensely unexpected that I teared up. I'd begun to think of myself as the Last Man. Or First Man. At the very least a Singular Man. I collected myself and edged through the party, gently nudging through the Liis' petals and leaves and stalks until I saw her, a tall human woman, dark-haired and green-eyed swathed in a green silk robe. I stared at her as if she were a mirage. It took her some seconds before she noticed me, and even then it was only because her Lii companion pointed me out. She startled. She laughed again; her voice had a husky depth to it. She gestured me over.

I willed myself to walk over slowly in what I hoped was a genteel and languid way. She handed me a pod of nectar. "Another Terran here on Stahvi?" she asked.

"Another Terran here on Stahvi," I said.

"Pity," she said. "I came here for the escape. Why are you here?"

"Business," I said. I smiled and leaned in a hair closer, conspiratorial. Flirtatious. I was horribly attracted. It had been nearly a Terran year of

living among aliens; the idea of sex with a mammal was extremely entic-
ing. "Banishment."

She raised her eyebrows. Her Lii companion whispered something to
her and sauntered off, graceful and fluid. "What's your name?"

"Gavin. Gavin Camayo."

She held her hand out to me. "Lydia Brightlake. Call me Lake," she
said. We traded inane chatter—where did you grow up? How do you
know the host of this garden? What about those Silvans? Just idle chatter the likes of which you really can only do with another human. It was
inordinately pleasant.

As the conversation went on, there was an increasing sense of familiarity. It tugged at me, nagged at me. The green of her eyes. The glint of
her black hair. The arrogant jut of her chin. The cadence of her voice.
These little things, these very small things began to knit together. It was
a shrewd disguise, truly, but when you've been so starved for human contact, and when a memory is so very indelible, disguises fall apart. "Lydia
Brightlake," I said. I'd interrupted her. She gave me a curious smile. "Lake,
I think you're the reason I was banished."

A strain of fear froze her expression. It's funny how transparent human
faces are when you've been immersed so long among the aliens. You have
to try so hard to read their cues, and then you come upon one of your
own and it's so easy. She covered her face with her hand. "Well. Shit."

"But you were a man!" I said.

She shrugged. She blushed. She grinned. "I flicker," she said.

"You flicker?"

"It's not my first time out of orbit."

"Versa bodyscaping?" She shrugged again. She sipped her nectar with
a canny smile. A dozen question crowded my tongue—isn't that illegal?
Expensive? An urban legend? What I asked instead was: "How?"

"How what?" asked Lake.

"How do they do it?"

"Oh." She cocked her head to the side. "Gavin, really, I'm no Versa. I
don't really know. Something about taking you all apart and putting you
back together again, tiny piece by tiny piece. They do…well. I don't know
what they do. It's beneath anything we can do, below even the cellular
level. It's like they break apart this tiny piece of reality—the tiny piece of
reality that is your body—and construct a new one. I don't know. I'm not

a scientist. I'm no Versa. It's not unpleasant, though. They're consummate professionals."

"How many times?" I looked her over; no scars, no telling marks anywhere. But she was still herself. Himself. The same person, but re-imagined. The same emerald-jade eyes. The same black hair. The same peculiarities of speech.

"Oh, I don't know. Six or seven. I flickered back and forth for that bastard Arthur three times—man, intersex, man. This is the first I've been a woman in some time." I wondered, when she said it, if Arthur's wife was one of these mercurial Terrans, these unmappable people who changed, who were such uncertainty, such flexibility incarnate. Probably not. The scandal would have kept him from marrying her.

She answered then a question I hadn't wanted to ask. She grinned at me. "Here on Stahvi," she said, "I flicker for myself."

THERE ARE LIMITS TO VERSA MEDICAL tech. They guard the secrets of their magic-like sciences, but they are not quite as god-like as they'd have us believe. Lake got me minor bodyscaping for free—she'd positioned herself as a Versa scaper's muse/walking advertisement. Every few months she'd shift a little—taller, or rounder, black-skinned, etc.—but she kept the green eyes and the black hair in every iteration. She never spoke of it, but I know from my own experience it was her choice. My first scape was to change my eye color to match her precise shade of green. Then I had the Versa scaper do my hair black. The Versa suggested a change to the shape of my nose and a correction to my slightly pigeon-toed stance, but something in me wouldn't let ver do it. As Lake would say it, I'm no Versa: I need some fixedness, some small tether to link who I've been with who I'll be. And so I've been a red-haired, white-skinned woman. And I've been a lean, black-haired something-in-between. And I've been a sharp-faced grey-eyed man, but in all those iterations I've had the nose and the pigeon toes with which I was born.

Having two of us on Stahvi drummed up more business for the Versa scaper, but ve was a hungry and ambitious sort, and there is an art to scaping that eludes my human mind. Ve came to Lake and me one day and proposed a set of scapes that would—in ver words—equalize us. The Versa took our ragged, mangy DNA and sculpted out of it twins. Ve gave me Lake's emerald-jade eyes and ink-black hair. Ve gave Lake my hawkish nose and wrong-angled feet. There was enough detritus in our genetic codes to match us on skin tone, on height, on build. We emerged from ver cocoons as mirror images, left and right.

The thing about finding another Terran on Stahvi back then was that as the two sole members of our species on the planet we were forced to choose: love each other deeply or hate each other on sight. Nothing in between was workable for either of our human minds; we each of us craved that extreme. Mercifully, we both turned to love. It would have been awkward but nothing more than that had we both turned to hate. I still shudder to think what it would have been like for one of us to love the other and the other to hate them in return. Lake and I were inseparable, were devoted, this is true. We'd shared a thousand kisses before we were equalized, and yet, something about the equalization, that strange magical-scientific twinning the Versa scaper pulled off, sparked something new. New and old—something forgotten but familiar. When we kissed the first time as a mirrored pair, as so identical and yet still different in our fundamental and imperceptible ways, it felt exactly like it had when he kissed me at midnight as that long-past year turned over. Something about it, some strange and charming taboo overturned, danced upon, celebrated and destroyed, at once lived in both that equalized kiss and the kiss on Arthur's doorstep. There is something in that tension between the sameness of us and the difference that pulls at me. Something that highlights the glorious randomness of life. Something in those kisses that makes me feel at once infinitesimally small and yet the center of the universe, and the unresolvable paradox of it is intoxicating.

We lay entwined that first night as made twins, in bodies that were still unfamiliar but which already felt like home. I told Lydia Brightlake I loved her. She stroked my new breasts and told me she loved me, too. And then she smiled. "Well. Well, really, I love us. I love creating us from nothing, from scratch. I love being us."

The Librarian's Dilemma

E. Saxey

JAS'S JOB WAS TO BRING LIBRARIES into the twenty-first century. St Simon's library hadn't left the seventeenth, yet.

Jas stood in a university quad, surrounded by stone buildings. In the centre was a huge yew whose branches brushed the walls. The wooden library door, ahead, was studded with nails.

The house Jas shared with his mother in Bradford would have fitted comfortably into this quad. Jas felt his principles—the anti-elitist, democratic ones that drew him to work in libraries—should have soured the sight. But they didn't. He felt out of place (too brown, too poor, too queer) but was still attracted.

The oak door opened. An older woman appeared in its shadow, straight-backed in dark clothes that swung about her like robes.

"Jaswinder? I'm the librarian for the Harrad Collection. You've brought a lot of luggage."

Jas was smuggling the future, in big suitcases. Digitisation equipment: expensive, and unique, and terribly heavy. They'd been hell to drag around on the long train journey (although had probably done wonders for his developing arm muscles). *The librarian hasn't asked for them,* his boss had said. *But you can change her mind. Just don't tell her you brought them with you.* "I wasn't sure what the weather would be like," Jas said.

"I'll send Fred to help."

She slipped back inside, and from the same door rocketed a figure in a suit, thin as a stick with thick-framed glasses and a mane of hair tossing around.

"Hand 'em over. I'm stronger than I look." A Scots accent. "I do all the shelving. Up and down the stairs, too—no lifts, the place is too old." He grabbed a case, swung it over his shoulder, staggered a little. "Follow me."

Up a stone staircase, into a room overlooking the quad. The yew tree pressed its fingers on the leaded glass window.

"Do I sleep here?"

"Yep. Student rooms. I'm down the corridor."

"Aren't you a librarian?"

"God, no. Who'd want to do that?"

"I do." His holiday job was a decent start, but Jas planned (when he'd finished his degree) to get properly chartered.

"You're young. You'll grow out of it."

Fred led Jas back to the library. A dim room, as long as one side of the huge quad. When the door opened, a knife of light stabbed across the floorboards. Tweedy readers cluster around the windows. Academics were strange. Any sane person would take a book outside, sit under the tree.

The librarian looked up from her desk near the door, shook back her bobbed grey hair.

"Jas. Call me Moira. Now, we have you for eight weeks?"

"Yes." *Or longer, if they need you,* Michelle-the-boss had said.

"You're going to tag our rare books, and connect each book to our catalogue record. You've had experience?"

"I tagged the incunabula in the founders' library in Lampeter." A miserable wet fortnight in Wales, but useful for the CV.

Moira laid a book on her desk. "Show me."

Jas eyed the book, conscious of being auditioned. Nice leather binding, useful crescent-moon gap between the sewn pages and the spine. He took from his bag a small plastic box and a slim long tool, like a sparkler. *Talk them through it,* Michelle reminded him.

"So these are the seeds." The box was full of flat beads, like white lentils. "And I pick one up…"

Dipping the sparkler in the box, giving it a theatrical stir, then tapping to dislodge all but one seed.

"Then we…" He slid the sparkler into the spine-gap of the book. Good: no knots of glue, no tearing threads. You wanted the invisible worm, from Blake's poem, to wriggle into the book and hide the seed there, in the spine or the cover. The benevolent reader would never notice, the malevolent reader would never be able to find the seed and remove it.

"And now you can never lose it." It was part of the sales patter, but heartfelt. In a traditional library books got lost, not just in a prosaic sense (like lost keys) but in a profound way (like lost souls)—misplaced, they became inert, never again to be useful.

This was a great time for a quick demonstration. *Find an excuse,* Michelle had said. *It'll hook them.*

"Can I show you..." Jas moved around the room, sprinkling seeds at different heights on the shelves. (They were fiddly, but you couldn't, *ipso facto,* lose them.)

This was the fun part. "Now, if you want to find something..."

Jas held his device up to the room. The screen showed dots of light sprinkled all around. Constellations. Jas knew why it worked: because librarians thought of themselves as being gods of a miniature cosmos.

"Each light is a book. And when you know which book you want..." Jas turned off all the seed-lights except for the one he'd just installed. A single light remained, the star over Bethlehem.

"Hmm. I suppose it could be useful," said the librarian.

Jas felt his smile congeal on his face.

"OKAY, LET'S DO PHILOSOPHERS," SAID FRED.

"Plato."

"Ooh, a toughie. Ockham! William of Ockham. Your turn."

"Morris. William Morris."

"Sartre!"

At Moira's instruction, Fred was helping Jas to seed the books. He was beaky, frenzied, seemed likely to jab a seed tool straight through a book cover. "I'm only working in this library until I get a post-doc job," he'd announced. Jas resented this slur on the profession, but Fred did help to pass the time with whispered word games. Without Fred, it would have been dull work; Jas never read the books he seeded, to avoid getting sucked in.

By lunch on the first day, they'd seeded a huge stack of texts.

"We need the catalogue," Jas whispered. "To match the seeds to records. How do I access it?"

Fred pointed to a beige terminal.

Jas read a peeling sticker announcing it had been inspected for safety. "Ten years ago?"

"Well, it passed!" Fred said. "What more do you want?"

When consulted, Moira searched under her desk and dragged out a laptop, maybe only five years old. "Don't take it out of the library."

It was ridiculously slow. The ancient kit was inexplicable, given that St Simon's was so well endowed. The library catalogue wasn't complex, you could run it on anything. Jas could load it on his phone, for goodness' sake.

After an hour of wrestling with the ancient laptop, he did just that, and the work went so much quicker he nearly cried with relief. He kept the laptop open in case anyone was watching.

On the dot of five o'clock Fred stood and clapped his hands. Every tweedy reader looked up, and half of them closed their books and donned their jackets. Fred the pied piper led them towards a pub on the seafront.

"Why do you want to be a librarian, then?" Fred asked Jas as they walked. "Isn't it a wee bit boring?"

Jas wondered if he was being tested. "There are radical librarians."

"Really?"

"Yeah, fighting restrictions. Freeing information." Jas admired them for all those things. What stole his heart was also the multicoloured hair, the facial piercings, and the fact that half of them seemed to be trans or queer. "Mostly in America," he admitted.

"If you say so. I'll get the drinks in. Connell, tell Jas about your research!"

Connell was a squat black professor from Los Angeles. He nodded his bald head sharply at Jas. "Trauma! War, civil conflict, interpersonal violence."

"Oh. Goodness."

One by one, the other researchers named their expertise.

"Italian Fascism."

"Madness. Sorry, I wouldn't say 'madness' normally, of course. But I'm eighteenth century, it's all *madness*, *lunacy*, all that outdated terminology."

"Medical ethics. Well, mostly when it goes wrong." That was a woman from Sweden.

"I suppose you could say...the occult?" A younger man wearing a pentagram necklace.

"Mass graves."

There was nobody else to speak. Say something! thought Jas. Anything! "Nazis?"

"Not really."

With a clunk, Fred set down his tray of pints.

Ritual grumbling commenced. Jas knew it had all been said before, because people took up one another's refrains.

"If I could take books back to my room..."

"And you're only working on early twentieth century, aren't you? They're not fragile..."

"...not fragile at all."

"And the chairs!"

"No back support! I have to do stretches..."

Prof. Connell murmured to Jas. "Hey, you're doing something technological with the library, Jas?"

"Yeah."

"Fantastic. Now, this place needs to open up a little, you know? An amazing collection. Should be available to the best people, twenty-four/seven. No offence to these guys! Are you going to shake things up?"

Jas nodded weakly.

WHEN HE NEXT SAW PROFESSOR CONNELL, the prof. was reading a book while sitting in the yew tree.

"Stop this at once." Moira's voice ricocheted off the walls of the quad.

"Okay, okay. Tell me which part I can't do. Is the tree the problem? Can I sit on the grass?"

Jas grinned, then un-grinned. Better not to appear partisan. Better not to be seen at all. He'd just arrived in the quad, and hung back.

"You've removed a book from the library. You signed a contract."

"Yeah, I'm not sure that contract's legal. Forgive me. Two months in a dark room could make anyone a little wild. Cabin fever. Jas?" He'd been spotted. "Take this book while I climb down?"

The professor leaned down from the branches to pass Jas the book: a slim gum-bound paperback from the 1970s. Then the professor dropped neatly onto the grass, and walked back into the library.

"Good morning, Jas." Moira fell into step beside him. "You've done counter work, haven't you?"

"Sorry?"

"You've worked on library counters."

"Oh, yeah."

"You've probably had moments like this."

"Mm." Students hiding books down their trousers. Tossing them in the air as they walked through the security sensor. "I reckoned it was their job to push it as far as they could, and my job to bat it back."

"It's not symmetrical, though, is it? If half the time the thieves win, and half the time we win, soon there's no library." Moira held the door. "Jas, I want all the books seeded. Not just the old ones."

"Yes." That doubled the project. Michelle would be delighted. "I mean— I'm studying, I start my course again in October."

"What are your grades like? You could study here at St Simon's, perhaps, and work in the Collection."

The casual offer, in the chill of the dark room, sent a shiver up Jas's neck. To *go to university*—to indulge in that old, expensive rite of passage. To use a real library, rather than downloading e-books.

Then there was the added appeal of starting in a new place. His friends, his mother, had been a life support. But to begin again, where people had always known him as Jas, was tempting.

Fred had been eavesdropping. "So, she said you could study here? Will you go for it?"

To distract him, Jas asked: "What are you researching?"

"The Gothic." Fred widened his eyes, tossed his hair.

"Isn't that old-fashioned?"

"It won't die! It's big in America right now. I'm working on getting myself a Stateside post-doc. Going to become a genius."

"Can you—I mean, you can't *plan* to be a genius."

"You need more than brains. You need funding."

MOIRA WAS CLEARLY EMBRACING TECHNOLOGY, so Jas decided to give her another demonstration.

"University of Salisbury—special collections. My boss designed this for them."

Moira prodded Jas's device, bringing up related lecture notes, an audio clip of two students debating.

"You could have something like this," Jas said. "Use work from the visiting researchers. Showcase what the library does."

Moira shook her head without taking her eyes off the device.

"This modernity," she said. Jas thought she was referring to something on the screen, until she continued: "This *modernisation*."

"Yes?"

"It happens, of course, but it's not inevitable. This project you're leading. It's incredibly useful. But it's not the leading wave of an unavoidable rising tide."

"Of course!" Jas tried to sound sympathetic. "Not every innovation suits every library."

"I hope you don't feel you're here under false pretences."

"No, no. I'm happy just tagging," Jas lied. "I just—I liked this." He pointed at the device, at the University of Salisbury's shining showcase.

"I like it too." Moira was faking regret. Dishonesty was contagious. "Perhaps if things were different." Then, sincere again, she held out a Post-it note. "Here's the number for St Simon's admissions. I told them you'd be in touch."

"...YOUR FATUOUS LITTLE DICTATORSHIP..."

Professor Connell had been shouting for a couple of minutes. Jas's hands had started to shake—he hated arguments—so he put down the seeding wand.

"What harm does it do anyone?" The professor was playing to the gallery, but getting no response. The madness expert shook her head regretfully, the occultist pursed his lips. "So that's it? No second chance?"

"You used your second chance weeks ago, Professor," replied Moira.

The professor scooped up his notebooks. Everyone found somewhere else to look as he stomped down the aisle, slammed the oak door behind him.

Jas scribbled on a piece of paper: *What was that about?* Pushed it towards Fred.

Fred mimed holding a box, squeezing: a camera. Except the Professor wouldn't have made that gesture—he'd have taken his snap with a discreet tap on his phone.

Back to America, Fred wrote. Utterly expelled.

"SO PHOTOGRAPHS AREN'T ALLOWED AT ALL?" Later, in the pub, Jas was still keeping his voice down.

"Nothing's allowed." Fred pulled out a sheet of crumpled paper. "Here's the contract researchers sign. Check which ones you've already broken."

No stealing, no smoking. Fair enough. No photocopying, no scanning. Well, it might damage the books. But for every three reasonable requests, there was a big ask.

The researcher will not discuss the Harrad Collection in person or on social media.

Texts from the Collection will not be added to referencing apps or software including (but not limited to) Zotero, EndNote, RefMe…

Modernity isn't inevitable, the librarian had said. She knew about social media and referencing software, but had decided to ban them. She wasn't an ageing dusty stereotype. She was well informed, and gatekeeping.

"I don't like it either," Fred said. "But I'm not going to climb a tree with a book up my arse to prove a point."

"I don't think anyone could expect you to do that."

"I'm out of here, anyway." Fred's exodus predictions had taken on a personal, insulting note for Jas. *This place that you want to get into?* Fred seemed to be saying. *I shun it. I'm better. I'm gone.*

"So you said."

"You should read up on the founder, Lady Harrad. She had some interesting principles."

Lady Harrad had been born in 1890, Jas remembered vaguely. Victorian Values didn't seem relevant here.

Jas felt Fred's hand fumbling with his own under the pub table. He felt a flush of embarrassment, then realised Fred was trying to slip a tiny object into his palm.

"Have a look at that."

"What—"

"There are more discreet ways to take photographs."

Jas remembered the thick-rimmed glasses Fred wore for reading.

IN HIS BEDROOM THAT EVENING, JAS phoned his boss.

"Jas! Great work so far."

"Michelle, did I sign a contract to work here?"

"The company signed one."

"Could you send me a copy? I want to make sure I'm sticking to it."

"Sure. Probably common sense, though."

But there was nothing common, or sensible, about the Harrad Collection.

Jas held Fred's gift. The sliver of plastic was almost weightless. He knew he shouldn't examine it. He'd lose his job, and any chance of studying here.

But a radical librarian had to be brave. Jas opened up Fred's gift.

The memory card held a dozen files, all photos of pages. Jas read a header at random: "Unlike Other Women." Intrigued, Jas read on.

The woman was Unlike Other Women because she wasn't a woman at all.

The page was from a transsexual autobiography. Jas knew the label was anachronistic, but the story felt so familiar. *I rarely found myself drawn to feminine ways, and as a child threw myself into games with hoops and trains.* The voice bubbled off the page. By the end of the first page, the narrator had become engaged but *could not rest while betrothed to Daniel, having no wifely feelings for him. I then lived ten years in Clacton under the name of Donald.*

"Lived under the name of Donald." What a world of activity that sentence glossed over. How had she—*he*—earned his keep, bought his clothes…

Jas checked the title of the book. *Accounts from the Patients at Woburn Sands.* Fred had also photographed the contents page, and there were twenty names: Constance, Jack, Alicia, Robert, JC. Were they all trans?

Published in 1878. A voice from history, a miracle.

MICHELLE, IN JAS'S MIND, SAID *SLOW down, hold back*. But Jas still cornered Moira the following morning for another demonstration. There were things in this collection too precious to stay boxed up. He'd known it objectively, but Fred's illicit snaps—Donald's story—had brought it home.

He needed to know where Moira stood.

Jas opened some images from the Lampeter website. "This was incredibly fragile, a Vulgate Bible from the twelfth century." Everyone liked illuminated manuscripts. "We scanned it without even opening it."

Moira didn't dismiss it out of hand. "How?"

"Michelle's inventions." He showed Moira pictures of the scanners. Sheets of graphene that slid in between pages, ultra-fast book flippers for the most robust texts, or ultrasound devices for the most fragile. "So now that book can never be lost, or destroyed, even if it's stolen or water-damaged…"

"Or burnt."

It felt wrong to mention fire, to a librarian. Like saying "Macbeth" to an actor. "Yes."

"Interesting."

He would pitch hard, now, while he had her attention. "And with a collection like this, it seems such a waste for only the readers who are physically present to see it. I'm not saying you should throw it open…" He wanted that with all his untrained anarchist librarian heart, but he could haggle. "You would still absolutely be able to control exactly who has access to the texts." She'd like that.

"So you see digitisation as a way to *circulate* the texts."

It was such a basic question that it confused Jas completely. "Yes." Of course, why else?

Moira sighed. "Jas, you are a very diligent young man. That's why I hope you'll work here for a long while, perhaps study here. But please understand, I will invest in any technology that means I *know where my books are*." Tapping her desktop with a bloodless fingernail. "And which means they cannot be destroyed. Anything that makes it harder to steal them, to photograph them, to gain access to them without my knowledge—I want that."

She wasn't interested in opening the library up. She wanted to close it down. Maybe she'd misunderstood.

"We live in such an amazingly connected world, now," Jas said. "It's such a part of scholarship, and learning, and…" Vainly throwing keywords at the librarian.

"You're right. In fact, I've been speaking to Michelle. She's agreed that you can advise me on this."

"Really?" A bloom of optimism.

"Building a security net, for a connected world. I'll tell you about some of the worst offenders of the last five years." Her eyes were bright at the thought of book thieves. Worse than that: library thieves. "You can tell me how you would have caught them."

"YEATS," SAID JAS. THEY WERE USING famous writers for the game, today.

Each touch they give / love is nearer death… Jas had read that Yeats poem when he was learning about the librarian's dilemma. It applied more to books than to lovers.

There were always two impulses in any librarian, any library, any collection: the desire to preserve a text, and the desire to make it available. Those two impulses were always at war. Each finger on a book lessened its lifespan.

But that was the marvellous thing about Jas's scanning work: now the whole world could read a book without damaging it, without even touching it. How many other professions built around a central paradox could say: we solved it?

"Wallace Stevens. Hey. Sleepyhead. Stevens."

Moira didn't seem to be conflicted at all about her collection. Preservation trumped access, for her, every time. She was committing an act of enclosure: taking things which could easily be in the public domain and building a wall round them.

There was a dark side to collecting books. A hoarding, acquisitive desire. To keep the books away from other people and their sticky fingers. You had to temper that desire, and use your knowledge to increase the knowledge of others. Without that, you weren't a librarian. You were just a hoarder.

"Stoker," said Jas. "Bram Stoker."

"Hey, not fair. That's my turf. Anything Gothic—mine. Anyway. Ayn Rand."

And now she wanted to put Jas's diligent young brain to keeping people out. Poacher turned gamekeeper.

"You coming to the pub?"

"Already?" The whole day gone, and he hadn't even tried to find the Woburn Sands book.

"ALL LIBRARIANS ARE EVIL," FRED ANNOUNCED, as they crossed the dark quad on the way home that night. "You want to be a librarian, Jas. It's because they *make a difference*, right?"

Jas shrugged. There was still a light burning in the library. At lunchtime he'd emailed his best essays to an admissions tutor at St Simon's, and he wouldn't let Fred's ramblings damage his chances.

Fred rolled on. "But librarians are supposed to be neutral, right? You want a book about raising Satan, the librarian's supposed to give it to you. So how can you be moral *and* neutral? They want to *make a difference*, but they don't say what difference they actually make."

"But you gave me that book."

Jas hadn't intended to say it. He was tipsy. He wanted to check if he had someone on his side. "That made a difference, to me."

"Oh, that was just queer solidarity. Hope you didn't mind. I mean, I'm not assuming... Y'know."

"I thought you were agreeing with me. Showing me something that should be shared—released."

"Nah. None of that hippy stuff. Just a present."

They climbed the stairs to Jas's room, and at the door, Fred said: "Hold on a moment." He reached behind Jas's head, speaking and moving so casually that Jas thought Fred was brushing fluff off his coat collar.

Fred laid his hand across the nape of Jas's neck and kissed him. His beer-tasting tongue parted Jas's lips and moved in a slow circle inside Jas's mouth. It was a bit much, but not unpleasant.

"Can I come in?" Fred asked.

"You're drunk."

"Have you met me? I'm always drunk."

They were both laughing. He could feel the upwards curve of Fred's lips, wished he could remember what Fred's face looked like, if he'd been attracted to him at all before this ambush.

"Look, come in, but maybe not..."

"Not for that."

"Maybe not."

"But maybe."

After all Fred's threats to leave, his sudden attempt to move closer was sexy. Sexier than his musty suit jacket. "Perhaps."

IT WAS HARD TO PLAN THE theft.

Jas found *Woburn Sands* the following day and read more of it in the library. It was too intense to read it in a dark public room during his lunch hour. It needed to be read on a windy beach, in a cafe in a city, on a bed, being charmed and buffeted by the voices from the past.

More importantly, it should be shared with the people who would be cheered by it, who were trying in the face of hostility to construct a history.

Jas checked the perimeter first: no door, no hatches. No means whereby he could slip the book into another bit of the building.

He argued with himself while he patrolled: I could get sacked.

I probably wouldn't.

This would be a ridiculous way to remove all hope of studying at St Simon's.

It's really important. It's the principle.

I'm a thief. When you steal from a library, you steal from everyone in the world.

That's such a pre-digital idea. A childish idea. I'm not a thief. I'll bring it back.

You'll keep it.

Shut up.

Jas looked at the windows. In most libraries, the windows were sealed. If you didn't have a central courtyard, you were condemned to swelter. Here, at least, they were open.

Jas set his book on a wide windowsill.

Then he worked for another half hour, to make it less suspicious.

"I'm going for lunch."

"Mind if I join you?" said Fred.

"Oh, I need to do some things."

Fred's poker-face rebuked Jas. It would be tactless, after last night, to fob him off. "Sorry. We could meet later?"

Fred shrugged, all bony shoulders and nonchalance. "If you like."

Jas forced a smile. His footsteps down the library aisle had never sounded louder. Moira was in her office. His heart slapped insistently, *something is wrong, something is wrong.*

Jas opened the library door, turned hard right along the wall, to the window where, on the sill, his prize waited for him. He scooped it up silently, slipped it into his bag and kept walking.

In his room, Jas slid the book under his mattress. No, that was the first place people would look.

He turned round and round, eyeing every crevice and seeing no hiding place. What had he done? A sackable offence, definitely a sackable offence.

Better to scan it, and take it back straight away. He popped the book into one of the slower flicker-scanners and watched it deftly turn the pages.

The door opened.

Jas tried to stand in front of the device.

Fred stood in the doorway.

"Cheeky," he observed. "Oh, no, don't faint on me…"

Jas sat on the edge of the bed and waited for the room to stop spinning.

"It's not enough," Jas said, when he was calmer. "I mean, it's not fair for me just to borrow a book that I want to read. There must be other books, useful to other people…"

"Aye."

"What should I do?"

"Well, what can you do? You can't take snapshots of everything."

"I've got these scanners. Really good scanners."

Fred raised his eyebrows. "Moira wouldn't like that."

"Do you think we could talk to the Vice Chancellor of the University?"

"'We'? Leave me out of it."

FOR THE NEXT FORTNIGHT, JAS WAS remarkably productive in both halves of his double life.

He set up the online security net Moira had requested. First, he cross-referenced the Harrad Collection catalogue against other library catalogues to find the really unusual books. Then he set up alerts, triggered if anyone mentioned one of these rare books online.

"That'll catch them," Moira said. It was the most satisfied he'd ever heard her.

After work, Jas smuggled texts out of the library. Ones that seemed to him to relate to queer history, a couple every day. He scanned them and returned them, too nervous even to read them. They went no further; he couldn't work out how to share them. It was a futile, minuscule act of rebellion.

Most evenings he ate dinner in the pub while Fred drank, and they slept in Fred's room together. And while Jas worked and stole and slept, he waited for an offer from St Simon's.

HE WOKE UP IN FRED'S ROOM, colder than usual. Fred's warm weight was absent.

Jas wondered if he should go back to his own bed. It was weird to be here on his own. The pillows smelled of cigarette smoke—it had seemed exotic and sexy as he'd fallen asleep, but now he didn't want to rest his face in it.

Jas walked as softly as he could to his own room.

There was a light shining under the closed door. He flung open the door, hoping to startle whoever was in there.

The surprises came in quick waves.

To find Fred in his room, when he'd just come from Fred's bed.

To see Fred juggling very competently one of the graphene scanners, clearly having used the slippery and delicate thing before. A flicker-scanner fanned a stack of five books in one corner of the room, and the ultra-sound machine hummed in another.

But mainly, Jas was startled by the scale of it. There had to be a hundred books stacked on the carpet. Fred alone had clearly carried them from the library, intending to scan and replace them tonight. Up and down the stairs, and no lifts. Fred was enthusiastic, manic at times, but Jas had never seen him so industrious.

Jas realised that Fred and Moira both scared him. But at least he knew what Moira wanted.

Fred sprang towards him. Wrapped his pyjama-clad arms round him.

"You were right. Information wants to be free," said Fred.

"Fred, why…" Fred had been awake for hours, Jas for only minutes. He couldn't think straight, and Fred talked over him.

"You've opened my eyes," said Fred.

"You've nicked my scanners."

"Borrowed. Just for tonight. But something's better than nothing, eh? Send a few books out into the world, like doves after the flood." Fred tightened his hold.

Jas spoke into Fred's mop of smoky hair. "You need to promise—
swear—you'll never do this again."

"Okay, okay."

"Have you shared any of it?"

"No."

"You have to wipe your memory cards, wipe everything. I'll help you
put the books back."

Up and down the stairs in the dark. Barefoot on stone, so as to make as
little noise as possible, so that each step was painful—like the little mer-
maid, he thought, as sleeplessness sent his brain off on strange tangents.

He was so bone-cold and bone-weary at the end of it that he never
wanted to see Fred again. But so much of both that he let him creep into
his bed and hold him.

"Promise. Never again." Jas knew his own lesser transgressions would
have to end, too. Even though they was hardly comparable to Fred's ef-
forts. No more scanning for either of them.

"I promise," said Fred.

An alert was triggered the next morning; something caught in
the new security net. An academic in America boasting about working
on a "lost" Gothic novel. It could be a coincidence. Jas didn't report it to
Moira.

Fred didn't turn up to work. Catching up on sleep, Jas guessed.

An email at midday from St Simon's made Jas an offer: a place on an
undergraduate degree, starting that autumn.

Jas prayed they'd never find out about the scanned books.

During the afternoon, a different fear crept over him. If he took up the
offer, would he be tied to Moira and the library indefinitely?

As Jas was leaving the library, that evening, Moira spoke. "Wait,
Jas."

She'd found out. About the alert Jas hadn't reported, or his thefts, or
Fred's misdeeds. She was going to sack him, prosecute him, have him
barred for life from all libraries.

Or she knew about his offer, and he was trapped.

"I've not been fair to you. Come with me."

Moira led Jas a long way into the library. Unlocked doors, revealed a dusty room. On a table lay metal guillotines, a pin-cushion stuck with three-inch needles. Moira was going to torture him. No, don't be daft.

"I do some small repairs, here. Have a seat."

She laid a book in front of him. Published in the 1940s, maroon cloth binding. He picked it up, automatically looking for the crevice in which to insert the tracking seed.

"The founder of the Collection."

Jas shifted his attention from the binding to the content. *A Life of Lady Harrad.* The contents page described the founder campaigning for women's suffrage; then for pacifism and the League of Nations; then against fascism, and in favour of self-government for India. An all-round good egg, Jas thought.

"Lady Harrad saw the book burnings in Berlin. Including the archives of the Hirschfeld institute." Did Moira know that Hirschfeld would strike a chord with him? Did everyone know he was queer? "She started the Collection after that."

Surely, then, she'd want the world to *use* the damn Collection. Not for it to sit and moulder in a stone room in an odd corner of a small country. He phrased it as mildly as he knew how. "So she knew it was important to—preserve ideas."

"She collected books to get them out of circulation."

Jas stared in disbelief at the frontispiece photograph of an Edwardian teenager, big eyes and swept-up hair.

"Anti-suffragette materials, fascist tracts," said Moira. "She boxed them up and sent them home to her mother and kept collecting."

Moira laid other books on the desk. Jas opened the covers carefully.

The Segregated City.

Motherhood in the Lower Classes.

Disordered Desire: Deportation as Solution.

"And the Collection kept collecting, after she died."

More volumes were added to the desk, modern ones. Virology, Anthropology, Economics.

It was horrible because the books wore all the trappings of legitimacy: smart fonts, cloth-bound covers, a familiar formal layout. Like a polite voice saying terrible things. And because Jas loved books, totally bloody loved books—it was like the voice of a friend in a nightmare.

Were all the texts in the Collection similarly awful? Had he been surrounded by walls crawling with malice, for weeks? But the book Jas had
found, the book from Woburn Sands—had Lady Harrad disapproved of
it? Why was it here? "There are good things, too."

"I don't doubt it. She didn't have time to read everything herself. And
fashions change, in politics, as in everything."

Jas took deep breaths, looked away from the books. "So why keep them
all?" he asked.

"For the same reason that we preserve the smallpox virus. They could be
useful to study. That's why we permit researchers to visit. But the books
shouldn't be allowed to spread."

Jas's head was swimming with objections. Paternalistic. Patronising.

"I suggest you take tomorrow," Moira offered, "to *look around*. Read the
books. Talk to the researchers. Ask them about their work: the unethical
medical experiments—the economists advocating enforced labour—the
novels that are as beautiful as Proust but, oh, five times as anti-Semitic.
See if they think *those* books should be available to the world."

She was defending herself heatedly against objections Jas hadn't even
raised. "Okay. I will." He needed the conversation to stop.

Moira sighed. " It's expensive to keep people out. Distance is a great
boon. That's why Lady Harrad lodged the Collection at St Simon's. It's
rather far from everywhere."

JAS WALKED ON THE BEACH FOR an hour to get his head straight. He
imagined the horrors of the Collection, and tried to reconcile that with
the dark, orderly library room. He heard the shingle growl as the waves
dragged it back, then saw the surf roil and crash.

When he was exhausted he turned back towards the university. Across
the beautiful quad, which his new knowledge still couldn't make ugly. Up
the stone stair, opening the door to his room.

The sight was so much as it had been last night that Jas wondered if
he'd become stuck in a loop of time. Fred, cross-legged on the bed, feeding books into scanners. More books, if anything, than before.

"Ah! Finally! You're back." Fred sprang up and moved from device to
device, clicking out memory cards.

"You promised…"

"I lied."

"You've been here all day?"

"Yep."

"But you were up all night, as well. You can't have slept..."

"I've hardly slept for two weeks, Jas. I've been in here every night. I'm on uppers. Didn't you bloody notice?"

"What are you doing?" He definitely wasn't releasing books like doves after the flood.

"I'm taking everything relevant from the Collection and I'm going to America. Where I'm starting a post-doc. I'm not smart enough to get it on my own. No, no, Jas—I know my limits. I have to research a *unique* resource. And I have to bring that resource with me." Fred tucked the memory cards into his breast pocket. "Nobody's even heard of half these texts. They're nasty stuff. Turn your hair white."

"This is all for your research?"

"Of course. Oh, and because information, it wants to be free, apparently."

"You set off the alarm I set up."

"One of my future colleagues. Got overexcited about one particular book. Idiot."

Jas tried to breathe evenly. He should tell Moira. But it was his own bedroom stacked with books, his own equipment (smuggled into the building) which had pirated them.

"Anyway, I'm off tomorrow," Fred announced. "But first: the final step."

"What?"

Fred's eyes sparkled.

"I burn the originals." Fred reached into his inside pocket.

Jas had a sudden vision of the room on fire, bindings blazing, leaded windows cracking in the heat.

Jas hit Fred.

He'd never done it before, and he did it badly. His knuckles jarred against Fred's cheek, instantly aching like they were broken. But at least he'd stopped Fred reaching for a lighter, or a bottle of petrol.

Fred reeled back, clutching his face. Laughing. "Good God, Jas, I'm not going to do that! Why would I need to do that? You're so bloody gullible!"

The side of his face was red, a spreading blotch, horrifying Jas.

"I wouldn't *burn* them. They're too bloody valuable. I mean, I've *sold* a lot of them. To cover my relocation costs. You wouldn't believe how much a neo-Nazi will pay for a—"

Jas hit him again. No ticking clock as an excuse, this time..

Fred fell, and lay on the floor, gulping.

"Sorry," said Jas automatically.

"Help me up, then."

Jas couldn't move. He could have helped skinny, frenetic Fred, the friend who was reaching up a hand to him. But Fred had metamorphosed himself into something untouchable. Revulsion welled up in Jas so strongly that it became awe.

The man at his feet was a library-thief. He had stolen from everyone in the world.

Chosen

Margarita Tenser

ON THE SEVENTH NIGHT OF THE new year, with snow piled up on the eaves and the spirits whistling out of doors, the Great Mother Goddess appeared before the youngest Miller child in a flash of light more brilliant than a thousand candles. Also, in the hayloft. The Goddess appeared to be a noblewoman of about forty, her brown hair tinged with grey, and kind wrinkles at the corners of her eyes, which had no colour, but swirled and stormed like the sky outside.

"Virginia," the Goddess said, in a voice that bypassed the brain and went straight to the skin on the back of the neck, a voice that was thick with both caring and discipline, a voice that smelled like pies. "You are of the blood royal, and you have been chosen for a glorious destiny."

"Um, it's Johnny now, actually," squeaked Johnny Miller, a tousle-headed brat who looked to be about eleven years of age. "What...what kind of destiny, milady?"

"You are to be my champion in mortal realms," intoned the Goddess. "You will fight for justice, defeat monsters, bring peace to the realm—what do you mean, it's Johnny now?"

"Er, sorry, milady," said Johnny. "Everyone's been calling me Johnny for a couple years now. I suppose they don't really gossip much in the realms of the gods."

The Goddess hesitated. "Do you mean that your mother dresses you as a boy so that your growing beauty doesn't bring trouble down upon your family?" she ventured.

"Um..." said Johnny.

"Or do you perhaps intend to bind your breasts and join the king's guard when you're older?" The Goddess brightened up at this.

"Beggin' your pardon, milady," said Johnny, hunching down slightly as though preparing for a blow. "I just like it, is all, milady. And my mum come round once our dad passed. Needs a son about the place."

"Oh," said the Goddess.

"And...and that's why I dunno about any destinies or nothing, milady..." Johnny said, hesitantly. "Someone needs to inherit the mill, right? None of our Jessy's boyfriends have really got what it takes, you know?"

The Goddess appeared nonplussed.

"But the blood of ancient queens—er, and kings—runs through your veins," she said.

"I know that, milady," said Johnny. "Lots of people round here have though, haven't they? The old duke wasn't none too quiet about his prerogative, was he?"

"Don't you want to take up sword against the injustices in this world?" the Goddess demanded, looming over him. Johnny thought he might have heard a crash of lightning outside, although the effect was rather spoiled by the wind already howling at the top of the available range of hearing.

He swallowed nervously. "Sword's a nobby weapon, isn't it?" he said. "I can hit some things with a stick for you, if you like." At this he gestured at the big icebreaker resting beside him in the hay.

"What is that?" asked the Goddess.

"Well, milady," Johnny said, "in a little bit the wind's going to die down and I've got to go outside with it and smash up the ice that's forming in the river around the big mill-wheel. Otherwise it'll get all gummed up and we'll have no use out of it till summer."

The Goddess stared at him for a bit.

"It's...it's an important job, milady," he said, scuffing his feet on the wooden floor. "My dad used to do it, before he went, and mum'd have some hot stew waiting for him when he got back. He used to say the spirits talked to him out of the wind."

"Well," the Goddess said finally, sitting down beside Johnny in the hay. She drew her skirts up around her primly and looked him in the eye.

"There may be some truth to that. There is an ancient, secret power in your bloodline, Vir- ah, Johnny. It does not," she sniffed, "Come from the old duke."

"Might as well do," muttered Johnny. "S'no way to hand out bloody destinies, an' Ginny Miller would've told you the same thing."

"Listen, child," said the Goddess, leaning in uncomfortably close and gripping Johnny firmly by the chin. He gulped. "I am offering you the opportunity to see marvellous things, to do marvellous things, to be renowned throughout the land. You could help so many people! You could perform wonders! You could *be* a wonder."

Johnny hadn't thought it possible for the wind to grow any louder, but now it was as though the walls of the stable had fallen down and the storm was beating directly onto his face. The Mother Goddess's fingers were twin spears of ice piercing his jaw, and she seemed to grow in a way not related to physical size until her face was a vast field of snow reflecting the sunlight into his eyes.

"Your ladyship," said Johnny, tears streaming as he squinted up at her through the blazing light. "I just want to grow up, inherit the mill, marry a pretty girl and raise some good-fer-naught aristocrat's bastard offspring like my father and probably his father before him. My dad was a good man. You tell me why should I get anything more than he did."

"You. Are. Chosen," thundered the Goddess, tightening her grip on him.

Johnny whimpered and tried to squirm away, but found his muscles refusing to obey him.

"Please…" he managed to get out through gritted teeth.

"You would defy me?" the Goddess demanded. "You would defy *me*?"

Motionless beneath the force of her rage, Johnny squeezed his eyes shut and waited to be struck by lightning or turned to stone. But instead, the noise and pressure abruptly stopped, and the Goddess's hand fell away from his aching face. With the invisible shackles he'd been bracing against suddenly gone, Johnny dropped back into the hay, ears ringing with the sudden silence.

He sat up and opened his eyes. The walls were still intact. The Goddess was standing with her back to him. She seemed to have returned to an approximately human size and shape.

"This is not how I thought that conversation would turn out," she said.

"Sorry," mumbled Johnny.

The Goddess turned around. The winter storm was hidden in her eyes again, and her face looked mostly human. And tired. "I don't need your sorrow," she said. "Events are afoot in the realms of the gods of which you know nothing and which you could not comprehend if you did. What I need is a champion."

"Oh," said Johnny, pulling himself together. "Um, have you considered Kate Thatcher? She lives just down…" He gestured in the general direction of the village.

The Goddess raised one perfect eyebrow at him. "Is she descended from the mage-queens of yore?"

"Common as muck," said Johnny. "Does a bit of secret reading, though."

"Hmm," said the Goddess. "I can maybe work with secret reading."

And then she vanished, simply, with no sound effects, although the hayloft felt imperceptibly more mundane than it had a second ago.

"Whew," said Johnny. Then he pulled his cloak on, hefted the icebreaker and went outside.

Where Monsters Dance

A. Merc Rustad

ONCE UPON A TIME THERE WAS a girl named Red, but since this isn't a fairy tale, that's a stupid way to begin.

Start here: You're sitting with your girlfriend Ashley after dance practice and she says, "They won't let me join the girls' dance team."

You punch the grass. The hill isn't bothered; its grass is more dead-brown than green, anyhow. "That's bullshit."

She shrugs and stares at her feet, toes digging into the ground. Her mascara is beginning to run, so you put an arm around her and pull her tight.

"It's bullshit," you say again, no less angry. You've seen her dance. She's good. She should be on the team.

Dancing is how you met. It was the first party you went to in this town, because your aunt's house was too suffocating in the quiet and you needed music blaring, a rhythmic beat in your chest. You needed to feel something. Ashley danced like a wild thing in the thumping strobe lights. You watched, entranced, and when she saw you, she beckoned. But you just shook your head. Maybe it was the longing in your eyes or your pixie cut or the party-vibe, but she swung her way over to you and asked if you wanted a drink. Watching Ashley dance was like finding an oxygen mask as the room filled with smoke.

(You haven't danced with anyone since your monster went away.)

"Hey Ashton!" someone, a guy, shouts from the bottom of the hill. One of the mass of the interchangeable bullypack. He starts making lewd gestures at you both, laughing.

Ashley presses her face harder into your shoulder. You flip the idiot the finger.

Ashley takes deep breaths and squeezes your hand between hers. "I just have to wait till I can afford surgery and—" Her voice cracks.

You hug your girlfriend tighter. She should still be able to join the girls' dance troupe. You have no one guilty nearby to punch out, so you hit the ground again.

I love you, Ash, is what you want to say, for support, because it's true—but you can't. Words have never been your domain. They belong to *him.*

You never told your mom you loved her, either. You don't believe in happy endings anymore.

This isn't a fairy tale.

ONCE UPON A TIME, WHEN YOU were a kid, you fell into an old abandoned well in the woods. You should've broken your arm or your neck, but you didn't. You landed on a monster instead.

"What are you doing here?" said a deep voice.

You looked up—and up and up—at the monster.

The monster was as big as your house (almost), covered in fluffy purple fur because purple was your favorite color. The monster had great big eyes and soft round ears like a teddy bear. When the monster smiled, you saw very, very big teeth.

"I ran away," you told the monster. It was one of the Bad Days. Daddy was shouting at Mommy. It hurt your ears.

"Why?" asked Monster.

"I'm scared." You pressed your face into Monster's poofy fur. "Don't wanna go back."

Monster hugged you while you cried. You knew the shouting was your fault. You'd asked if you could take ballet lessons. Mommy said yes; Daddy said no.

"I'll protect you," Monster said.

"On Bad Days too?"

"Always," said Monster. "That's what monsters are for."

You took Monster home and let Monster live under your bed so you wouldn't be afraid of the dark.

This was when you thought fairy tales were real. Then maybe you'd be a princess in shining armor riding a palomino horse to save your stuffed animals from the evil king.

And besides, even when Bad Days happened, fairy tales got happy endings.

Like this:

It was a Bad Day. Mommy was crying and saying "Stop, stop, please stop!" but Daddy kept hitting her.

So you got really mad. You ran up and kicked Daddy in the leg. Your shoes had hard toes because Monster was teaching you how to dance after bedtime. "Leave her alone!"

Daddy's face went as red as your favorite hoodie. "You little bitch."

You ran to your room and dove under the bed. "Help, Monster!"

Monster's warm, furry arm wrapped around you. "You're safe, Red."

Then Daddy's face appeared all scrunched up mad. "I'm gonna teach you a lesson in respect, you little brat."

Monster growled.

"Go away or Monster will bite you," you told him.

Daddy thrust both hands under the bed to grab you. You squirmed back into Monster's protective fur.

Monster's mouth opened wide and bit off both Daddy's hands.

Daddy screamed and rolled around on the floor, hugging his arms to his chest.

Monster smiled with red teeth, and you smiled back.

But it was just a chapter ending, and the fairy tale went on. (You didn't know how dark most fairy tales were, back when you were small.)

Daddy leaned in the doorway of your bedroom later. When he stayed outside the room, his hands came back. If he came inside the room, they disappeared, because Monster had bitten them off. He stopped hitting Mommy when you told him you would let Monster eat him all up if he didn't.

(He didn't, not really—he just made sure you didn't see.)

You sat cross-legged on the floor playing Go-Fish with your favorite plush rabbit, Mr. Bunny. Monster watched from under the bed.

"I'm going to kill it," Daddy said in his Normal Voice. "Your monster. I'm going kill all of them. Just you wait."

"Go Fish," you said to Mr. Bunny, but your hand quivered as you picked a card.

When Daddy walked away, you crawled under the bed and tugged Monster's ear. "I don't want Daddy to kill you."

Monster pulled you close with one arm. "He can't harm us in this world, Red. Don't worry."

You sniffed, relieved. "Can we dance, Monster?"

Monster smiled. "Whenever you wish."

You bounced up and down with excitement, and pulled Monster by the hand into the ballroom. Under the bed was like a tent, full of space for your stuffed animals and toys. It even had a dance floor where Monster gave you lessons.

Monster took your hands and began to hum, a lullaby that had become your favorite music. You hummed along with Monster, your feet tapping to the beat.

You pulled Monster along to the music, spinning and dipping and leaping. Your feet hardly touched the ground. It was like the time Daddy took you to the amusement park and you got to ride the grown up roller-coaster, only a million billion times better. The music soared through you and you felt like you could fly.

The dance floor blurred around you, became an open glade full of trees and a bright sunny sky. It smelled like lilacs and cotton candy. You loved when Monster made it look like outside. You danced wildly, swept away in the movement and the music.

Letting go of Monster, you twirled faster and faster across the grass. You sprinted onto a fallen birch log and jumped into the air. Monster caught you and lifted you up, higher and higher until you thought you could peel the sky open with your fingertips.

The dance ended.

Monster set you down, back in the ballroom under your bed. You laughed, out of breath, and hugged Monster tight. "I love dancing!"

"It is something no one can ever take from you, Red," Monster said.

(Daddy's words were long forgotten by the time you went to bed.)

You DON'T SEE ASHLEY AFTER TRACK practice on Friday. She texted you she'd meet you on the hill. You're taking her to dinner (even if it's just McDonald's because you can't afford much more) to celebrate the year you've been dating.

But she's not there. Storm clouds roll in, a cold October wind kicking the trees into a gold-brown frenzy.

Your phone dings. Voicemail, although you don't see any missed calls. You drop your duffel bag with your change of clothes and dial your voice mailbox to listen.

It's Ashley's voice.

"Red, it's me—oh God, I don't know what's going on. There's this—it's huge, Red, some giant animal but it's nothing—Jesus, let go of me!" Ashley's screaming. "Let go! Help! It's going for the woods—"

And the message stops. Your voicemail asks you in a monotone if you'd like to save, repeat, or delete the message.

You shove your phone in your pocket and run.

Someone—something—has kidnapped your girlfriend, and you've got to get her back.

For a moment you wish Monster was here. Monster could've carried you faster than you can run. You can't swallow down the dry, crunchy fear that you won't be *able* to help.

(Monster isn't here. Monster never will be here again.)

Up ahead, the forest looms. It's just the rumbling clouds, the lack of daylight. The woods aren't some creepy, mystical landscape. You could get lost, sure. But your phone has GPS—your aunt insisted on it so you could always find your way home.

Wind moans through the treetops, and it sounds like desperate voices. At the corner of your eye, you notice a ribbon of gray in the trees, but it's not a cloud or a bird. It's a hole, as if you're staring at a movie screen and a patch of static ripples across the picture.

It hurts your eyes to stare at the hole. You look away, shaking, and as soon as you do, the memory blurs, fuzzily distorting until you aren't sure what you were just looking at.

One thing's always clear, though: Ashley.

You wipe your sweaty palms on your jeans and step into the woods. There, not a yard inside the dark treeshadow, you see a glimmer of color. A red thread—it matches Ashley's favorite wool sweater. It's caught on a branch and unravels deeper into the woods.

She came this way. You follow it as it twists and spins through trees, a wobbling path stretching into the heart of the forest.

You're almost running now, so you can't stop when the ground disappears.

It's a long way down into the dark river below.

YOU WERE THIRTEEN WHEN MOM OD'D and your stepdad—fuck, why'd you ever call him Daddy?—left. At first you thought *thank God he's gone*, but at night, you lay awake trying not to panic that he would come back.

(He'd spoken in his Normal Voice when you called him at work, hardly able to speak, because Mom wasn't breathing. "What did you do to your mother, girl?")

You had this aunt, some relative you'd only met once, who took you in. You moved to some backwards little town in the middle of nowhere. At least there were woods around, so much forested land you weren't allowed to wander too close in case you stepped off the trail and got lost.

You didn't care about the goddamn trees at first. Your mom was dead. You were stuck here. Friends were hard to come by for the new girl from the cities, the one who liked other girls and loved to dance by herself to music no one else had on their iPods.

"Why didn't you protect her too?" you asked. Monster sat on the bed next to you, no longer as big as a house, fur darker, magenta and sleek, not the poof-ball you remembered as a kid. "You could have saved her! She's all the family I had!"

Monster looked down. "She didn't believe in us."

"You're supposed to be my friend, Monster. You should have saved her!"

Monster sat silently as you pummeled your fists against the thick fur until your knuckles hurt and your face burned from tears. Blaming your monster was better than blaming yourself. You hadn't seen Mom shoot up in months. You'd thought she was getting better, that the support group meetings were working, that the new job with the nice guy she'd gone out for drinks with were helping, that your stepdad being gone more and more was returning the world to normal.

(Nice lies, weren't they.)

"I'm sorry, Red," Monster said, wiping sticky hair from your face with one claw. "There was nothing I could do."

That's the thing about monsters. They're real—of course they're real. But you have to accept that before they can come out of the shadows.

"Well, if you can't do anything, then I don't need you." You were so angry you felt like you were about to explode. You hoped you would. POOF and done. Then you could stop hurting inside. "Go away, Monster."

Monster flinched. "Red…"

"I said go away!" You shoved Monster as hard as you could, and Monster flew off the bed and slammed into the wall. Cracks rippled along the sheetrock. You didn't care if your aunt saw the damage. "I don't want to see you again."

Monster's head bowed and Monster's whole body shrank until your monster disappeared altogether.

You flung yourself on the bed and screamed into the pillows.

YOU PULL YOURSELF FROM THE RIVER, shivering, hair plastered to your face. You're not sure how far the current carried you. You're good at track because it gives you an excuse to run, to move, to feel wind comb your hair—your legs are strong, and so are your lungs.

You're still in the woods. Maybe this forest goes on forever. Except—there's the thread of red wool, curling up from tangled deadwood and winding through the trees.

Ashley.

You brush mud from your hands and look up.

An immaculately dressed wolf sits on a sycamore branch, swinging his legs. His suit is rich burgundy, pinstriped with black. His fur is glossy gray, neatly combed, and he smiles as he hops down and offers you a courtly bow.

"Good evening," says the wolf. "What brings you here?"

You've never been scared of monsters. And since this isn't a fairy tale, you have nothing to fear from a big bad wolf in the woods.

"My girlfriend was kidnapped," you say. "I'm going to get her back."

The wolf rubs a claw along the lapel of his suit. Some undefined light source gleams off the polished nails. "Are you, now?"

You fold your arms. "And no asshole in a cheap suit is going to stop me, either."

"Do you like it?" The wolf smiles wider. "It was tailor-made. I made him sew it for me before I ate him."

You're not going to take this bullshit. You nurse the anger like a personal white dwarf star; maybe one day it will cool with nothing to fuel it, but now? Now it's dense and bright and hot. "Get out of my way."

The wolf glides around you and you turn to follow his gaze. "You must pay my toll to pass," says the wolf.

You bet he doesn't take plastic, and your wallet's pretty empty as it is. What if he demands riddles or magic or games you can't win? You throw at him the only thing you hope might work.

"I'll pay you with a secret," you say.

The wolf's eyes glint like sequins. "And what kind of secret is worth safe passage into our land?"

You clench your hands to stop them trembling. This is a bad idea. But what else do you have? You can't bring yourself to dance again, even with another monster. "It's a secret I've never told anyone."

The wolf's ears prick towards you. "No one?"

"Ever." You swallow hard. "Aren't monsters supposed to like secrets?"

"The one I love is made from secrets and shadow," the wolf says. "But what will you do if I do not *like* this secret?"

"Suck it up and deal," you snap before you think better of it. You brace yourself, ready to run or fight back if the wolf attacks you.

But the wolf only throws back his head and howls with laughter. "I think I will like whatever you share with me," the wolf says, smoothing his lapel again. "Very well. A secret for your safe passage."

He leans close until you smell the river and hot sand and summer air after a rainstorm in his fur.

Words stick like toothpicks in your throat. You don't want this secret and you don't want anyone to ever know, but you already made a deal.

You take a deep breath, then whisper in the wolf's ear.

Once upon a time, when you just started sixth grade, the cool girls cornered you and your best friend Terra by the lockers. Your heartbeat jumped, because you had a crush on Vanessa, the clique leader, and now she was speaking to you.

"Hey, Red. Want to hang out this weekend? I'm having a party Friday."

She knew you existed. You blushed. "Yeah! I mean, I'd like—"

"Assuming," Vanessa went on, "you're not going to go on about 'monsters' again like a two year old. Terra says that's all you ever talk about."

You glanced at Terra. You'd told her about Monster, about dancing, and she hung on every word; you'd told her she could find a monster of her own, too, so she wouldn't be scared all the time.

Vanessa tossed her hair. "Well? Is it true?"

You shrugged, looking at the floor. If you told the truth, Vanessa would mock you forever. You didn't want school to be hell for another year in a row. "There's no such thing as monsters."

Vanessa leaned close. "I didn't hear you."

"Monsters aren't real," you said again, not expecting it to be that hard. "It's just a bunch of bullshit for little kids."

Vanessa smirked. "Obviously."

Terra's mouth hung open, shock in her eyes, but you ignored her and followed Vanessa and the other girls instead.

A week later, Terra's family moved out of state unexpectedly, and you never saw her again. You never knew if she found her monster.

(Maybe she believed you that monsters aren't real.)

THE WOLF SIGHS AND HALF-SHUTS HIS eyes. "You carry so much pain in your heart."

You shake your head, face burning, and remember where you are. You wish you could forget the shame of that secret as easily. "Let me pass."

"I can do more than that," the wolf says. "I know where your lady love has been taken."

You stare hard at the wolf, trying to tell if he's lying. His bright eyes and brighter teeth give nothing away. "Where's that?"

"Ah," he says with a smile. "Answers must be paid for."

"What do you want in return for telling me?"

"Your help, lady knight."

You realize in sudden panic that you've lost sight of the telltale thread. There's nothing caught any longer among the branches.

If Monster were here now, Monster would know where to go, like the day Monster carried you out of the woods. (You can't let yourself miss your monster. It's always better to stay angry.)

"Enough," you tell the wolf. "If you help me get my girlfriend back and let us get out of here, I'll help you in return. Okay?"

The wolf bows. "Very well."

"Where's Ashley?"

"The Hall," the wolf says. "Our home."

"Who took her there?"

"Kin," says the wolf. "At the bidding of the new king."

The wolf grabs your elbow and tugs you sideways, off the path. You yank your arm free, about to curse him out, when he points at where you were standing.

"Look."

There's a hole in the air where you were. It's the size of a baseball and there's *nothing* on the other side. Not darkness, really, but an absence of anything that sends shooting pain up your neck and behind your eyes.

You retreat, bumping into the wolf. "I saw…" The recollection is still fuzzy. You frown and concentrate. "There was one by the woods in my world."

The wolf snaps off a branch as thick as his arm, then pokes it through the hole. The branch disappears and the hole grows a half inch wider. It sits there, ragged edges flapping as if in a soft breeze. Up above you see more holes poking through the endless twilight-lit treetops.

You hug yourself. "What are they?"

The wolf sighs. "Emptiness. Entropy. An end. That is what the king is doing—he is destroying our world. And yours."

They aren't separate. You asked Monster about this, once. They coexist beside each other, overlapping and easily crossed if you believe you can. Yours is not a nice world. But it's still yours, and Ashley's, and your aunt's. The world of monsters is just as important. Without one, the other can't exist.

You hunch your shoulders. Your stepdad left holes in your life you don't know how to sew shut. Your mom's death. The loss of your dance. You tried to dance again, after you and Ashley were dating for a few weeks, but as soon as you struck a pose and Ashley turned on a CD, your muscles locked and you started shaking. *Monster isn't here.* You curled up on Ashley's bed and hid your head under the pillows, refusing to move even though she promised she wouldn't ask you to dance with her again. You didn't have words to tell her it wasn't her fault.

You can't freeze up again. You won't lose her the way you lost Terra or Monster.

"Show me where the Hall is," you tell the wolf.

He offers his arm and you loop your elbow through his.

THE FOREST GROWS DARKER AS YOU walk alongside the big, not-so-bad wolf. He gracefully dodges the holes that appear faster among the tree-tops and in the ground, eating away the world.

"Who's this king?" you ask. You try not to clutch the wolf's arm harder than necessary. You've already asked how far the Hall is. The wolf said it was as far as it needed to be, and no more.

"A man self-titled so," says the wolf. "He beguiled his way into the Hall; he spoke with such charm and smooth words, we let him join us. Many lost travelers may find their way in. Perhaps not all leave again." His teeth gleam. "But he brought a weapon with him. It is a small knife made of all the words that have ever been used to harm another. It is power unlike any we can match." The wolf points at a hole, but you don't look at it too long. "With each cut, the false king destroys pieces of our world and our kin."

"You can't kick him out?" You want to run, to drag the wolf along behind you. Ashley can't wait, not if there is a wicked king holding her prisoner.

The wolf's ears droop. "The ones who tried are no more. The queen is…gone. He will not stop, lady knight."

And the wolf thinks you can help? Shit. The angry part of you wants to blow it off, take Ashley and go home, let the monsters deal with it. Isn't that what they're for? Monster lived under your bed and protected you. But the guilty part of you knows it wasn't Monster's fault you were hurt when your mom died. Monster would do anything for you, but there are some things even monsters can't fix.

And you sent Monster away.

Right in front of you, huge arched doors shimmer into sight.

"Welcome to our home," says the wolf.

The Hall is made of whispers and mirrors and filled with monsters. There are more than you can ever count. They dance to a haunting, un-known melody that grows slower and slower, perpetual motion winding down. Dusk hangs from the ceiling; dawn winds through the founda-tions. Only stars light this place.

"One of us ate the sun," the wolf says, "and another ate the moon. But it's impolite to remember who devoured which, now isn't it?" And when he smiles, you can almost see sunlight glimmering at the back of his throat.

For a moment, you can't breathe. This place is what you always believed (secretly) heaven was like.

The monsters are beautiful and terrible. Not one is alike. Some have glossy fur and coarse manes, some are covered in shimmering feathers and scales. Some have horns or claws or antlers or teeth. The monsters have bright eyes and some have no eyes. There are monsters made from shadow and monsters made from light. Smooth skin and armored pelts. Some monsters have skeletons, or exoskeletons, and some only pretend.

The dance floor stretches out in all directions to the horizon lines. You rub your eyes hard. This place feels like *home*.

"Here," says the wolf, and offers you a dance card. "It never fills up, so you may dance until the world ends."

You tuck the card in your pocket. You need to find Ashley first. "Where's my girlfriend?"

The wolf points at a dais that floats above the monsters, luminescent stairs trailing down all six sides.

Ashley's sitting there, hunched with her knees pulled against her chest. For a second, she's all you can see. Ashley: quirky, smart, dedicated Ashley, who was the first to make you feel welcome in the new town, who's going to be an EMT when she graduates, who takes care of her younger sisters while her single mom works three jobs. Her sweater is only a few threads tied around one wrist now. Her jeans are muddy and her make-up little more than messy streaks. Your heart lurches.

"Hurry," the wolf murmurs. "Before the music stops."

You weave your way towards the stairs. The dais is translucent at the edges, and a carpet made of a white material mutes the light near the middle. You can't see anyone else on it. Just Ashley.

A monster made from metal angles, sharp and contrasted, sweeps by with a glass cougar in its embrace. Their bodies reflect the light in geometric patterns. A brilliantly painted girl made from ivy dances with a metallic velociraptor, and they smile at you as you pass.

Your breath comes faster. Your body longs to move, join the music and *dance*, but you can't. You can't lose sight of Ashley.

Closer now. You want to yell to your girlfriend to jump. You'll catch her. But you don't know who else is up there. You dash up the steps, hope thumping along with your heart. You stop short at the last step when you see what awaits you.

The king.

And Monster.

You gasp. Monster is thin, fur ragged and patchy. Monster's eyes are dull and won't look at you.

The king sits on a throne. A thick, heavy chain tied around Monster's neck holds Monster down at the king's feet. That's blood matting Monster's fur. Bones cover the dais: pale and dark and silver and translucent. But bones all the same.

You glare at the king, the asshole who married your mother then ran off to do *this* to your monsters.

He's got his hands now, but they aren't his—they look sawed from someone else and stapled on with undulating threads. He holds a pistol in one hand and a knife in the other. He points the gun at Ashley.

Your stepdad smirks. "Not so tough now, are you? I get your boyfriend and your freaks—" he kicks Monster and Monster flinches "—and what can you do?"

"Let Ashley go," you say, but your voice cracks.

"Why?" He speaks in his Normal Voice, calm and confident and it makes you want to *listen*. Like when you were little, before the Bad Days, when he would read you stories and buy you presents and candy and make you laugh with funny faces. "I'm doing what I said I would. It's your fault, girl. It has always been your fault."

You shake your head. That's bullshit.

"Don't believe me?" The king leans forward. "Where were you when your mom killed herself?"

"It was an accident—"

"No."

That one syllable is like a sledgehammer in your stomach. There is so much *hatred* in his voice, you can't catch your breath.

"No, she did it on purpose. You might have gotten away with anything you wanted because of that beast you had." He kicks Monster again. "She started getting ideas she could do the same, and we couldn't have that, could we? I'm in charge. She had to learn that. If you hadn't hidden behind your monsters, your mother wouldn't have thought she needed to escape. We could have been a family."

You stumble back a step. The realization sinks cold in your stomach. You usurped his power and he couldn't bear it.

"I didn't…" But you can't go on.

"Don't listen to him, Red," Ashley shouts. "It's not true!"

"One more word and you join my wife," the king says, his finger on the trigger.

You stand there, shaking, trying not to think how much *sense* his words make.

The music—it's softer now, weaker. And it's coming from Monster's throat.

Ashley locks her jaw and stares unblinking at you. *Don't listen.*

You swallow hard. The melody drifts through your fingers and toes. It's the lullaby Monster sang to you when you were very small.

If you believe the false king, he'll win. He'll take everything away, like he's tried to do all your life. You can't endure losing Ashley. And you can't see Monster go away again.

You put a foot on the dais floor. A bone crunches under your shoe. Perhaps you can find a way to heal Monster, because you want your monster back so badly it hurts. You want to tell Monster you're sorry, so sorry.

But how do you find your own words when the king owns so many? You couldn't tell Ashley you loved her. You couldn't tell your mom. You lied to Terra. And what if Monster doesn't want you back?

You look at Ashley again.

You can't fight the king. He has a gun and a knife. But with Monster at your side, you have a chance. If Monster will forgive you.

"Monster?" you breathe.

One of Monster's ears twitch. Very slowly, Monster looks up and meets your eyes. You hold out your hands.

"Please come back," you whisper. "I need you."

"And now," says the king, "let's turn off this fucking music."

You lunge forward—

The king shoots your monster in the head.

Monster's body goes limp and the music dies.

ONCE UPON A TIME, WHEN YOU were very small, you fell off a skateboard and scraped both knees raw. Mommy was drinking, and Daddy wasn't home, so you climbed on the sink in the bathroom and looked for Band-Aids all by yourself. But you couldn't find any.

You tried not to cry when you crawled under the bed and told Monster.

Monster pulled two pieces of fur off one hand and made bright purple Band-Aids for you. You gave Monster a hug.

You sat together on a huge beanbag chair, which you couldn't have in your room or Daddy would take it away.

"Do you ever get owies?" you asked.

Monster nodded. "We all do. But you know what makes them feel better?"

"Dancing?" you asked, because that was your favorite thing in the world and you were going to be a ballerina princess astronaut veterinarian when you grew up.

Monster smiled. "Yes, Red. We dance."

You cradle Monster's head, but Monster's eyes remain closed. You keep shaking Monster, not caring that there is blood all over your hands and jeans. Monster's body remains limp, so much lighter than you remember, and the chain remains dark and heavy around Monster's neck.

The anger isn't there now. It's gone cold, like your white dwarf has burned out and turned into a black hole, sucking away everything inside you.

You felt like this at Mom's funeral, and you remember punching one of the nameless mourners who showed up to pay useless respects. You don't remember who that was, just a sudden crack as your fist met a nose, and then shouting, maybe you, maybe the idiot you punched—shouting for people to get the fuck away from you. Because you were alone, and everyone made it worse by pretending you weren't.

The king laughs, jerking your attention up.

Ashley stares at you wide-eyed, a hand crammed against her mouth.

All around you, the Hall is still. None of the monsters are dancing any longer. In the starlight, holes appear above them.

You're not sure when the wolf showed up, standing at one side of the throne. There's a shadow-monster at the wolf's side, wispy and long like a feathery snake. The wolf curls an arm around the shadow-monster.

You kiss Monster's forehead, lay Monster's head gently on the floor, and stand. You don't know what to do. If this were a fairy tale, a kiss would bring Monster back to life. All you get is the taste of fur.

You focus on what really matters—you focus on Ashley. You focus on the living monsters around you.

Dance takes away the pain, Monster said once.

You won't let the king take any more of your monsters. You won't let him hurt your family again.

You begin to hum softly, the same music Monster sang. You know this melody. It builds in your chest and fills your throat. You've never had a voice for singing, but it doesn't matter. The music is *there.*

Your limbs are stiff and heavy at first, your feet clumsy. Like when you were first learning the steps and rhythm and how to let the music flow around you, become part of you. If the dance is what keeps the holes from devouring your worlds, then you will *dance.*

The king frowns. "What are you doing?"

You step over the bones but don't avoid the blood. Your feet are red.

The holes grow wider. You feel the air being sucked up and out, a rush of wind that pulls your hair in all directions. It stirs Monster's fur.

For a moment, you can't see through tears. You want your monster *back.* You dance faster, harder, flinging yourself into the music with all your fury. It burns and you welcome the heat and the pain.

Nothing around you moves.

The king leaps to his feet. "Shut up!"

Then the wolf begins to hum along with you. The shadow-monster joins him.

The king aims the gun at the wolf's head.

You kick off the dais and sail through the air. You aim for the king's arm, but you spin too fast and suddenly you're between him and the wolf.

You don't hear the gunshot over the music. There's a pain in your arm and it fades to nothing as you dance. Red ribbons of blood spin around you as the music swells.

You move like silk in the wind. Faster and faster you dance, your heart-beat the only rhythm you need. Your feet are weightless and sure. It is when you dance that you know you're *alive.*

"Stop or I will kill him!" the king screams. He wields the knife above Ashley. The gun lies far from the throne, swept aside in your wake.

But the knife. Its blade glimmers, every horrible word you and Ashley have ever been called, and so many more, twisting inside the metal. It almost touches Ashley's check, and you know what will happen if that goddamned blade even scrapes her skin. She'll disappear.

Your steps falter.

A thick, rusty wire muzzle appears around the wolf's face, and heavy chains coil about the shadow-monster, pulling it to the ground.

Agony flares in your arm.

All around you, the monsters waver and fall. Breath comes ragged in your lungs. You try to hold onto the song, but the music slips away as your body overwhelms you with pain.

"Bind her," the king tells the wolf. Then, to you, "And if you take one more step, I will cut your boyfriend's throat."

You stare in numb shock at the blood spreading across your shirt. You crash to one knee.

Ashley's expression hardens into fury. "You aren't gonna hurt Red anymore." Ashley twists away from the king and slams her heel into his crotch.

The king gasps and doubles over. Ashley rolls to the side as the knife comes down. The blade cuts into the floor. Bones pour into the tear in the world. Ashley scrambles backwards. In a blur, the wolf scoops the chained shadow-monster into his arms. You lurch on your hands and knees. The dais groans, bending at the edges. The whole structure will implode inward in minutes.

You grab Monster's limp body and hold on. Ashley staggers towards you, her hair full of twigs and her face pale with shock. But she keeps her balance on the warping floor.

The king crawls to the gun and snatches it as bones cascade past him into the hole. The knife has fallen through, gone forever. He raises the gun at Ashley's back.

"Ashley, look out!" you scream.

Glass explodes behind her. She whirls. The glass cougar crouches between Ashley and the king, one arm shattered by the bullet meant for her. You stare at the large shard of glass embedded in your leg.

Across the dais, the ivy girl vaults onto the platform beside the metallic velociraptor with glowing red eyes. A rainbow-colored tentacle monster heaves itself onto one corner of the dais. All along the edges, monsters climb and jump and fly onto the platform.

The king whirls, pointing the gun wildly, but it has no more bullets.

"Enough," says the cougar. Translucent blood drips from its arm, glittering among the shards of glass. "You will not harm us any longer."

Ashley clasps your good arm. "Come on," she whispers. You can feel her shaking. "We need to stop this."

The wolf crouches by your side. He still holds the shadow-monster in one arm; he easily picks up Monster in the other. "I will guard your friend."

You don't want to let go. But Ashley pulls you to your feet as the wolf holds Monster tight.

"Will you dance with me, Red?" Ashley asks.

"Yes," you tell her. And before you can silence yourself, you add, "I love you, Ash."

She grips your hands tight. Your words mean what you want them to; her smile in response is enough.

Together, you and your girlfriend hum the music once more.

The world is heavy. You struggle against the inexplicable weight, against the icy pain in your leg and the burning in your arm. Ashley holds you steady, holds you close.

You remember every time you danced with Monster. Every time you danced by yourself, wild and unchecked and free. Every time you wished you had the courage to dance with Ashley.

Faster and faster you move now. With the music, with the dance, you can pull closed the holes in the world.

"Dance with us!" you call to monsters. "The music is not over!"

Ashley laughs. The monsters roar.

Light blurs around you. There is a tremendous cracking sound, metal splitting and bursting, and the chains around the shadow monster burst into sparkling light. The wolf's wire muzzle crumbles. The cougar's glass ripples smooth into an unbroken mirror-shine; the shard vanishes from your leg.

The starlight catches the music and echoes it back. One by one, the holes crinkle and snap shut.

"You cannot do this!" the king screams, but he is alone and unarmed. His words go unheeded.

You whirl with Ashley in front of the throne. The king charges at you with fists raised. He gets no more than two steps.

"Enough," says the wolf. He and the shadow-monster hold the king's arms behind his back.

You pause, leaning on Ashley for support.

The wolf looks at you. "What, pray, shall we do with this one?"

The king looks around, his terror unmasked.

All the monsters watch you and wait.

"I never want to see him again," you say to the wolf. "The rest is up to you."

The wolf laughs and the shadow-monster purrs and shows very sharp teeth. They drag the false king away. You never see him again.

Pain flares sharp in your leg and arm. You stagger, and only with Ashley supporting you can you stay upright. You're suddenly so tired.

"God," Ashley says, "Red, you need to sit down, I—oh Jesus, I don't even have my first aid kit with me."

It doesn't matter. Light shimmers along the floor, repairing the dais, and the most beautiful monster you have ever seen rises from it.

She's covered in black and cobalt feathers, her face made of mirrors, and her eyes are dark like the sky. She's taller and more terrible and more glorious than anything you've ever seen, and you know at once she's a queen.

"Thank you," says the queen of the monsters. "He chained me first with his poisoned words and so gained power, but you have freed us all. And you have begun the dance once more."

"Red!" Ashley's voice, so distant.

You think of bad cell reception and wonder if you still have your phone. You slip, falling backwards.

Strong arms catch you. "Red?" says a different voice, deeper and bigger than Ashley's.

Monster is holding you.

Fur poofy and silky purple once more, grown to the size of a house (almost), Monster is just like you remember. And Monster is *here*.

"Monster?"

Monster smiles, holding you close in one arm. With the other hand, Monster pulls out tufts of fur and bandages your arm and leg.

Ashley kisses you and you pull her close.

Monster does not disappear. You throw your arms around Monster and Monster hugs you back and you know it will be okay.

For the first time in your life, it will be okay.

The queen of the monsters tilts a hand and the gates appear. Through them, you see a path through the woods. At the edge of the woods stands the hill with its dead-brown grass, and the school beyond. There are no more holes in the October sky.

"Do we have to leave?" Ashley asks, wiping her face with the back of a hand.

You look between Monster and the queen. You hate the stories where the heroes grow up and are banished, everything they grew to love ripped from them for no reason.

You fight to find your voice, and not let your words be muted again. "Please don't send us away," you whisper.

"You may always come and go as you please," says the queen. "You are forever welcomed here."

Monster nods. "There will always be room for you in the dance."

Ashley grins. You let your breath out at last. There's cool, calm relief in your chest where the usual anger is. You lean back against Monster. You'll have time to go back and call your aunt to reassure her you're fine. There's still time to take Ashley on a date for your anniversary.

Ashley rests her head on your shoulder. You squeeze your girlfriend's hand, and Monster's too. They hold you tight. The three of you watch as the monsters dance.

This isn't a fairy tale. But that doesn't mean you can't have a happy ending.

Be Not Unequally Yoked

Alexis A. Hunter

THINGS USED TO BE PURE INSIDE me. Separated. When I was a boy, I was wholly a boy. When I was a horse, I was wholly a horse.

Things used to be simple inside me. I was all one thing or I was all another. And the two only got close when the change was happening.

But things aren't so simple anymore. The lines inside me feel blurry, more and more every day. And as I sit here across from that pretty Beiler girl, all I can think about is how she smells like dew-damp clover. She's got eyes as bright as bluebells, a smile like sunshine and I know that should make me feel something, but all I can think of is that smell.

It makes me hungry. I press my hands over my stomach to keep the rumbling quiet. My shoulders twitch and I imagine rolling over, scrubbing my sunburned back against thick sweet grass and the dry Michigan soil beneath.

A few dozen boys and girls pack the Stoltzfus' barn, all chattering like blue jays. All laughing as the Sunday singing comes to an end. The smell of musty alfalfa hay wafts down from the loft. Two draft mares in the far stalls snort softly and munch on sticky-sweet molasses grain.

The Beiler girl—Katie?—is speaking. My face feels hot as I lean forward, head cocked sideways. "What's that now?"

She smiles, her face going probably the same shade as mine as the kids around us start rising. "I said, you're Abram Fisher's son, jah?"

"Jah," I say, and stand with the crowd of dark-clad teenagers. I'm a full head taller than most everyone here. Standing makes it more noticeable. I feel a dozen eyes on me and fight the urge to bolt. "Jah," I say again. "I'm Joash."

She sticks a hand out, still smiling. "I'm Katie."

I take her hand in mine, feeling the calluses on her palms scrape the calluses on mine. She doesn't let go right away, so I do it for her, shoving my hand awkwardly back in my pocket.

Katie's talking again, but there's laughter and chaos all around us. The boys are showing off, flexing muscles hidden by somber blues and blacks, harnessed by suspenders. They heft the well-worn benches and stack them along the barn wall, jostling each other like good-natured colts.

I promised Dat I would look for a good girl to settle down with. And I reckon Katie's as good as they come, but the horse in me tramples through my head and it's hard to think of much else.

My gaze lands on Daniel Yoder, follows him as he lifts a bench over his head. He's the only one near my age—the two of us have outgrown terms like "boy" and "kid." Near outgrown Sunday singing, too.

Little Katie of the clover turns away and I realize I've been ignoring her something awful. I trip over an apology, but she's already disappeared into the mingled pack of youngsters. They're all pairing off, and I stand alone.

I brace myself with a shaky hand on the barn's support beam. There's a painful emptiness deep in my gut, an emptiness that's got nothing to do with being hungry. Least not for food. It's got everything to do with feeling walled off. Hindered. Strapped down.

Everybody's shuffling out the barn doors and I follow the kids out into the yard. There, dozens of buggies and horses wait. All I can see is the leather straps, the gleaming bits of metal jammed between strong teeth. I hear every faint snort and whinny, catch every hoof scraped in annoyance against the earth.

It's wrong. It's all wrong.

I just stand there watching as Katie lets another boy take her home. I don't know his name. Truth is, I don't know most of their names. Our family only moved here a few months ago, and I haven't exactly tried to get to know these kids. Weren't for Dat, I'd never have come out tonight in the first place.

Daniel Yoder brushes past. His shoulder catches mine and something like lightning zips between us. He stops, laughs and pats my back. "Sorry 'bout that, Fisher."

"Joash," I say, instinctively. Fighting the trembling of my body, I offer my hand for a shake. "And...no trouble."

His grip is firm. Warm. The wind picks up behind him and drives his scent into me. Horse-hair and sweat. My heart beats unsteady, and my stomach's all churned up like butter.

"Joash," he says. "Good to meet ya."

He's already turned away by the time I reply. "Jah...you, too."

He drapes his arm around the shoulders of Rachel, a plump girl with a hearty laugh. They make their way to his buggy where he helps her inside. I watch their hands link, watch them smile at each other, but mostly all I see is Daniel.

I don't understand what's inside me. I want back the simple division of my two selves. I been this way—half horse, half human—most my life. Mam says it started when I was only five. I have no memory of that first change, but I sure remember my first time in horseflesh. It's a crisp memory, cold and clear like frost on the grass.

The moonlight pales the skin of my upturned palm. I stare at the surface, remember the warmth of Daniel's grip, and I shudder. I bolt forward, down the dirt road toward home. There's no light in the Stoltzfus' house, but I don't trust them not to be watching. I gotta get some place safe before it overtakes me.

Before she overtakes me.

I'm breathing harsh, but it's not the running that does it to me. It's Daniel. His skin against mine, his voice warm like a sunrise, and those eyes—flashing in my memory a cornflower blue... And there's a panic and I—

I plunge off the side of the road, slosh through a ditch and into a thin tree-line. Just a little bit of cover. I collapse and the change hits me like it always does.

Real sudden. Real uncontrollable. The panic is second only to the pain. I clench down to smother a scream. It hurts down to the bone. Sometimes I feel this invisible instrument scraping at marrow, unravelling me. Jabbed between joints, levering my bones apart.

My skin stretches. Burns. There is a lingering moment of agonized anticipation as I wait for it to rip like thin cotton. When it does, I am barely able to keep my silence. Skin gives way to thick, tough horsehide. I rake my fingers through the soft soil, desperate for some anchor.

"Father, please," I gasp, before the change takes away my voice. My prayers become whinnies. My hands become hooves. My clothes split and rip as the other part of me emerges, full in the flesh.

When it's over, she stands there for a long moment. Her name is Belle; she's been with me, part of me for as long as I can remember. She shakes her massive head; her flaxen mane slaps against her neck. A fly buzzes somewhere close and her tail twitches over tawny haunches. Pain recedes. Fear lingers, though it didn't use to.

She waits. I wait.

And finally, it comes.

It's a rush. Power. She bursts forward, out into the freshly churned soil of the Stoltzfus' fields. Thick haunches propel her forward. Hooves reach for more ground. The wind combs invisible fingers through her coarse mane and tail.

Inside her, I give myself over to animal abandon. Here, everything is okay. There are no rules and frowning elders. There are no demands to find a spouse, to choose the church or the outside world. There is only sweat and the strain of muscle, and the wind and the grass, and the power.

Belle snorts uneasily. Slackens her pace and cocks her head to the side. There's a fearful sensation, creeping in, and I am sick with it instead of lost in the mare's power. She slides to an abrupt halt and whirls. There is nothing but the wind behind her, nothing but the crickets and their serenade. Her hooves churn the soil as she skitters to the side again, always looking behind.

What's wrong? It has never felt like this before.

We are both disturbed by the sensation that she's dragging something along behind her. An invisible buggy, a burden—and at that moment, it hits us, as one.

She's carrying me. She always has, but now she feels it.

Our forms used to be pure inside her. Separated. When she was a horse, she was wholly a horse. When she was a boy, she was wholly a boy. She was all one thing or she was all another.

But things aren't so simple anymore. The lines inside her feel blurry.

PALE STREAKS OF LIGHT ARE BEGINNING to bleed into the sky outside our barn. I am on my hands and knees in the straw of my stall. A neat pile of somber-colored clothes waits on a worn bench beside me and, next to it, a bucket of water and ladle.

Mam is a *gut* woman. Too *gut* for me.

When my sides quit heaving and I can finally breathe evenly, I rise on shaky legs like a newborn foal. I scoop up handfuls of water from the bucket and scrub away the sweat and grime on my chest, shoulders, and thighs. Pulling on the coarse black pants feels like a sin. They scratch against my renewed skin and the horse in me shudders. The plain white shirt clings to my still damp chest as I slide the suspenders over my shoulders with a grimace.

Mam's smell—mostly flour, a hint of vanilla and a whole lot of fresh-baked-bread—reaches me before I hear her step behind me. She leans against the outside of the stall, peering around carefully. Our eyes meet and shame instantly fills me, a hot sensation spreading from stomach to face in a flash.

There are so many questions and tentative hopes in the lines of her face. I avoid her gaze and it's all the answer she needs. Still, she steps closer. "Did ya meet anyone then, son?"

Yes. Daniel's face floods my mind—the squared jaw, the slightly bent nose and that playful smile. I inhale sharply and pull Mam to me so she won't see my face.

Mam clings like a child. Used to be, she was taller than me. Bigger than me. But that was many years ago. Now she feels too thin, too fragile. And I bear guilt for that, too. In Pennsylvania we were surrounded by loved ones—her and Dat's cousins and sisters, brothers and grandparents.

But then I saw that Zook boy thrashing his horse. All I could see was the whites of that creature's eyes. I could feel its panic and pain. Feel the harness and the buggy traces hemming it in on both sides, and it was scared and he kept striking it with the whip and...

"Joash?" Mam pulls back enough to look into my face. "You okay, boy? You're shaking."

She blinks tears from her faded blue eyes. I shake my head. Mam and Dat have been there for me, all my life; they've made sacrifices for my sake. I even told them about Belle. But how can I tell them about the two halves merging? About my lustful thoughts for Daniel Yoder?

"I just feel poorly for failing you, Mam. I know ya miss all—"

"Shh," she chides, sliding an arm around me and guiding me out of the stall. "We best put the past behind us and thank the Lord for the blessings of today and tomorrow. I raised you better than to be dwelling on things such as can't be changed."

Things such as can't be changed.

I do my best to put them evil thoughts behind me as I enter the kitchen with Mam. We take up our familiar places at the counter and I help her get breakfast ready for Dat. I lose myself in the comforting smells and sounds of this place: the crackle of bread's still-warm crust as I slice through it, the sizzle and pop of bacon, the whiffs of smoke leaking from the wood-stove's flue.

Only when the door bangs shut behind me am I pulled out of this momentary calm. Dat scrapes muck off his boots on the mat. His eyes are dark, watching me, brows pushing down in a frown as he hangs his hat on a peg. He's a big man, dusky of hair and eyes. His skin is bronzed from hours of labor beneath the sun, and all these colors makes the bland white walls of our home seem blander.

"Been out all night, boy," he says, his voice a thunder-rumble of judgment. "Take that as a good sign?"

He wants me to find a girl like Katie Beiler, ask to take her home in my buggy—only I never bring a buggy, 'cause I can't stand hooking old Mae up to one. Instead, I'm spending my *rumspringa* stalling and changing shapes in the night. Sometimes I think he'd give up the world for my sin to be drinking, smoking, or anything other than what it is: bone-deep and unshakable.

He huffs at my silent admission and stomps into the dining room.

"C'mon now," Mam says gently. I help her carry breakfast to the thick cherrywood table, handcrafted by Mam's father. We set out the serving dishes: piles of greasy bacon, rolls of spicy sausage, the still-warm braid of friendship bread, eggs scrambled the way Dat likes. I fill our glasses with chilled milk from our Jersey cow, Daisy. And Dat's eyes follow me, a constant silent reprimand. He lets me help Mam in a way that most Amish would find shameful. Women's work.

But if you're half mare and half man, what does that make you? Where does that put your God-given roles and responsibilities as laid down in the Bible and the Ordnung?

Dat offers a prayer and we tuck into our meal.

My silverware lies untouched; I eat with my fingers. The taste of metal in my mouth brings back bitter memories of the day Deacon Zook found me in my horse-form and tacked me up. I shiver at the memory, almost glad when Dat speaks.

"Can't put off the plowin' anymore."

The horse in me twitches. "That so?"

He's trying to ask without asking. "Wouldn't be *gut* to start out wrong. Best give the People time to get used to us, 'fore we go adopting peculiar ways again."

My hands clench under the table. Mam's eyes are on us. Tension whirls around us like smoke off pine brush.

"Mae's too old for that kind of work," I say. An image flashes in my mind—old Mae harnessed up straining as she drags the plow. Muscles bunching, hooves slipping in the soil.

"Joash, we got to be careful—" Dat starts.

I stand. My knees jar the table. Milk splashes out of my glass. With shaking hands, I use my napkin to clean up the mess. "It ain't right," I whisper. "I can't..."

Most times, I control the change. But the need is always inside me, sometimes burning hot and sometimes just embers in my belly. Whenever I get tore up with emotions, she surges to the front of my mind. Same thing happens when I go too long without letting her out—like with the Deacon that time. Never should'a turned mid-day like that; I learned my lesson well.

Dat's standing now, too. He's got his hands out as if to show he isn't going to hurt me. He's treating me like the animal inside me. Careful not to spook me.

My eyes are wet when I meet his gaze. "Please, Dat..."

His jaw clenches as he steps for the door. "So be it. Best hope Mr. Knowlton's got time to tend to our work then." His heavy tread sounds his retreat through the kitchen. The door slams and I settle shakily back on the bench.

Dat's off to hire an *English* farmer and his tractor. The Ordnung isn't specific about hiring your fieldwork out, but I know what kind of disapproval the act will bring down upon my family's head. We used the English when necessary, but they're still outsiders.

My family's given almost everything for me.

Come next Sunday Singing, I'm going to ask to take Katie Beiler home. It's the right thing to do.

Isn't it?

THE STEADY CLIP-CLOP OF HOOVES AND the rattle of buggy wheels signal the arrival of our neighbors. My fingers freeze up, still carefully holding the needle. Mam's stopped her quilting, too, and we listen to the muffled chatter of masculine voices.

The kitchen door opens and I scramble back from the quilt.

It's only Dat. "Put down your woman's work now. I need ya."

I move to the window and peer out. A dozen buggies and strapped-up horses. I wince. When I catch sight of Daniel amongst a group of young men our age, my heart stutters. I straighten quickly and face Dat. "Mam needs me—" I'd been helping her sew the wedding quilt. Mam was always more kind, open, and understanding about my peculiarities.

Dat grips my sleeve in one strong hand and lowers his voice. "I ain't asking, boy. I did what you wanted and hired out the fieldwork, now you gotta at least act like you might be a man."

Mam inhales sharply, but doesn't speak against her husband. I reel back from his words, but he's already dragging me toward the door. I shake him loose to pull my boots on. When he closes the door behind us, he does it nonchalantly, as if nothing is wrong.

It isn't normal for Amish families to keep secrets this big. The weight of this settles on me as I tuck my hat down against the sun.

The young men are gathered around the skeleton of a barn we've been in the process of raising. Bare blond rafters and stacks of sheet metal wait for us.

"Hullo, Joash!" Daniel calls. The group parts, allows me in. They nod a welcome, but I can feel the distance even in that expression. Most of them are bearded—a sign of their marriages. Daniel and I are the only two clean-shaven men.

"Hello," I offer back, mustering a smile.

The group passes back and forth some friendly banter as if I'm not even there. I can't keep my eyes off Daniel as he joins right in. There isn't a scrap of fear or awkwardness in him. It's like God took all the strength and courage of a self-assured stallion and wove it into this man standing before me. My face flushes hot and I wipe sweat out of my eyes.

On the roof, the entire unit moves in tandem, laughing and sweating and striving together. I fumble with the sheet metal. It's hot and the edges are sharp. I nearly let a piece slide down off the rafters, but Daniel catches it in time.

"Ach, you act like you never roofed a barn before, Joash," he says, smiling.

"Jah, been a while," I lie. I grip the rafter between my thighs and help him hold the sheet as a few other fellows begin bolting it down.

"Here." Daniel steps across the rafters as if he's skipping over a puddle and offers me a pair of gloves from his back pocket. "Helps with the edges."

Our fingers brush as I accept the gloves. For a heartbeat, we remain that way, hands touching under the safety of the garment, and our eyes meet. Something sharp and wistful passes through me. I want him—really and truly, in a way that terrifies me. I keep telling myself it's just the horse in me, but I don't know anymore. Daniel's lips curve in a gentle smile, like he knows, like he sees the hidden parts inside me. But then he breaks the contact, retreats to his spot on the roof.

"Th-thanks," I say, then clear my throat. Normally the gloves would feel unnatural—and I can hear Belle echoing her distaste in my mind—but today they feel like a gift. Like a sign of…something that can never be.

We work through the heat of the afternoon. I lose myself in watching Daniel. He works quickly, chattering with a lightness I envy. The muscles under his tanned forearms bunch and cord as he hefts the sheet metal up over the rafters. The other men in their white shirts and dark pants blur around us until I am completely lost in the rhythm of Daniel's words, the marvel of his strong hands.

Someone nudges my shoulder and I jump.

"Fisher, you gonna help us or what?" I blink, blush, and realize that they've all moved on to the next panel. They're all looking at me.

"I-I'm sorry. The sun…"

Dat's dark-eyed frown lingers on me from the other side of the roof; Daniel's still laughing, his cornflower-blue eyes twinkling like something magical. I'm all mixed up and it's hard to focus on keeping my footing.

When the laughter settles down, a few of the men around me start humming hymns from the Ausbund. The words of praise to God usually have a lulling effect on me, but I hear Deacon Ezra Beiler, Katie's father, ask a question of my father.

"So what 'cause you got for hiring them English tractors, Abram?"

The humming drifts into silence. Now there is only the warping cry of sheet metal and the steady breathing of the men around me. My body tenses as I peek at Dat on the other slope of the roof.

He settles back on his heels, meets my gaze briefly before looking to Deacon Beiler. "We's still settling in. Our mare is gettin' too old for that kind of work and I ain't had the time to get a new one."

A moment's silence. My pulse pounds through my temple at the lie my father told. I yearn to fly apart, to fly into Belle, and leave behind the burdens of this world.

I WALKED KATIE BEILER HOME FROM singing. She asked why I didn't have a buggy.

Seems like I have to lie more and more every day. I thought about marriage, the way the lies would pile up like the husks of dead leaves.

She's a true beauty—not just in the coils of wheat-blond hair under her kapp and those bluebell eyes always seeking mine—but in her heart and soul. She has a gentle way with animals and seems especially fond of her *dat*'s dairy cows. She told me, as we walked, of a time when she'd helped one of the cows with a difficult birth. Her eyes glittered with unashamed pride as she told me of tying twine to the babe's front legs and pulling with the cow's contractions.

"I named him Jonah," she said with an easy laugh. She laughs like that often and speaks kind of everyone. In that way, she is so similar to Daniel. But of course, she isn't.

But I won't be selfish. And life is all sacrifice, all struggle. I'll join the church, let them baptize me, pray they never find out what I am. I'll lie to Katie—assuming she accepts me as her husband. I'll lie with Katie in one bed and raise a family and pray they're not cursed like me.

I used to pray for God to take this thorn out of my flesh. I used to ask him why he did this to me. And I used to be afraid that maybe he didn't make me this way. Maybe I did something when I was little, so bad it cursed me.

As I step onto our porch, I square my shoulders. There's a soft flickering light from the lantern in the dining room. Did Mam wait up for me again? Standing outside the door, I try to summon up strength like Daniel's got. No more thoughts of him. No more. You just gotta shut that off. My eyes sting. I blink back the tears, try to shove back Belle as she noses her consciousness into mine. We want something more than what we're about to choose.

We want more than a lie of a life with Katie Beiler.

We want more than pretending to be one of these people, and all the while hiding our true self.

But this is what we must do.

Mam and Dat are huddled around the lantern at the table, their hands linked. They both look up and even in the wan light I can see Mam's puffy, red-rimmed eyes. Dat's jaw keeps working in the way that tells me he, too, is near tears.

"Mam? Dat? What's—"

"Sit down," Dat says, and he doesn't sound angry. He sounds tired, and somehow that's worse.

I obey. Fear pulses through me and I remember the way they looked when they told me we had to leave Hickory Hollow. It was my fault then. Is it my fault again?

"Bishop Stoltzfus came by this evening," Dat says.

"Why?" My voice croaks and I'm suddenly parched.

Mam's shaking, but she won't speak. She bows her head, graying strands of hair escaping her kapp.

"He gave us a warning 'bout using the English tractors," Dat continues. There's still no anger in his dark eyes. They reflect the flame, they do not harbor it. "Says it's not in line with the spirit of the Ordnung. He thinks we do it for the convenience. 'If any would not work, neither should he eat.'"

"I-if we don't stop—" Mam says, but can't finish.

I scoot down the bench so my knees brush hers and I rest a hand on her arm. "I'm sorry, Mam. I'm so sorry." She doesn't need to finish. If we don't stop, we'll be cast out. Again.

Mam draws herself up when she sees my tears. She straightens her shoulders. "We can find another home. We can try again. One of those less...them modern orders, where—"

"No." My whisper stops her.

"That's not all," Dat says. "Bishop says you got to choose your path before the week's out. He had to tell Daniel Yoder the same thing."

The utterance of Daniel's name makes me flinch. So we've both got to choose. Conflicting thoughts surge through me and the trembling begins in my hands; I remember and long for the surety of hooves.

Squeezing Mam's hand gently, I stand. "Use the horse, then." It's hard to speak when I'm trembling like this. My vision is blurry, but I catch the surprise in Dat's voice.

"What?"

"No more tractors."

"Are you sure, Joash?" Mam sounds as broken as I feel. Gratitude and love flood my chest, and they are warm feelings, but they are not enough.

"Jah, I'm sure. And I'll join the church. Bishop ain't gotta worry about that."

I've got to get outside before Belle tears me apart.

BELLE REARS AND SCRAPES HER HOOVES against the sky. We fly across the fields, mindless of the corn and wheat shoots we trample. I try to lose myself in the rhythmic pounding of her hooves.

Despite a recent rain, the night is steamy and hot. We shift and slide on the slick soil as we run. Sweat froths on our neck, our chest. Belle no longer flinches or skitters away, trying to see her burden. We are becoming one.

And we're both wondering how we're going to carry this lie for the rest of our lives.

We stretch low over the ground, avoiding Amish and English homes alike. We streak toward the trees surrounding Barrowman's Pond. The thought of cool water, washing over our steaming body and soothing our feverish minds, is appetizing, like sweet clover calling.

I am trying not to think of how I will ask Katie to marry me when Belle pulls up sharp and snorts in surprise. We stand at the edge of the pond, surrounded by creaking trees. Cattail fronds bob around the water. A young man surfaces, splashing and triggering a cascade of ripples around him.

We do not move, Belle and I.

We are pierced. Our heart beats too fast, our breath comes too quickly as we recognize the man in the water.

Daniel Yoder tilts his head to the side as he sees us. He stands and the water comes only to his waist, leaving his bare chest dripping under the pale moonlight. The sight burns deep inside me, inside us both. With Belle at the helm, my feelings are amplified. She trembles.

"Well, hullo there," Daniel says. "You slip out of somebody's pasture?"

Belle snorts. Scrapes her paw greedily through the mud. She wants to bolt into the water, but for the first time, I am fighting her, trying to wrangle her back.

Daniel steps toward us. His clothes are piled in a heap on top of a nearby boulder. Our gaze rolls over the muscles of his chest, the strong shoulders and forearms, the abs rippling down to...

Daniel pulls on his trousers. His suspenders loop over his bare, wet shoulders. Belle snorts and shakes her head. He smiles as he rubs his hand down the length of our face. He caresses our muzzle and laughs when Belle nuzzles her head against his hard chest. His skin is surprisingly soft. He slides his hands down our neck and we tremble. The slow slide of his skin against ours makes every part of us feel painfully awakened. It should be enough—this gentle touch—but it isn't. She needs more. Panic shoots through me as she presses our body into his.

His edges are sharp against us, his touch playing against my hunger and I—

I need more and there's a panic and I—

Belle screams a protest as we begin unravelling. Our vision blurs, pain seeping in on every front as we collapse in the wet clay. Daniel stumbles back and the removal of his touch eases off some of my panic, but it's not enough. My fear is redoubled as Belle's bones grind down. Pressure in my chest, in my head. No, no! Not in front of him.

He doesn't run. I can hardly see him through the tears in my eyes— eyes that are being squeezed and pushed and compressed into the proper size to fit my shrinking skull. Rough horsehide sloughs off in peels, as if grated away by an invisible hand. The strength of my hooves is lost to trembling fingers. When at last my world stops blurring, when my body stills, I am curled up in the mud. Belle's last whinny twists into words, "God, please!"

Silence.

I can't raise my eyes. The mud is cool against my new, naked skin. My breathing is wet and thick, shuddery.

Daniel steps nearer and I am forced to look up. I try to brace for disgust, for horror, for any number of judgmental expressions I have pictured a thousand times. Instead, there is only awe in the clean lines of his face. His eyes are wide, glittering by the moonlight as he crouches down and carefully extends one shaking hand.

"...Joash?" His voice is breathy.

My stomach churns as I wipe tears from my face. "Daniel." I sit back on my haunches, hands struggling to hide myself. He glances down, then away. There's color in his face, as if he's just worked a full day under the heat of the sun. He whirls to his pile of clothes and returns quickly with his shirt. I accept it when he presses it into my hands.

"Here, to..."

I cover myself and whisper a raspy thanks. Another few heartbeats of silence. We stare at each other and I am sick with dread. I shiver with it.

"I-I'm sorry you..." I start, but the words escape me. "I'm sorry."

He's already shaking his head. "I find myself speechless, Joash. And I tell you that is not a frequent thing!" He laughs, and the sound is a little skittish, but still warm. "I don't even know what to say."

I drop my head. If I could, I would turn and flee, but his shirt cannot hide the truth of me. "I know. It's...horrible. I think I am cursed—"

"No." He kneels beside me, laying his hand on my shoulder. I shiver, but he doesn't pull away. His eyes are full of an earnestness that strikes me in the chest. "It is a wonder, brother." That light in his eyes, that awe! "Truly. I knew our God was a God of wonders, but this..." He laughs again and it is a merry sound that washes over my bruises and my fears. "Joash, it cannot be a curse. It is a sign of the Lord's power."

"Y-you don't think I am...wrong? An unclean thing?" My hand rises to his shoulder, emboldened by his touch.

"An unclean thing? More like a miracle. It is a *gut* thing, do you not think? A gift to be embraced, welcomed, even. I—"

I cannot stop the tears. I sag against him, my forehead against his bare shoulder, and I am powerless under the sway of this relief. Belle is, for once, at peace within me. We are both still, even as our shoulders shake with all that has been held back and pressed down. Daniel's hand still rests gently on my shoulder and he does not pull away. His warmth is overwhelming; I feel his breath on my neck and only when the heat of my attraction rises do I pull away, necessarily.

"I'm sorry," I say again, wiping my face.

He squeezes my shoulder and stands. "Do not be. I have very many questions for you, Joash. I would ask them all, but I have to get back."

The thought of him leaving rips at my insides. I start to rise, then stop, clutching his shirt against me. "I-I could take you…carry you, wherever you need go."

His head cocks to the side as he considers me for a moment. I fear my voice was too eager, my expression too hungry. Then a smile cracks his face and he nods. "Jah, if it wouldn't trouble you?"

Heat rises up my neck as I surrender to Belle again. The change is slower this time, but no less painful. I am aware of Daniel's marveling eyes upon me as my bones are leveraged apart, as they groan and lengthen. Pain blinds me, a half-human, half-horse cry escaping my lips. My skin shudders, then gives, an audible rip that rises into the night air.

Within moments, my weakness becomes strength. My flesh becomes hide. I am strong and sturdy and I rise to see his shining face. He laughs again and scoops up the rest of his clothes. When he returns to us, he stands at our side. "May I?"

When we bob our head, forelock dancing over our eyes, he grabs a fistful of our mane in one hand. We've never tolerated a person on our back. That one time under the harness was enough. But there is no suppressing leather now, no metal bit between our teeth.

There is only Daniel. He climbs on our back and speaks softly, "You are a wonder of God, Joash, and a *gut* man."

The next minutes pass in a slow blur. It is hard to feel guilty for enjoying Daniel when he is so near, when his touch is constantly on my neck. My neck. Because Belle and I are the same now, or soon will be. The lines inside me dissolve like sugar in water. This is my powerful body. These are my strong hooves, my wild gaiety and fierce exuberance for life. Yet, there are still parts of me that are afraid. There are parts of me that still reprimand me for this sin. I am at once happy and miserable.

But I am one. I am whole. I am wholly man and wholly horse.

Why did it take Daniel to bring me to this conclusion? His knees hug the barrel of my sides and his hands are bunched in my mane and it feels so right, and I am no longer a secret. He beheld me and he did not turn away. He saw in me the handiwork of God, not the abomination I have always deemed myself. He accepted me and if he can accept that, perhaps… Perhaps I could stay. I could live a lie for the rest of our community if only I knew Daniel knew and cared, if only I… If I could tell him…

I begin to carry him home, but he directs me elsewhere. We trot down dusty dirt lanes, lined with sentinel-straight oak trees. We move under the moon, then under the branching shadows of trees.

We reach a home I do not recognize. My heart beats quicker as I try to find words to express how he moves me, how I am constantly lost in thoughts of him. I am still grasping the edges of these slippery words when the door opens and Rachel slips out. When she nears, I see joy in her face. Daniel slides off my back, still shirtless, and pulls her into an embrace. They whisper back and forth, affirming vows that will soon be spoken in front of everyone.

Daniel kisses Rachel and a cry, both equine and human in its torment, wrenches from my lips as I stumble back. Daniel flinches, turns, and our eyes meet. My sides rise and fall unsteadily as he disentangles himself from the girl and steps to my side. He brushes his fingers against the side of my face and there is something like an apology on the fullness of his lips. A shadow flickers over his strong cheekbones.

"I'm…I'm sorry, Joash." His voice is low, so she cannot hear.

I sway, but keep my feet. I nicker softly and brush my head against his shoulder. He turns, drapes an arm over my head, and the warm susurrus of his voice and breath flood my neck.

"I can't," he says. "You need something I haven't got in me. I don't… But I meant it back there, brother. This is a *gut* thing. You are a *gut* thing. You mustn't forget that."

Through the rumbles of pain, thundering inside me, I nuzzle his chest. I enjoy the touch for just a moment longer.

And then I turn and trot away. It takes every ounce of resolve I have to leave him behind, but I do not turn and I do not look back. Still, he fills my thoughts. I let his words echo in my head. It's hard to think through the pain, but something in me feels alive and awake, almost hopeful.

Daniel welcomed the truth about me. I can't be with him, but I can take his words with me. Beyond the cornfields and Sunday singings, I will find someplace both man and mare can call home. This world is big, bigger than Amish and English put together. Shadows litter the path ahead, and I do not know the way. A thrill of fear almost makes me almost want to turn back.

Almost.

Instead I race under the moonlight. The packed dirt roads are solid as a rock beneath my hooves.

I can still feel the imprint of Daniel's body against mine.

Maybe I always will.

The Thing on the Cheerleading Squad

Molly Tanzer

"BIBLE CAMP WAS RAD, NATALIE! COMING together in God like that…at the end, we all made a pledge to live the Gospel after we went back into the world, where temptation and sin are everywhere. And you know what? I'm really going to try." Veronica Waite tossed her mane of dark curls, revealing more of her new off-the-shoulder Esprit sweatshirt. "So, what did *you* do all summer?"

"I worked at the daycare at First Methodist," mumbled Natalie, shoving her face into her faded Trapper Keeper. "I…wanted to earn some money."

Veronica blushed. She should've remembered; her father had said something about Natalie working at the church.

Natalie's family's finances were often the subject of prayer meetings at First Methodist. Everyone talked about it. It was probably mortifying.

"How did that go?" Veronica asked, trying to sound encouraging. She and Natalie had been friends they were kids. True, they'd grown apart during their first two years of high school, but they'd still seen a lot of one another, both being flyers on the JV cheerleading squad. "I bet it was great, huh?"

Natalie shut her Trapper Keeper with more force than necessary. "The other aides were nice, but the kids were pretty rotten."

"'Suffer little children, for of such is the kingdom of heaven,'" quoted Veronica piously.

Natalie flushed. "I didn't mean like that," she snapped. "You weren't there, all right? Cleaning up puke, and stopping them from fighting and whatever. It was just babysitting, even if it was in a church."

"Take a chill pill." Veronica rolled her eyes as she toyed with the cross that hung around her neck on a delicate chain of real gold. "What did you need the stupid money for, anyways? Prom's not till next year."

"Well, varsity cheerleaders have to travel and stuff," said Natalie.

"Oh…"

"What?" Natalie was getting super worked up; she looked like she might cry. "I'm a reserve, aren't I? I'll be coming to all the practices… I might have to sub, if someone gets injured."

"I wasn't thinking about that," said Veronica quickly. Natalie hadn't made varsity, but Miss Van Helder was too kind to keep her on the JV squad. "You're right."

The bus slowed. Veronica craned her neck; this was her cousin Asenath's stop. The doors opened with a squeal, then shut with another, but in between the two, Asenath didn't get on.

"I hope Asenath's okay," mused Veronica, grateful to have something to talk about besides cheerleading.

"Shouldn't you know?" From her tone, it seemed Natalie was still sore.

"Daddy and Uncle Ephraim don't talk much," admitted Veronica. "I only see Asenath at school."

"Well, *whatever*. I'm sure she just got a ride. We'll see her at practice."

True—Asenath wouldn't miss cheerleading practice. She didn't just love it; she was the best. She'd been the star of JV since their first week on the squad and would probably be Team Captain next year. And it wasn't just because she was an amazing flyer in spite of her height. She worked hard, and made sure to be friendly and kind to everyone.

Privately, Veronica felt her cousin's aspirations to popularity were a result of the rumors that haunted her family—her mother had left when she was just a girl and her father was a real weirdo. Some said Ephraim Waite was a Satanist; others said he was just a creep. Victoria's daddy wouldn't elaborate on any of it. He just said that Uncle Ephraim had "chosen his path," implying strongly it was one that led straight to Hell.

Which, of course, meant Uncle Ephraim wasn't the kind of father who gave his daughter rides to school. Veronica fell into an uneasy silence until they pulled into the Miskatonic High parking lot.

There must really be a first time for everything, thought Veronica, for there was Uncle Ephraim's blue BMW. It was strange, though—peering out the window, Veronica saw a boy and some dirty-looking punk girl with blue hair leaning on the driver's side window, laughing and smoking cigarettes. The boy leaned in for a kiss.

"Oh, *gross,*" she said, disgusted. "Who are those losers? They shouldn't be doing...*that.* I'm going to talk to them."

"Suit yourself," said Natalie, joining the throng of students clambering off the bus without a backwards glance. Veronica was surprised—she had no idea what the girl was so upset about.

The fresh air of Miskatonic High's parking lot was a welcome change from the stuffy school bus, but Veronica made a show of coughing and waving her hand in front of her face as she approached the hooligans practically grinding on one another, pressed against Uncle Ephraim's car. The girl had at least seven rings in her left ear and was wearing a plaid skirt obviously from Goodwill. It was pilling and had some prep school's crest close to the hem. The dark-haired guy was wearing a Members Only jacket and Wayfarers. When he finally came up for air, Veronica cleared her throat loudly.

"Do you know whose car that is?" She put as much distain into her voice as she possibly could.

"Yeah, *mine,*" said the boy, lowering his Wayfarers with one long, smooth finger. Then he laughed. "Oh, hey, Veronica."

It couldn't be—and yet, it was! Veronica had no words as she realized the boy was not actually a boy, but her cousin Asenath. Over the summer, she'd cut her hair and bought herself a new wardrobe, but it was definitely her.

Veronica felt heat rising to her cheeks. Asenath looked great. If she'd been a boy, Veronica would have called her a hunk—*dreamy,* even.

But she wasn't a boy. And while the Bible might not be all that specific on this kind of issue, her camp counselors had made it clear there was no uncertainty about the matter whatsoever.

"Asenath, what gives?" asked Veronica, wrinkling her nose. "You look weird."

"And I was just going to say how nicely you'd filled out over the summer."

"Don't be obscene. Were you kissing her?"

"Jealous?" Asenath winked at her as the bell rang. "Better run. Wouldn't want to be late."

"What about you?" Asenath had always been a perfect student.

"You only live once," said Asenath and went back to sucking face.

Veronica was shocked, but the pair were ignoring her, so her only option was to retreat, embarrassed and furious. Who did Asenath think she was? What she was doing, it wasn't right—socially, academically, or spiritually. Veronica felt a brief flash of guilt. Asenath had applied for the Bible Camp scholarship, as her father wouldn't send her, but Veronica had told her father Dougie Smithers was a better fit. But Dougie Smithers had ignored her all summer, and now…

Vexed, Veronica threw herself down into a random desk just as the late bell rang, barely paying attention to the teacher, who began calling roll. Her fingers snaked up to the chain around her neck. The cross felt hard and cold under her fingertips.

Her daddy always told her to pray at times of great confusion. Veronica asked Jesus to guide her, but no answer came.

ASENATH WAS IN GIFTED, SO VERONICA hadn't expected to see her during the school day—but it did surprise her when, after school, Ms. Van Helder came onto the field and told everyone that Asenath had quit the team.

"What? Why?" asked Beth Townsend, the Varsity captain. "Is she okay?"

"She's taking on a different role this year, is all," said Ms. Van Helder. The woman seemed amused by the team's dismay. "Don't worry. She'll still be involved with school spirit. But enough chit-chat. Go warm up. Fifty jumping jacks, then get to stretching. The Warriors are playing Kingsport in a month!"

After its awkward beginning, practice actually went okay. Everyone was eager to get back to drills and to discuss routines during breaks. Beth agreed that Veronica's idea of using "Girls Ain't Nothing but Trouble" would be totally fresh for a halftime performance and Ms. Van Helder said she'd consider it.

Towards the end, Ms. Van Helder had them try some basic stunting. Veronica was one of the more experienced JV flyers, so some of the veteran varsity bases agreed to try an elevator with her. "One, Two, Three,

Up!" they cried, pushing her skyward. As she rose, Veronica tensed her abs and thighs, sweating and trembling; keeping her focus and her balance, she lifted her hands, only to feel the spots wobble.

"Holy crap!" said one. Veronica felt her feet moving apart as the bases lost their concentration.

"Let me down!" she called, not enthusiastic about the prospect of an injury on literally her first day.

That got their attention and Veronica felt her feet touch solid ground without an incident. Once she was on the grass, she saw just what had caused the commotion.

It was Asenath.

Veronica's cousin seemed determined to make a spectacle of herself this year. Instead of wearing Miskatonic's green-and-black varsity warm-ups, she had donned the school mascot's uniform. Her dark hair was hidden by a centurion's galea, her chest behind a breastplate. She carried a shield and sword. Greaves glistened on her shins, but her long thighs were exposed—the segmented skirt, intended for a boy, was almost indecently short on her.

"She looks amazing," observed Beth. To Veronica's chagrin, the rest of the team seemed to agree, almost falling all over themselves in their haste to greet her.

"As I said, Asenath will still be promoting school spirit this year," said Ms. Van Helder. "Since Ernie graduated, the position was open, and Asenath's enthusiasm and athletic ability made her application most impressive."

"Thanks!" said Asenath. "Should be fun, everyone. Miz V and I already talked about how it might be cool if I did some stunts in this getup. What do you think?"

"That would be super!" enthused Amanda Slider.

"Awesome!" agreed Natalie. That bitch needed to shut up. She wasn't even on the varsity team.

"I don't know," said Veronica, raising her voice a little. The squad quieted down, surprised. "If she's not coming to practice, stunting could be a safety issue."

"Ms. Van Helder thinks it's fine." Asenath's cool tone just further stoked the flames of Veronica's temper.

"Ms. Van Helder won't be lifting you," she snapped.

"What's your deal, Veronica?" asked Asenath.

"What's *your* deal?" she shrieked. "What on earth happened to you over the summer? You've changed—and *not* for the better."

A hideous sound coming from the direction of the bleachers distracted them all. Veronica turned and saw an old man sitting in the stands, doubled over laughing. Though the day was warm, he was dressed in a heavy overcoat and he clutched a Miskatonic High pennant in his withered hand.

"Shit," swore Asenath. "Sorry... I told Dad he could come if he kept quiet."

Veronica took a second look, shocked—her uncle was unrecognizable. She'd never have known it was him; he looked as though he'd aged years over just a few months, or as if he'd suffered some terrible illness.

"I'd better..."

"Do what you need to do," said Ms. Van Helder, glaring at Veronica for some reason. Asenath took off toward the bleachers, her long legs covering the ground within moments. She confronted the old man, then led him away.

"Let's call it a day," said Ms. Van Helder. "Back to work tomorrow. And Veronica?"

"Yes?" Veronica lagged behind the others.

"Try to be patient with Asenath? She's been having...family troubles."

In Veronica's opinion, that didn't excuse anything. Asenath had never not had family troubles. Just the same, she nodded.

With a heavy heart Veronica changed and went out to wait for her mother by the front doors of Miskatonic High. Asenath was in the parking lot, bundling her father into her car, clearly having words with him. She'd changed back into her outfit from that morning; she looked ferocious and intimidating as she shoved the old creep into the passenger's side seat.

"Not unless you can control yourself!" she shouted angrily, slamming the door in his face after he whined something at her that Veronica couldn't hear.

Then Asenath noticed her cousin sitting there as she came around to the driver's side. Veronica, remembering Ms. Van Helder's admonition, timidly raised her hand in a greeting. Asenath laughed, blew her a kiss as she slid into the driver's seat. She pulled away just as Veronica's mother drove up.

"How was your first day?" her mother called out the window.

"Great, Mom," lied Veronica. "Really great."

VERONICA, MINDFUL OF HER BIBLE CAMP pledge, tried to forgive Asenath for her antics—she really did—but it became increasingly difficult, given how her cousin seemed to want nothing more than to shock the whole school. Every day, she came in wearing a different appalling outfit—tweed blazers and slacks, Hawaiian shirts and brightly-colored shorts, leather jackets and jeans—and with some new girl on her arm, inevitably giggling like it wasn't social and spiritual suicide for her to go out with a woman. Veronica was mortified, and the worst part was, she didn't even have cheering as a respite. Whenever Asenath showed up in her mascot's outfit to practice, the girls went crazy, mobbing her like she was the captain of the football team. Veronica thought that was sick, but she couldn't say anything—Beth, the team captain, had gone out with Asenath a few times. "She's the best-looking boy in school," was her only comment when Veronica remarked on the queerness of it all.

Interestingly enough, for once, the cheerleaders were in the minority in terms of popular opinion; they might coo over Asenath, but the rest of Miskatonic High did not. Girls whispered whenever she walked by; guys shouted epithets. Veronica sensed Asenath was enjoying the attention and would have been more than happy to let Asenath reap what she sowed, just like in Galatians...except Asenath's refusal to act normally began to reflect poorly on her.

"You a dyke, too, Veronica?" shouted Dougie Smithers. The entire lunchroom heard him, given the laughter this sparkling wit produced. Veronica pushed away her half-finished pack of Handi-Snacks, the yellow cheese and buttery crackers now sawdust in her mouth. "Is it true that this Saturday, you're gonna go cruising for chicks together?"

Veronica refused to acknowledge him, but in her heart, she was seething. It shouldn't be like this. She was certain no other varsity cheerleader had ever dealt with such scorn from her peers. Pretending to ignore Dougie and the rest, she put on her Walkman and grabbed her notebook. The rhymes of DJ Jazzy Jeff and the Fresh Prince became her world as she scribbled down some ideas for the new varsity routine. Then, the notes blurred before her eyes when she had a sudden vision of her cousin prancing onto the field in her costume, proudly flaunting the inevitable catcalls and boos to stunt alongside the *real* cheerleaders.

She'd tried to forgive. She'd tried to forget. She'd been cordial to her, offering to let Asenath borrow her more feminine clothes if she needed to, and prayed for her in church, in the hopes that God would touch Asenath's heart and help her return to the fold. But nothing had worked. Something had caused Asenath to give up everything—her popularity, her straight-A average, her faith, the cheerleading squad—and Veronica couldn't imagine what it could be.

Dougie slid onto the bench beside her, grabbing a cracker out of her Handi-Snack.

"Hey," he said, grabbing Veronica's headphones. "When you lick it, does it look like this?" And he pantomimed something obscene.

"Beware, ladies—he's clearly no expert." Asenath grabbed the boy by the collar and slung him off the bench. Dougie landed hard on his tail-bone on the linoleum floor of the cafeteria with a thump and then a howl. The laughter was more sporadic than before. Veronica did not take part in it. "Sorry if he was bothering you, Veronica, but everyone knows I don't cruise for chicks—they come cruising for *me*."

"You're disgusting." For some reason, Veronica was angrier with Asenath than Dougie. She shoved her notebook into her backpack, snatched her headphones away from the boy still writhing on the ground, and stalked out of the lunchroom.

Once the door slammed behind her, Veronica totally lost it. She slumped against the lockers, tears running down her face. When the school board had announced their decision to integrate sex ed into the health curriculum last year, her daddy had threatened to put her in private school. Veronica had begged and pleaded to remain at Miskatonic because of her friends, because of cheering. Maybe this was her punishment for not being obedient to her father's will.

"Hey."

It was Asenath. Veronica dashed the tears from her eyes.

"What do *you* want?"

"To talk to you." Asenath came closer. Today, she was wearing a button-down men's Oxford tucked into high-waisted Guess jeans that somehow made her long legs look longer. "I'm sorry about what happened back there. Dougie's a real jerk. But —"

"You're sorry?" snarled Veronica. "Oh, great! I'm super-excited that you're *sorry* for ruining my life, Asenath!"

"What?"

"People tease me all the time about…about being like *you*." As she said it, Veronica knew how petty she sounded, but that just made her angrier. "And you've ruined cheering, too, prancing around in that stupid costume. They'll shout us off the field the moment they see you!"

Asenath laughed in her face. "That's all it takes to ruin your life?"

"What happened to you, Asenath? You used to be so nice. You used to care about important things, like school and cheering—and what people thought about you." Veronica shook her head. "Now…it's like…you just can't be bothered."

"What happened to me?" Asenath grinned mirthlessly. "*Life* happened. The real world intruded on the fantastical dream-lie that is high school. Sorry if that's *inconveniencing* you, Veronica. Me? I'm having a great time."

Veronica rolled her eyes. "So, what—you're Laura Palmer now?"

"Maybe Bobby Briggs." Asenath lowered her voice. "I wasn't the one who went looking for darkness. Somebody…*showed* it to me." The taller girl leaned in closer, planting her hand on the lockers behind Veronica, bracing herself on them, looming over her cousin. She smelled like cigarette smoke and peppermint gum. "You don't know what's out there, Veronica—the sad thing is, you don't even know what's *here*, in Arkham. You went to Bible Camp, just like your daddy wanted you to…sang your little songs, prayed your little prayers. Well, baby girl, sing and pray all you want, because it doesn't fucking matter."

"What do you mean?"

"I'll tell you what *I* did on my summer vacation." Her cousin's intensity was startling. Her prominent brown eyes were shining like stars as her lips pulled back from her white teeth. Veronica couldn't help but compare her to the mild-mannered, sweet-tempered girl she had once been. "I looked into a well of absolute darkness, a well without a bottom, full to the brim with writhing whispers blacker than the darkness. I looked—and I *listened*."

"What…what was in the well?"

"Laughter. It laughed at me. The darkness, I mean. A hole full of nothing, *absolute* nothing, and it *laughed* at me."

"What did you do?"

Asenath stood up, looking around as if to see if anyone had witnessed
her losing her cool. "Doesn't matter. But I tell you what…after that, I
decided to live every day like it was my last, and I advise you to do the
same. There's no heaven. There's no hell. There's only you, me and this."
She gestured to the hallway. "The things beyond this world don't give a
shit what you do—if you pray, if you're good, or if you're bad, according
to some outdated notions of propriety."

"You don't sound like yourself," said Veronica.

Asenath shook her head. "I've always been this way. The only thing
that's changed is that I know it's not worth hiding it."

The bell rang, and students poured out of the cafeteria. Veronica flinched
away from Asenath, instinctively, which made the other girl laugh.

"See you around, *Veronica*," she said.

VERONICA BARELY PAID ATTENTION TO HER classes the rest of the day.
Asenath's speech had shaken her. What she really needed was a good,
hard practice to drive everything from her mind, but of course, Asenath
showed up, to everyone's delight but hers.

Asenath seemed full of a savage fury that day. Her jumps were high, her
kicks, higher. The term "flyer" had never been so apropos. She seemed to
hover above everyone when she was lifted and hang in the air for an un-
naturally long time on the dismounts. Ms. Van Helder was so enthusiastic about her prospects toward the end of practice, she suggested Asenath
try a scorpion instead of a full liberty after being popped up.

As Asenath executed the move perfectly, Veronica turned away, re-
minding herself that jealousy was a sin. Uncle Ephraim was sitting on
the lowest bleacher. He was always in attendance when Asenath came to
practice, gaunt and horrible in his big weird coat, a Miskatonic pennant
clutched in his clawlike hands.

After his outburst the first day, he had remained largely silent, hunched
into himself and watching them all with unwavering attention, but today, he seemed agitated. He shifted on his seat, twitching. The sight of
Asenath in a scorpion further perturbed him. When she fell into the

basketed hands of her fellow cheerleaders, he uttered a grotesque, bubbling cry.

Veronica was the only one who heard him, so she was the only one unsurprised when he began to holler and snort as Asenath tried the move a second time. Asenath wobbled and fell; her cohorts caught her, but there was no saving her from the old man's wrath.

"Thief!" he cried, staggering toward her. "Mine! It's *mine!*"

"Asenath," said Ms. Van Helder, as Asenath stood unsteadily, "are you—is he—"

"It's fine," said Asenath, through gritted teeth.

"Thief! Wolf in sheep's clothing!" The old man drew nearer, but Asenath wasn't waiting around—she began to advance on him. "Give it back—it's mine!"

"Shut up!" she snapped, grabbing his arm.

"Mine!" he cried, running his crabbed hand down her smooth arm.

"Maybe it was, but not anymore!" she shouted in his face.

"Asenath, your father's not well," said Ms. Van Helder, putting her hand on the girl's other arm. "You should—"

"Don't touch me!" cried Asenath, wrenching herself free of both their grasps. Her father, unsteady on his feet, fell to the ground with a heart-wrenching yelp.

"Asenath!" Ms. Van Helder was shocked.

"None of you have any idea about anything!" she screamed, and took off running toward the locker room.

A moment passed where they waited to see if Asenath would return. She did not. "Come on, Mr. Waite, let's get you home," said Ms. Van Helder, helping Ephraim to his feet. "I'm sorry. I don't know what's gotten into her."

"She stole it," he mewed. "She's a thief."

"Ms. Van Helder...I could take him home." Veronica felt bad for her uncle, the latest victim of Asenath's troubling metamorphosis. Perhaps, if she got him alone, she could talk to him. Maybe he needed help from the Church, or from her father, to deal with his wayward daughter.

"Do you have a car?"

"No, but it's not far. Maybe a mile. I mean, he walked here, didn't he?" Veronica took the man's hand. "Can you walk home with me? Are you strong enough, Uncle Ephraim?"

At first, he shook his head no, then something about his expression changed—brightened, maybe.

"Not far," he whispered, apparently agreeing with her.

The sound of a car peeling out of the parking lot made them all look to see Asenath's dramatic departure. She wasn't heading in the direction of her house.

"Better get him home," said Ms. Van Helder.

Uncle Ephraim nodded his enthusiasm.

VERONICA HAD NEVER BEEN A REGULAR visitor at Asenath's house; not only did her daddy think she should "limit her contact" with her cousin and uncle, the place was just spooky, with its peeling paint and sagging roof. Her father also said the only reason their neighborhood's home-owner's association hadn't served Ephraim a notice was because of his intervention.

Uncle Ephraim had a key hidden somewhere in the deep pockets of his coat. Veronica got the door open and helped him inside.

"Can I get you something to drink?" she said, taking off his coat. It was very warm in the house, and dark; the blinds were all shut and the golden bars of afternoon sunlight that fell over the carpet through the slats didn't so much brighten the room as they showed the dust motes swirling in the air.

He nodded and shuffled toward a chair in the living room that shared his shabby, ill-used appearance. "Please," he mumbled. "Water."

There were no clean cups, so Veronica rinsed out a glass and got him some water with ice. She brought it into the living room and set it beside his elbow on a little tray table.

"I'll leave my number," she said uncertainly, "in case she doesn't—I mean, I'm sure Asenath will be home soon."

"*Asenath...*"

"She drove away," said Veronica. "But she was just angry. She'll be back."

"Stay." Uncle Ephraim pointed to the couch. "Please."

Veronica really, really didn't want to stay, but didn't feel like she had much of a choice. "Okay," she said. "Should I...turn on the TV?"

"Read to me." The suggestion of a whine in his unsteady voice stopped Veronica's protest in her throat.

"What should I read?"

"Upstairs," he said. "*Secrets.* Under Asenath's mattress."

"I shouldn't..."

"I hid it there."

Veronica's skin prickled as she wondered just what in the world Uncle Ephraim had stashed under his daughter's mattress. What if it was a girlie mag, or something even more disgusting? She decided she might as well do as he said. If it was really bad, she'd give it to Asenath and tell her to get rid of it.

The stairs were dark and cramped. Veronica took them two at a time, but she hesitated before grabbing the knob of Asenath's bedroom, unsure what she might find inside.

Like Asenath, the room was...different. The antique vanity Veronica had always coveted was still there, but Asenath's beloved Kaboodle full of makeup no longer sat upon it, nor did the shelves hold the toys and dolls she had brought over to Veronica's when they were younger. The strange thing was, nothing had replaced the missing items. It felt bare in there, denuded, stripped of its essence as if it had been bleached.

Veronica shut the door open behind her, unsure what she was feeling. Sadness over the loss of a friend, yes, but there was anger, too. They hadn't just grown apart naturally, she and her cousin. Asenath had chosen this path, no matter what she said.

It made her uncomfortable, being in Asenath's private space, so Veronica screwed up her courage and plunged her arm between his mattress and the bedspring. She rooted around until her hands closed on a slender volume.

"*Hieron Aigypton,*" she read slowly, running her fingers over the tooled leather of the cover. "By Ana...Anacharsis." She'd never heard of it. It looked very old.

She opened it to the first page, curious to see what it was Uncle Ephraim wanted her to read to him. "*Hieron Aigypton, or Egyptian Rites,*" she read. "Being an unflinching translation of the dreaded rituals detailed by Anacharsis, who was born a woman, lived as a man, and died neither." She flipped another page. "*Weird.*"

Veronica knew that "rituals" were nothing her daddy would approve of, but just the same, Uncle Ephraim had requested this book... Veronica pursed her lips, but went back downstairs with it.

"Let us rejoice in the true story of one called Narcissus, whose will was stronger than any alchemy," she read aloud, after Uncle Ephraim requested she read from the first chapter. After that first line, it became a story—one she vaguely remembered from school, about a beautiful boy who became a flower and the nymph who loved him until she became only an echo.

"I, Anacharsis, went to that glen, where the first narcissus sprouted. There I found Echo, who told me his final words. These were they…"

The language was strange to her. As Veronica mumbled her way through the stanzas, her vision began to blur. At first, she thought it was just the warmth of the room—she was sweating through her warmups—but then her eyes focused and saw only blackness.

She was somewhere that was nowhere, standing at the edge of something that was nothing. Inside the nothing was more nothing, but a denser nothing that writhed—and *laughed*.

"Asenath," she whispered, horrified. She couldn't tear her eyes from the abyss. Her cousin hadn't been lying! Did that mean she had read this book? Seen the sights it offered? Horrified, Veronica regretted all the cruel things she had said to Asenath, all the comments she'd made behind her cousin's back. It was no wonder the girl had turned away from God—they said He was all-powerful, but Veronica couldn't believe He had ever been here, at the edge of wherever she was. She wept, knowing He was less than she had believed, if He existed at all.

Asenath said she had turned away, backed away—Veronica needed to find the will to do the same. But try as she might, she could not tear her eyes from the sight. She felt her foot move. It was no longer her foot. She took a step forward, not back. The laughter became louder, and when she went over the edge, it consumed her.

WHEN VERONICA AWOKE, SHE FELT SORE and nauseated. She groaned, dry-mouthed and cold, and realized she lying was on the floor.

"You're awake." A woman spoke to her. Veronica opened her eyes, hoping Asenath had come home. But it wasn't Asenath.

It was *her*. Veronica Waite was standing there in her black-and-green skirt and Miskatonic warmup jacket, staring at her.

"What?" she mumbled, not in her own voice but Uncle Ephraim's.

"You're weaker than your cousin," she said, or rather, someone said with her voice, as she helped herself up and into a chair. "Asenath resisted all my arts. I couldn't take her body. She wouldn't let me, even though I raised it, fed it, clothed it, for seventeen long years! It was *mine*. The little thief stole it and after she saw what I was about, she made it nearly impossible for me to try again with someone else. But I managed to hide the book, just in case. Good thing *you* came along, my little niece, or I might have been trapped in that awful body for the rest of my days."

"Uncle?" Veronica was so confused; it was so difficult to do anything, even speak. Her jaws were made of lead. "How…"

"Don't worry about it. You don't need to know," he said coolly, out of her own lips. "Thank you, Veronica. You always were *such* a sweetheart."

The sound of a key in the lock silenced them. Asenath came through the front door, looking sheepish. The smell of food wafted into the living room.

"Sorry I took off like—oh, hi Veronica," said Asenath. She was carrying takeout from somewhere in her arms. "Ms. V said you took Dad home for me…thanks."

"No worries," said Veronica brightly, as Veronica watched in mute horror. "It was the least I could do. I've been such a bitch. Can you forgive me?"

"Of course," said Asenath instantly. "Veronica…I'm so sorry I've been making trouble for you at school. But you have to understand…"

"You don't owe me any explanations," said Veronica warmly. "I'm just glad we're friends again."

"I brought home dinner. Can you stay?"

"No," said Veronica. "Mommy and Daddy want me home, I'm sure. Maybe next week?"

"Sounds good," said Asenath. "Hey—this was really cool of you. Dad and I…after his…his stroke, he…"

"It's okay." Veronica leaned in and hugged Asenath tightly. "See you tomorrow?"

"Yeah," said Asenath. "Tomorrow."

Veronica tossed her hair and strode out of the house, waving once before walking down the street toward her home. Veronica watched her go, barely able to make her mouth move.

"Thief," she muttered, hoping Asenath would understand.

"Shut up, Dad," said Asenath, throwing dinner on the table. "You've already lost TV privileges with that little display you put on at practice today. Don't make it worse for yourself." She crossed her arms. "You know damn well what I'm capable of."

"Stolen…" Veronica tried to swallow the spit pooling in her mouth, but just dribbled all over herself.

"No more cheer practice for you," said Asenath. "And if you keep *that* up, I'll tell our home care worker you're just too much for a teenage girl to manage—understand? Ugh, stop *crying*." She made a disgusted sound in the back of her throat. "You and I both know you brought this on yourself."

Kin, Painted

Penny Stirling

Watercolour.

I BRUSH WATER IN THIN LINES down my right arm before adding green pigment. Colour spreads down each lane. I twist my arm to surface tension's extent and then past it, letting the paint escape.

Think how lovely I could be covered in watercolours. Gradients with geometric patterns, perhaps, or precise stripes with thought-provoking colour-mixing drips. Now and then a performance piece, using my own sweat to blur and degrade my body's art.

No I sloppily write in water across the smeared lines as disrelish seethes inside me, shaking my arm—*no*—and washing the brush—*no*—and writing *no* until my arm is clean.

I am running out of paints to try.

Red, pink, orange.

OLDER BROTHER WEARS THE DUCHESS'S PRIZE-WINNING roses, witch-tattooed to bloom and wither on a weekly cycle. When she entertains guests—usually inside but in her garden on warm summer days—he wears naught but a sculpted skirt to wander as a flower vase.

Every night he covers his roses with thick strokes of rainbow paints—more dollops than a coat—that do not dry but instead smear and mix and splatter as his body slides and rubs against the duchess's eldest son. Since the betrothal ceremony they are no longer allowed to flirt in public, but no one knows that the duchess's son prefers paint to engagement rings if they're both clean and proper before morning.

"Will you go with him when he marries?" I ask Older Brother as he checks the garden's roses for pests.

Of course. "You could take over my duties," he signs, winking. The betrothed lady doesn't care for roses, he later confides. The duchess won't allow it, he frets. But, he muses, if *someone else* could be roses, even un-witched ones, she just might.

I imagine being beset with roses, scentless yet still cloying, and I demur. After all, I am mid-puberty; our parents would never allow me tattoos yet. Even though he assures me he jests, I dream of their tattooed thorns slicing my skin.

Black, white.

FATHER'S BACK IS A CHESSBOARD, HIS chest backgammon, repainted every day. In his younger days his legs were strong and he could kneel or stand, bent over, for an entire game but now he lies on a divan while the duchess and her mother play games on him. When the duchess's children were younger his arms were often covered in tic-tac-toe grids.

Sorting threads for his next embroidery project, he asks me how I'll paint myself. I don't know. I keep trying different things but…

"You'll figure it out," he says with a voice so full of trust and confidence it makes my stomach hurt the nights I lie awake staring so unsure at my unvarnished flesh.

Fountain pen ink.

PAINT I WRITE ON THE BACK of my hand. *Paint. Paint.* The black ink spiders.

I don't paint. I don't paint. Will I paint? Paint. Paint. Paint. Paint.

My pen has a thin nib and it takes a long time for the ink to overlap and coalesce into incoherency. It feels better than paint on my skin, but still it does not satisfy, does not reveal to me the pride I see on my parents' and siblings' faces.

Something must, surely. There has to be something that will bring joy to my skin and meaning to my life. I want, so much, to belong within my family not just in appearance or assurance. And yet I have tried so many paints. Will my façade be of happiness rather than pigment?

Silver, sepia.

MOTHER MOST NIGHTS WEARS GLASS SHARD garlands over stripes of reflective paint and dances, surrounded by lanterns and brocade mirrors, for the duchess. But on the eve of the new year she instead uses a mirror to ink faces of departed family, friends, respected enemies and honoured royalty onto her head and body. As the bells of midnight and the words of "Auld Lang Syne" usher in the new year, nestled between braziers she removes jacket and shirt then touches each face and whispers their names, her remembrance unheard but not unnoticed amongst the celebrations.

"What if I don't paint myself?" I ask one day after previewing her new choreography. "What if I disappoint and find no paint that suits me? What if I am no colour but my skin's?"

She smiles, shakes her head, and hugs me tight, stroking my hair like she would when I was a child waking from a nightmare. "Just because we all paint ourselves doesn't mean that you *must*, my love," she says and promises me I could never disappoint her.

(As a young dancer she had witched her painted stripes to undulate and coruscate as she moved—a performance I would love to see, but she gave up those routines upon deciding to continue courting Father. Magic residue on her arms sent him into anaphylactic shock during their first tryst. This eschewal of witched paints was one of many disappointments Grandmother never forgave.)

Mother's assurances only make me more anxious.

Navy, midnight, umber.

ELDEST SISTER IS PAINTED CAMOUFLAGE DURING her nightly patrols of the estate, her muscles dyed with rumours and nuisance for poachers. Before breakfast—her dinner—she trains, and when dawn is early I sometimes watch her lift weights and such.

"What will you *do* if you don't paint?" she asks as she checks her wrist strapping. "You hate studying, you can't witch, you lack the endurance for a trade, you'd detest marriage. Are you going to dust shelves or cut lawns? Really? When you could earn your keep by just getting the twins to paint you as illusion and sitting around all day? There's a lot of people'd be envious of the chance for an easy job." She jabs at her punching bag, eyes narrowed at a target I can't see. "Paint is a tool. It can grant us what we desire, but it doesn't require being loved to do so."

What is it that Eldest Sister desires? A frame and future never perfectible due to inherited hypersensitivity, their semblance only possible through hard work, no matter what designs she might try to paint on her body.

Gold.

AFTER THE WEDDING OF THE DUCHESS'S eldest son, hours after his new wife has roused and made an appearance, servants go to wake him—and find Older Brother too, both of them still a union of limbs and paint, drying and sticky. But though solvent separates them, the duchess does not. When the young husband and wife depart for her mothers' country, it is not only her retinue that accompanies them. There were handprints in the paint, a maid tells me, too small for either man.

In exchange for Older Brother the duchess is sent a gardener and seedlings. Before the wedding's first anniversary we have beautiful kangaroo paws growing in the glasshouse. I feel the allure of committing their colours and strange shapes to my flesh, of never worrying again about how to paint my skin, but when I imagine them persisting in six or sixteen years' time I feel only cold.

"Follow your heart," Older Brother bade me, but of course a man whose lust was suddenly rewarded would.

Graphite pencil.

PAINT I WRITE ON MY LEFT leg with the flat of the lead. *Paint. Is this my paint?* I continue until there is more smudge than words on my leg and then, biting my lower lip, *paint* I write in the smeared graphite with an eraser.

I stare at the new *paint*—an absence, not paint at all—for a long while.

Replica palettes.

YOUNGER SISTER-BROTHER AND YOUNGER BROTHER ARE prodigies, fraternal twins with identical talent: the duchess's pride. They painted before they could talk, she tells her guests; pity they can't test their genius with witched-paint. Their favourite performance is painting one another invisible, colours and patterns carefully matched to wallpaper or painting behind, but they are too talented for stagnation.

After pleading one day to borrow me they turn my body into a contest, two halves of a van Gogh recreation. "Which side wins?" they ask

anyone passing by, and I restate for those who don't understand sign language. My left is Younger Sister-Brother's painting, my right is Younger
Brother's. No one praises one more than the other.

"Tomorrow da Vinci?" they ask and it is tempting to give in to the
thought of paint without predilection, of appreciation without effort, but
I tell them no, not tomorrow. I cannot imagine my happiness in their
paint. But maybe sometime, I relent, because their matching disconsolate
expressions are masterpieces unto themselves.

Flesh brown, chestnut brown.

MOTHER'S TWIN VISITS AFTER ZIR LATEST exhibition and gifts her an
unsold melancholic study of a beachgoer's rainy afternoon. Four years
ago ze was commissioned for a portrait of the duchess but has been
too busy with success and its opportunities; ze may not have taken to
painting zir skin, but paint is still essential to zir. Now at last ze's come,
promising the delay's experience will mean greater art, showering us with
accumulated trinkets from the cities ze's visited.

After the night's patrol and breakfast Eldest Sister talks with zir about
those cities where no one would know enough about a newcomer to
misremember their past, where physical martial arts have a dedicated
following even amongst the multitude of magic-enhanced fighting styles.
Before lunch and schooling Younger Sister-Brother and Younger Brother,
ecstatic in the presence of a trained and established artist, get critiques on
their recreations and illusions with Mother translating. Come evening ze
shares card games and stories with Older Sister, and once she has gone to
bed ze talks with Mother and Father late into the night.

It is while the light is good in the afternoons that we watch ze work on
the duchess's portrait, sketching her posed and painting her eerily lifelike.
How strange zir paint is in comparison to everyone else's: more properly
artistic and yet less creative in zir technical prowess. Within me stirs an
appreciation for what my parents and siblings accomplish with neither
formal training nor traditional canvases, for how their paints display their
practicality, personality and pride.

Even though I might no longer take for granted the beauty and skill
that have surrounded me my whole life, when Younger Sister-Brother
and Younger Brother paint on me a replica of the new portrait—to great
applause by both its artist and the duchess—I feel no inspiring surge of

feelings towards the pigment on my skin, no sudden revelation or desire
to replace my siblings' work with my own paints.

It is later, contemplating my family's creativity in removing paint from
canvas, that inspiration arrives and brushes aside ingrained ideas of what
paint and art can be.

Tissue paper.

PAINT I CUT OUT—THE INSIDE OF the *a* a bit wonky—and lightly affix to
my right arm with water drops. The dye in the paper runs a bit. Next I
tear the paper sheets into small squares and overlay them into the word
paint, water-gluing each square into a mass on my left foot, but upon
standing up I see that distance smudges the torn edges and that layering
variegates the saturation too much like watercolours.

So back to the scissors for sharp, exact squares. This time *paint* I mosaic,
and when again I stand and check my foot it looks unlike anything my
family paints. It's not perfect, not yet, but it's the closest I've been so far.

I will get there. I will.

Azure, sapphire.

OLDER SISTER MIXES FLOATING PAINT BATHS and every day dips herself
into new patterns. She favours swirls and zigzags on her limbs, impre-
cisely styled by brushwork and paint added to the bath, but for her torso
she creates impressionist scenes. This week she has been illustrating *Don-
keyskin.* I sit with her to see how she details the dresses.

"I don't understand why you all paint," I admit.

She can't really explain why she chose these paints, she says, and taps
my nose with a dress-the-colour-of-sky-marbled brush. It was, you know,
"it just felt right," or something. And continues to, she supposes.

Plum, grey, copper.

FOR THE DUCHESS'S EVENING PARTIES FATHER shows off his makeup.
His gaming boards' colours and lines are simple and strict; his face is
where his expressiveness is displayed. Smokey look is his favourite, a
meticulous blend of liner, mascara and four or five eyeshadows together
with contouring and layers of lipstick and gloss. Backgammon is always
played in the evening, so that his face is not upside down and ignored.

As he dabs concealer across my acne, so the twins won't complain of hues clashing with the *Starry Night* they'll reproduce on me tonight, I ask him to write *paint* across my cheeks before foundation is added.

"It'll be too—wait, I know," he says, and after some comparing of eyeshadows selects a neutral shade. Using his smallest brush—without questioning or deprecating—he writes the word on my eyelids and then covers it evenly.

Houndstooth, argyle.

THE FIRST WHO SEES MY PAINT is Eldest Sister. When she promises not to laugh I remove my jacket and reveal bared arms covered in layers of tissue paper, pencil and ink all spelling *paint* over and over. There are no patterns, there is no overall picture or purpose. Just *paint paint paint*, sparse enough in some areas to read individual letters and elsewhere too cacophonous to see anything but accumulation. She regards it with surprise.

"What… What do you think?"

"I think you'll make everyone proud," she says, and smiles and hugs me. "I hope it brings you closer to your dreams."

When I begin to cry in relief and automatically wipe my cheeks with the back of my hand, smearing ink and graphite, she still smiles but she doesn't laugh. Cleaning the mess from my face she tells me she used to do the same constantly and then, after a pause and with a low voice, says that if I also promise not to laugh she too has something to share.

(It was not a secret, as such, but it was significant to say it aloud.)

Later, after a weekend trip to town buying his first binders and new clothes, he gifts me a box full of patterned fabric squares, bright stiff paper sheets, jewellery wire, beads, drafting tape, calligraphy pens, and crayons.

Luminous.

OVER OLDER SISTER'S SHADOWY DROWNING SCENE from *The Nixie of the Mill-Pond* I chart constellations for the duchess's youngest child, bed-bound with joint pain. We stand in eir darkened room and teach the winter sky from the glowing stars on Older Sister's body: swan and hare beneath breast and the huntsman's horrified face, centaur and scorpion touching hip and the nixie's legs. The paint is witched and I wear long sleeves and long gloves, but the duchess's youngest has no allergy and soon eir cheeks are covered in luminescent celestial bodies.

"What do you think about me learning witching?" asks Older Sister. She points to her abdomen. Her illustrations have been getting less impressionist. "Imagine the water moving, bubbles rising, the huntsman's fingers twitching."

I grimace at the thought and the duchess's youngest begins offering even more grotesque animation ideas. It'll be a lot of hard work—she knows—but Mother could teach her. And she would have to be careful around us. Unless…

"Of course I won't stay here my whole life."

One sibling gone already and now two more planning to leave. Almost all of my time is spent with family. What will I *do* when we are scattered?

(What…? What will I do? What would I do if we did not scatter?)

She speaks of living alone or with a kindred creator to fully develop her painting, that she'd love to write her own stories to illustrate. Her fervour slowly turns my possessiveness to shame. "Of course," she adds, smiling at me until I realise how glum I look, "that is years away."

Blood, cochineal.

GRANDFATHER WITCH-PAINTED THE DEAD'S FACES ON vellum that the then-duke dropped into fire. Weak magic, enough for ghosts to sing in the new year before they faded away, until the duke died and Grandfather followed his will's last request.

The duchess tells the story best when she's drunk on chocolate rum balls and gin, mimicking everyone's voices and going on long tangents: Grandfather, experimenting with witched-ink more potent than normal, drew the face of the deceased duke on his own skin and let the ghost possess him. The duke (our duchess's own grandfather) spent nine long corporeal hours—until dawn burnt up his spirit—gossiping about his husband's new partner, insulting his heir's redecorations and being so boorishly true-to-life that everyone began taking credit for his death.

Grandfather never taught Mother how to summon the dead with either flesh or vellum, but with most of her children inheriting Father's allergies, magic-tinged smoke is not something she would risk.

"She could have been a fine witch," the duchess once said, shrugging, and I dreamed of what a life hypersensitive to paint rather than magic would be like.

Chalk.

AS THE TWINS SKETCH ON ME to puzzle out a new perspective illusion, I have nothing to do but watch them. They are so engrossed in their craft and childhoods that even next month is too far away to plan for, and I wonder if they will be prodigies at deciding on their futures too. Surely their skills are too great to compromise with raising families. But what if I am the last here—if preserving an art form I only connect with through distortion and passing it on to spouse (*ugh*) and family is my default future? I spent so much time believing that the right paint would result in happiness and now, having only just found my skin's façade, I learn it is...maybe not even that important a decision. I once decided against effortlessness due to certain consequences; what antipathies will be endurable when faced with loneliness?

But what else is there for someone like me?

No one ever told me growing up would be so difficult.

"Look," signs Younger Sister-Brother, pointing to the word *paint* newly drawn on my stomach. The letters are oddly warped with a shadow nonsensical from my viewing angle, but Younger Brother sees it three-dimensional and claps in delight.

My future is still years away, though, and I am not alone. Not yet.

Sun yellow, royal blue, tomato red.

MAIL BRINGS KNITTED SCARVES, FLOWER SEEDS and semi-worsted Merino wool yarn from Older Brother and his lovers. We spend an afternoon dyeing skeins as well as Eldest Brother's hand when his glove tears and—after he threatens to douse the twins with dye in reply to their teasing that it's camouflage-enriching—several garments and Younger Sister-Brother's right elbow. Later the duchess's mother teaches me how to crochet. As I master tension she freehand crochets everlastings to fill her vases until the real ones bloom, and she tells me of a time when the duchess nearly drowned following a treasure map drawn on my grandmother.

E was a bestiary, she explains, covered in tattoos of birds, beasts and fish local and legendary. Most were tame, stationary, but a few were witched-ink. On that day a kelpie had smudged the painted map, luring the duchess to the pond's centre. I ask for more stories of my grandmother, as Mother only speaks of em with rancour. "Come seek my wolpertinger," e'd say with a coquettish smile, but only two people ever found it, my grandfather and—

Suddenly the duchess's mother remembers her audience and, cheeks flushed, asks to see how my stitch decreases are looking.

Paint I crochet with a simple chain once my swatches are deemed adequate, and *paint paint paint* I crochet in shell stitch, and herringbone and Tunisian and crocodile and every other stitch the duchess's mother teaches me, alongside gloves and blankets. I tie the woollen *paint*s around my legs and wallow in the texture.

What will Eldest Brother and Older Sister send me after they leave? And without my siblings' painted bodies here will my not-painted *paint*s be senseless and vapid? An adolescent's folly only tolerated on faith that I'll mature into someone more practical or visually pleasing?

Finding my paint was supposed to make me happy, wasn't it?

Agouti, tan.

WITH FERRETS AND THE DUCHESS'S TWO daughters, Mother and I go rabbiting. If Older Sister is to learn witching she will need a reliable source of bones; it might as well bring decent meat too. Hopefully when we return she'll have finished their enclosure. Next will be planting extra herbs and setting up fermentation barrels, and then eventually comes a day I won't be able to watch Older Sister illustrate her body for fear of anaphylaxis.

"Everyone knows what they'll do with their lives," I say when the duchess's daughters have run ahead to find burrows. "When should I?"

Mother *hmm*s and thinks for a while. "In a few years you'll find that is usually not true, or doesn't matter. But, look, some people are... Are you worried about your paint? You don't have to... I know you've worried, but just because you've found a paint you like—or don't dislike—doesn't mean that's it forever." She talks of how she's considering moving on from dancing. Maybe shadow puppets? Older Sister's interest in magic has got her thinking about it again. Puppets and lights, witched to move and dance, just imagine it. Easier to keep away from Father and the rest of us than witched-paint, too, and—

"I don't *have* any skills or interests like that."

She *tch*s. "Neither did I, at your age."

Sunrise, bruises.

NEXT MONTH IS ELDEST BROTHER'S FAREWELL. I've been waking up early to spend time with him. Everyone's been so supportive, even being happy that he'll give up paints because that will let him focus on forging his own path. He explains this as encouragement to never fret or hesitate should I wish to replace or cease my skin's veneer.

He's always made time for me, always tried to help me even if occupied or unqualified. And here I am, having reciprocated so little yet once again seeking to impose my inadequacies on him. He's stretching his calves, facing away and unable to see how much I've wrung my hands, when I finally manage, "Can I have a go?"

"Finally sick of just watching? Great!"

He talks me through warm-up exercises, wrist strapping, good posture and, finally, how to hit the punching bag. After several weary minutes I say I'm not sure about this, and when I turn around he's smiling and holding a pair of wooden swords. I've never seen him with *two* swords before. Is there anyone Mother hasn't talked to about this? (No. No, there is not. Within a week even the new gardener I don't know is casually telling me about their job and hobbies.)

"Remember you'd ask what I'd do if I didn't paint?" I copy his movements to jab and swipe with the sword. "You never asked what I'd do if I *did* paint."

He corrects my foot placement. "None of us has ever had easy answers, you know, but I think you'll find your desire. Looking for it can't hurt. And if you think it's not here, you'll always be welcome wherever I end up."

Eldest Brother's one of the few who doesn't tell me I'm *just a kid, don't worry.* For that I'll miss him all the more.

Collage.

I AM A REFLECTION OF MY family, an interpretation of painted flesh illegible without their paradigm behind me. Where one would expect paint to bring function, art, story, beauty or tribute, instead there is just de-scription—and a false one at that.

Paint in ink, *paint* in fabric, *paint* in beads, in paper, wool, fur, chalk, pencil, tape, eyeliner. *Paint* in crosshatch, *paint* in negative space, *paint* in pointillism, in mosaic, stamp, outline, calligraphy. *Paint* in layers and *paint* in discord and *paint* in anything but paint.

And one *paint* in dried chocolate sauce on my right arm because the duchess's younger daughter cannot be entirely rebuffed on her birthday. At first she proposed lipstick on my neck, ignoring previous rejections and that my attraction deficiency continues, and I almost acquiesced to the enticement of pragmatism and effortlessness.

The duchess takes me around the party, showing me off to guests for my debut. Some recognise me and what I've done. I'm all grown up now, aren't I clever, they'd assumed I'd go into tattoos. Some don't, confused or guessing I'm a joke, and then the duchess explains witheringly the charm and genius of my *paint*ed body until they apologise profusely, hoping invitation to her next party has been re-secured.

Obvious pride, approval and relief surround me. My family and the duchess are happy, and I am—I'm neither all grown up nor happy, not yet, but I suppose I'm growing into it. If I can find a way to paint my skin without paint, to conform without feigning comfort…then maybe finding something to strive for, to enjoy and love and pass the time with once family has dispersed, won't be impossible?

Future I will write. *Happiness* I will paint.

The Contributors

Nino Cipri is a queer and genderqueer writer living in Chicago. Nino is a graduate of the 2014 Clarion Writers' Workshop, which they attended with the help of an Illinois Arts Council Professional Development grant. Their writing has been published or is forthcoming in Tor.com, *Fireside Fiction, Betwixt, Daily Science Fiction, In The Fray, Autostraddle,* and *Gozamos.* A multidisciplinary artist, Nino has also written plays, screenplays, and radio features; performed as a dancer, actor, and puppeteer; and worked as a backstage theater tech.

Holly Heisey launched their writing career in sixth grade when they wrote their class play, a medieval fantasy. It was love at first dragon. Since then, their short fiction has appeared in Orson Scott Card's *InterGalactic Medicine Show, Escape Pod, The Doomsday Chronicles,* and *Clockwork Phoenix 5.* A freelance designer by day, Holly lives in upstate New York with Larry and Moe, their two pet cacti, and they are currently at work on a science fantasy epic. You can find them online at hollyheisey.com.

Alexis A. Hunter revels in the endless possibilities of speculative fiction. Over fifty of her short stories have appeared in magazines such as *Shimmer, Apex, Fantastic Stories of the Imagination,* and more. To learn more, visit www.alexisahunter.com.

Everett Maroon is a memoirist, pop culture commentator, and speculative fiction writer. He has a B.A. in English from Syracuse University and went through an English literature master's program there. He is a member of the Pacific Northwest Writer's Association. His young adult series, *The Time Guardians,* is forthcoming from Lethe Press.

Jack Hollis Marr is an English writer of speculative fiction and poetry whose work has appeared in *Stone Telling, Goblin Fruit*, and *The Future Fire*. He frequently writes on issues of gender, sexuality, and disability, juxtaposed with mythic and folkloric motifs.

A. Merc Rustad is a queer transmasculine non-binary writer who lives in the Midwest United States. Their stories have appeared or are forthcoming in *Lightspeed, Fireside Fiction, Apex, Escape Pod, Shimmer, Cicada, The Best American Science Fiction and Fantasy 2015* and *Wilde Stories 2016*. In addition to breaking readers' hearts, Merc likes to play video games, watch movies, read comics, and wear awesome hats. You can find Merc on Twitter @Merc_Rustad or their website: http://amercrustad.com.

Pronouns: they/them/their. *B R Sanders* is a white, genderqueer writer who lives and works in Denver, CO, with their family and two cats. B writes about queer elves, mostly. B tweets @B_R_Sanders.

E. Saxey is an ungendered Londoner who works in universities. Their fiction has appeared in *Daily Science Fiction, Apex Magazine, Queers Destroy Science Fiction* and in anthologies including *Tales from the Vatican Vaults* (Robinson) and *The Lowest Heaven* (Jurassic London).

Benjanun Sriduangkaew is a bee who dreams of strange cities and beautiful futures. Her fiction has appeared in *Clarkesworld*, Tor.com, *Apex Magazine, Beneath Ceaseless Skies* and the *Heiresses of Russ: The Year's Best Lesbian Speculative Fiction* series. Her first novella, *Scale-Bright*, was nominated for the British Science Fiction Association award.

Penny Stirling lives in Perth, Western Australia. Ou enjoys embroidering cross-stitch and blackwork pixel art, video games, and collecting notebooks. Ou write speculative stories and poems and has been published in *Interfictions, Limininality*, and *Strange Horisons*. More details can be found at pennystirling.com.

Bonnie Jo Stufflebeam's fiction and poetry has appeared in over fifty magazines and anthologies including *The Toast, Clarkesworld, PRISM International, Lightspeed*, and Everyman's Library's *Monster Verse*. She recently released an audio fiction-jazz collaborative album, *Strange Monsters*, centered around the theme of women's voices. She's been reprinted in French and Polish, for numerous podcasts, and on the popular science blog io9. She earned an MFA in Creative Writing from University of Southern Maine's Stonecoast Program and created and curates the annual Art & Words Collaborative Show in Fort Worth, Texas. She is active on Twitter @BonnieJoStuffle and on her website bonniejostufflebeam.com.

Bogi Takács is a Hungarian Jewish agender person currently living in the U.S. Eir speculative fiction, poetry and nonfiction have been published in a variety of venues like *Clarkesworld*, *Apex*, *Strange Horizons* and *Glittership*. E posts SFF story and poem recommendations on Twitter under #diversestories and #diversepoems. You can follow Bogi on Twitter at @bogiperson or visit eir website at prezzey.net.

Molly Tanzer lives in Boulder, Colorado along the front range of the Mountains of Madness, or maybe just the Flatirons. A professional writer of literary horror and fantasy both long and short form, Tanzer's first collection, *A Pretty Mouth*, was nominated for the Sydney J. Bounds and the Wonderland Book Award. Tanzer is also the author of *Rumbullion and Other Liminal Libations*, a collection of short stories with associated drinks, and the acclaimed Weird Western *Vermilion* (Word Horde). Tanzer is a Hong Kong cinema enthusiast, a former academic, and an avid hiker. Find her at @molly_the_tanz.

Margarita Tenser is a Ukrainian-born Aussie with a large comic book collection, an intense relationship with punctuation, and a pixie haircut, provided the pixie was dragged through a hedge backwards. Her work has been published in *Strange Horizons*, *Vitality Magazine*, and *Voiceworks*.

E. Catherine Tobler has never ridden a thunderbird into the heavens, but it's not for a lack of trying. Her fiction has appeared in *Clarkesworld*, *Lightspeed*, and *Beneath Ceaseless Skies*. In June, *The Kraken Sea*, a novella set in her travelling circus universe, will be available from Apex Book Company. Follow her on Twitter @ECthetwit or her website, ecatherine.com.

The Editor

In the best of all timelines, *K.M. Szpara* lives in Baltimore, Maryland, with his black cat and miniature poodle. He has a Master of Theological Studies from Harvard Divinity School, which he totally uses at his day job as a paralegal. On nights and weekends, Kelly advances his queer agenda by writing science fiction and fantasy novels. His short fiction appears in *Lightspeed*, *Shimmer*, and *Glittership*. You can find him on Twitter at @KMSzpara.

Publication Credits

CPSIA information can be obtained
at www.ICGtesting.com
Printed in the USA
LVOW10s1528140217
524243LV00002B/411/P

9 781590 216170